DEATH IN THE RISING SUN

JOHN CREASEY

Death in the Rising Sun

A DOCTOR PALFREY THRILLER

WALKER AND COMPANY
New York

First published in the United States of America in 1976 by the Walker Publishing Company, Inc.

Published simultaneously in Canada by Fitzhenry & Whiteside, Limited, Toronto.

ISBN: 0-8027-5338-8

Library of Congress Catalog Card Number: 75-34828

Printed in the United States of America.

10 9 8 7 6 5 4 3 2 1

1 : Dr. Palfrey Forsees Difficulties

PALFREY's right hand strayed to his forehead, and he began to twist a few strands of his light brown hair around his finger. He was sitting back in a large armchair, his long legs stretched out, and a cigarette burning low in a holder.

In front of him the Marquis of Brett sat at a wide, flat-topped mahogany desk, so highly polished that it reflected the silver inkstand, a blotting-pad with silver corners, a telephone and Brett's thin, veined hands, the fingers of which were resting lightly on the desk.

Palfrey pulled the strands of hair straight up from his forehead, and broke the silence.

'One great difficulty which I foresee is that I don't know a word of Japanese,' he said. 'Nor does Stefan.'

'Your German is fluent,' Brett pointed out, 'and you will probably be able to fall back on broken English. A surprising number of Japanese can speak English, and most Germans have a smattering. In any case, your guide can act as an interpreter.'

'I don't know that I would like to trust an interpreter,' objected Palfrey.

'Orishu is quite trustworthy. What you mean is that you don't want to go to Japan,' said Brett, bluntly.

'I certainly do not!' Palfrey released his hair and patted it down. His forehead was broad and his blue eyes were large, but their expression was a little vague, in spite of his sudden animation.

'I can think of nothing I want to do less than go to the Land of the Rising Sun. I know I asked for something to do,' he added reproachfully, 'but I didn't dream of a proposition like this. I don't like any of it. I don't particularly want to be in Tokyo when the Americans reach there. Between you and me,' he added warmly, 'I have had my share of being bombed, too. Iron nerves at breaking point, and all that.'

Brett smiled.

'All right, Sap! I didn't think you'd like the suggestion and

I didn't hold out any hope that you would accept, but I had to try. When are you and Drusilla going to get married?'

'That's another of the difficulties,' said Palfrey. 'We hoped to sneak off one day this summer and commit the fell deed. If I go to Japan there won't be more than one chance in two of my returning.' He looked up: 'That's about right, isn't it?'

'About,' admitted Brett, 'and that's why I was hesitant about asking you to take the job. Forget it, Sap!'

'I dislike the ingenuous expression in your eyes,' Palfrey informed him. 'When does the excursion start?'

'It should start next week.'

'How long can I have to decide?'

'Forty-eight hours,' said Brett, abruptly. He took a small envelope from a drawer in his desk and handed it over. 'You might like to take this to reflect upon.'

Palfrey had a solitary lunch at his club, choosing a corner where he was not likely to be seen, for he did not feel like indulging in small-talk. He felt wretched because Brett had chosen to put the proposition to him at a time when Drusilla Blair was out of London. True, she was due to meet him at Claridges for tea, but the three hours until four o'clock stretched like a limitless vista in front of him, and he knew that he would not be able to think about anything except Brett's suggestion. He did not feel any happier because it was partly his own fault. Goaded by a conscience which Drusilla and his friends said would one day be the death of him, he had asked Brett whether there were any little jobs he could do in the next few weeks.

'Weeks,' he told himself now. 'Not months, confound him!'

Few of the members of the Carilon Club knew the truth about him, although many knew that he was a doctor of considerable reputation, and that he had visited parts of Occupied Europe, during the war, to try to save the lives of important members of the resistance movement. Thus, at all events, the newspapers had declared only a few weeks before, when his photograph had appeared on the front pages of the picture papers, and a highly coloured story had brought him a few days of intensely disliked notoriety.

The truth was very different; he *had* helped to save the lives of men and women who were now playing important parts in the rebuilding of their countries, but he had also led a little band of people through some of the most dangerous and hair-raising adventures, both in Europe and Africa. Of the original members of that party, which consisted of representatives from

Russia and Washington as well as Drusilla, Brian Debenham and himself, only three were left fit for further work. Alec Conroy, the American, had been killed near Algiers; Debenham had lost an arm and was not yet fully recovered from a Scandinavian ordeal; and others had been lost to them. Of the old guard, only Stefan Andromovitch and he would be able to go to Japan, for this was certainly no task for Drusilla.

He spent the afternoon in the almost deserted smoking-room, looking through the contents of the envelope Brett had given him. They only confirmed what Brett had told him. At half past three he went to Claridges and waited near the entrance until, at two minutes to four, a taxi pulled up and he saw Drusilla's face at the window. Drusilla was one of the few women of his acquaintance who looked graceful even when she was getting out of a taxi, and that was the more remarkable because she was nearly as tall as he.

She wore a flowered silk dress and a wide-brimmed straw hat trimmed with the same material.

Half and hour later he led the way into his Wimpole Street flat. His name was still on a brass plate on the street door, but he had long since stopped practising in England.

'Sweet—that smiling, cunning, unlovable creature whom we know as the Marquis of Brett wants me to go to Japan.'

'Sap, don't joke!' Drusilla protested.

'I sometimes wish I had not been christenend Stanislaus Alexander,' said Palfrey. 'I know that S A P spells Sap, but it's getting to be something of a boomerang. If you call me Sap often enough I shall have softening of the brain, and accept—that appears to be Brett's *modus operandi* this time. He actually told me that I would be a fool if I accepted, and made it clear that he thought I was that kind of a fool.'

Drusilla did not smile, and the healthy glow on her cheeks could not hide their pallor. Yet all she said was, 'Why on earth does he want you to go there?'

'That's the rub.' Palfrey shrugged. 'There's a good reason. Japan, fair island of everlasting blight, offers attractions to certain gentlemen of whom we have heard. German gentlemen, that is. No one quite knows how they've managed it, but several members of the Nazi hierarchy have fled to Japan. We want them all, alive-oh!'

'But when Japan's beaten——'

'—They'll obviously try to arrange for as many men as possible to escape the misguided Allied desire for justice and retribution. We—you and I, my darling—have spent a lot of time in Europe trying to dig out Nazis who thought they were safe for life, and by the grace of God we prized some out of their fastnesses. Yes, we've done things like this before, and someone will have to keep on doing them. There's no argument about that, is there?'

'No,' Drusilla agreed quietly.

'If that isn't enough, there are other good reasons for an expedition to Japan,' went on Palfrey. 'They have toddled off with a substantial part of the treasures of the countries they overran. The sum total is fantastic. Jewels taken from every temple in Burma, Malaya, Indo-China and all like homelands have been looted, but they're still in existence and only the Japs know where.'

Drusilla said: 'You're going, aren't you?'

'I haven't said so.' Palfrey frowned. 'I didn't know about it until this morning, and it rather knocked me sideways. However, I'm trying to face the facts. The facts are that a large number of Germans remain loose in Europe and that the idea of preparing for another war of world domination is not, to their minds, fantastic. It isn't fantastic to the Japanese, either. After the accursed accumulation of horrors we've witnessed in the past few years, any man with any kind of conscience must——'

'Your conscience!' exclaimed Drusilla. The words seemed to be wrung from her.

'I'm really sorry about it,' said Palfrey, soberly. 'The trouble is, it won't lie down. The question I've got to try to answer within the next forty-three hours is whether by accepting I can, perhaps, put a few more nails in the coffin of world domination. Don't tell me that it's dead and buried. Only the mentally deficient will ever believe that, until we have had the experience of a few decades of peace untroubled by rumours of war. Too many powerful individuals, clever, unscrupulous, and possessed of quite diabolical cunning, are loose in the world, and Brett has an assurance from Moscow that many of them are in Japan, or else are passing through. Moscow is still at peace with Japan, and knows more about what's happening there than we do. Can I spike a few wheels?'

Drusilla, whose colour was back, said nothing, but leaned forward and took a cigarette.

'I've managed to in the past, with luck,' murmured Palfrey. 'There's no good reason why I shouldn't do so again. There's no legitimate reason why I should refuse to try. Any man who puts his personal longings—and God knows how I long to marry you and settle down, my darling!—before the common good is stoking up a nice warm fire in the nether regions for himself.'

He slid forward in his chair until he was on one knee in front of Drusilla. He took her hands in his and looked up into her eyes. 'Darling,' he said, 'I am the complete coward. I don't want to go. The thought of it frightens me. The thought of having to make a decision is a nightmare, and I don't even want to decide. Decide for me, will you?'

The room was very quiet.

In Drusilla's eyes were tears which she did not try to blink away. Her pressure on his hands was very tight, and seemed to grow tighter. She was breathing heavily, and looking down at him, as if she wanted to have a vivid picture of every feature of that beloved face. As he looked at her, knowing what she was going through, she had never seemed more lovely nor more desirable. Her lips were parted and quivering slightly, and twice she tried to speak, but the words would not come.

Palfrey broke the silence very gently.

'So your conscience is as troublesome as mine?'

'Sap . . .' Drusilla's voice trailed off, and he kept silent. When at last she spoke again her voice was sharper. 'I thought all the danger was over, and if any man deserves a rest from it, you do. I came back thinking that we could begin to settle down, to lead a natural life—I think I *hate* the Marquis!'

After another long pause, she added quietly:

'If you go. I shall go.'

'Now, 'Silla——'

'Presumably you will be going to Japan under the guise of a German refugee,' said Drusilla, 'and there must be some Nazis who would be loyal enough to take their wives with them. And, what is more,' she went on, 'I am not going to traipse about Japan or any part of the Far East as your fiancée! When are you leaving?'

'The Marquis says I would need to start within a week. But, 'Silla——'

'Look here.' Drusilla tightened her grip still further: 'I have been abroad with you before and I have worked abroad on my own. I am not a sweet innocent. Nothing the Japanese can show me in the way of horrors can outdo what I have seen in Europe. Everything you have said applies to me as much as to you. I hate the thought of going, but I won't let you go alone.'

Silence fell again, and when she broke it there was a note of urgency in her voice. 'Sap, say something! Don't look at me like that, say something *now*!'

'It's so difficult to know what to say,' said Palfrey. 'You're quite right. We could get married and travel as man and wife. I won't insult you by saying you would be in the way. The fact remains that you might sometimes be left on your own, and the Japanese aren't renowned for their chivalry towards European women. They will have the upper hand; we shall, as German refugees, be dependent on their goodwill. They may extract a high price.' He paused, then added: 'Facts. We can't blink at them.'

'I shall not let you go alone, if I can help it,' said Drusilla. 'That's final, Sap.'

It was useless to say that Brett might object; it was not likely that he would forbid Drusilla to make the journey if she were really bent on going. It was a fact, too, that she might become a valuable addition to the ranks of the party which would set out.

Palfrey released her hands, and stood up.

'I feel as if I've been run over by a tank,' he said. 'I suppose you know that if we go to see the Marquis he'll give us his blessing? There's no point in thinking that we may have found a way of outwitting him.'

'I don't want to find a way,' said Drusilla. 'I——Sap!'

'H'mm?'

'Do you know that we've decided to get married *this week*?'

'Have we got quite so far as that?' asked Palfrey, and then as she stood up he swept her into his arms.

Soon they were laughing and their eyes were filled with excitement; and before long Palfrey was on the telephone to the Marquis of Brett. He had made no mistake about Brett's reaction.

They were to travel by a devious route to China and fly in a Nazi aircraft to Japan. In Japan, they would rely on their German papers to ensure a sympathetic welcome—as well as the jewels they would take with them. For the reports which Brett, as chief of Z.5, had received about the German refugees now going in increasing numbers to Japan, suggested that only those who could pay for their safety were likely to get it. The chief difficulty was to provide themselves with false identities which would pass the Japanese authorities, and with this problem Palfrey wrestled as he ploughed a way through the countless little problems in connection with the wedding.

Two days after the decision had been reached, Drusilla came in from shopping and found him sitting back with his legs crossed and the smoke from a cigarette curling into his eye, his holder neglected.

'Well!' she exclaimed.

'Thoughts,' said Palfrey, hastily. 'Deep thoughts, demanding the utmost concentration. What have you bought?'

'Nothing to help you concentrate,' said Drusilla.

'Shrew! Can you tell me,' he demanded 'why on earth the Marquis insisted on this reception and a wedding with all the furbelows? He's been so decent about it that I hadn't the heart to insist on a registrar's office and a quiet coffee and bun afterwards, but why on earth we are burdened with all this as well as preparing for the eternal, I don't know.'

'It's a funny thing.' Drusilla sat down: 'but I've been wondering about that, too. This afternoon I've been to the dressmaker's to have a white dress altered for me, and the Marquis came in, full of eager solicitude. Just a little *too* full, I thought. I wonder if he knew that this would happen, if he really wanted us both to go.'

'Oh, he'd hardly go that far.'

'I'm not so sure,' said Drusilla. 'He's a pet, but I think he would sacrifice his best friend if he thought that it was going to help. Don't you agree?'

'I do, but I don't see how a big wedding is going to make any difference. He——' Palfrey stopped short. *'Don't* I though!' he gasped. *'Don't* I? 'Silla, that man has Richelieu beaten to a frazzle! I saw a paragraph——' He hurried across the room and seized *The Times,* spread it out on the table and turned over the pages. Drusilla stood beside him. 'There!' cried Palfrey. 'And I thought it was a piece of unintelligent guesswork on the part of the social editor. Listen!

'We understand that Dr. Alexander Palfrey, whose marriage to Miss Drusilla Blair will take place on Thursday, will revisit the scene of a war-time mission on the Italian Riviera, for their honeymoon, which will be indefinite.'

Palfrey shook his head in admiration.

'The old fox! That will be read in Tokyo before we leave. Any suspicion that might have been aroused by our joint absence from London, at this time, will receive its *congé*. I'll bet you that the Marquis wanted a big show so that word of it would get down under. I wonder if they've put this out on the radio at all?'

'They'd never put social chat on the radio,' Drusilla objected.

'I'm not so sure,' said Palfrey.

Later, he went to the offices of the *Daily Cry,* where certain members of the staff listened to all broadcasts from home stations under the title of the *Radio Research Department*. Any doubts he had of Brett's manœuvre were dissipated when he saw the broad beam on the face of one of his friends there.

'You are becoming headline news, Sap,' that worthy said; 'they've even thought it worth while putting a note about you on the European News Service.'

'Only European?' asked Palfrey, hopefully.

'Don't say you want to let it go round the whole world,' said his friend, 'or I'll think it's gone to your head.'

'I just wanted to know exactly what I have to complain about,' said Palfrey. 'Not even a honeymoon is sacred—I thought better of the B.B.C.'

He was smiling as he left, but the smile faded as he strolled along Fleet Street. He was prepared to admit that the manœuvre was justified, and by restricting it to the European Service Brett had made sure that it would only reach Japan indirectly. On the other hand, was it wise to emphasise that he and Drusilla would be out of the country? Brett rarely made mistakes, but he might have been carried away by his enthusiasm for this project.

Palfrey knew how thorough were the preparations for the journey. Brett would leave nothing undone. All their clothes and their luggage would be German, the markings on their clothes would have the initials relative to their assumed names. They would learn by heart the 'route' by which they were supposed to travel from Germany itself, and ahead of them would go the information that they had escaped and were on the way to Japan. Yet he was not too happy.

The Japanese had pulled some incredible howlers in the course of their extensive espionage work, but they had a passion for detail, not unlike that of the Germans. Photographs of Palfrey and all those who had worked with him in the past would be in Tokyo, with a full list of habits, appearances, and general information. If suspicion were aroused, the danger would become acute.

Then an idea flashed through his mind, and he looked round for a taxi. Within a few minutes, he was speeding towards the London offices of the War Crimes Commission. He was well known there and if his manner caused a stir, no time was lost in taking him to the *Photograph Files* section. There were thousands of photographs all neatly filed in steel cabinets, and he had no idea where to start looking. He only knew that he wanted to find a German on the books of the Commission who did not look unlike himself.

After two hours of fruitles searching, he telephoned Drusilla.

'Darling ,where *have* you been?' she demanded, distractedly. 'I——'

'Drop everything you're doing and come here,' Palfrey urged. 'I think I've found a way of making the odds a bit easier. Rush, darling!'

'But I don't know where you are!'

'Oh, I'm going really crazy,' said Palfrey, and told her.

He wanted a respite from the photographs of Germans and Italians, Bulgarians, Rumanians and Finns. And another idea, resulting from the first, made him hurry out of the room and into the larger general office, where fifty men and women were working. In one corner, at a large desk, was a very small elderly man—with a photographic memory. He was reputed to know more Germans by name than anyone else in England. He looked up at Palfrey with a tight-lipped smile.

'I thought perhaps you would ask me to help you, Doctor!'

'I was an ass not to have thought of it before,' confessed Palfrey. 'Can you show me the photographs of all Nazies over six feet five in height?'

'Six feet *five*!'

'Yes,' said Palfrey. 'There can't be many of them, but——'

'I will see what I can do.' The little man looked disappointed. 'How quickly do you want the information?'

'Within twenty-four hours,' said Palfrey.

'Oh, *that* will be easy,' he was assured.

By the time Drusilla arrived, Palfrey was again at work with the photographs, and the little man was in one corner, casting occasional glances towards him. The filing-room was large and Palfrey was able to whisper to Drusilla what he wanted.

'But why?' asked Drusilla. 'You aren't likely to find a man who looks just like you.'

'We can't expect miracles, a rough likeness will do.'

'I don't see——'

'Listen, angel,' said Palfrey, with a broad smile. 'If we can find a notorious Nazi who might be mistaken for me, I can masquerade as that gentleman. Then, in that far, far distant land, I can say that, disguised as Dr. Palfrey, I made my way through Allied occupied countries. That's the answer to "How did you get here?" and also the answer to "You look like Dr. Palfrey, of ill fame." I'm asking our little friend, there, to find us a Nazi of a size with Stefan, too. Satisfied?'

'We *must* find one!' Drusilla was suddenly excited. 'Where shall I look?'

2 : New Delhi

PALFREY lay in the pleasant state between waking and sleeping. Drusilla had slipped down in bed and only her nose, eyes and forehead showed above the sheet, with her dark hair, untidy and adorable, on her pillow. Palfrey could hear her soft breathing. Now and again he looked at her, and a beatific smile curved his lips. Hazy thoughts passed through his mind.

The wedding, the *Wedding March,* sweet-voiced boys in the full church-choir, the soft voice of the dean who had performed the ceremony, his own voice saying 'I will'; and Drusilla's, quiet and husky; the reception which was crowded beyond his expectations, the smile on Brett's face—and then the hurried journey to Euston, from where they were supposed to be travelling before they left England, and a quick journey back from London to this sleepy hotel in Kingston for a precious week-end.

This was Sunday; next day they were to leave on the first stage of their journey.

Drusilla stirred, and after a moment, sleepily pushed the sheet away from her chin. She blinked. Palfrey smiled at her until she opened one eye, hesitantly.

'Have you been awake long?'

'I haven't slept a wink,' said Palfrey, untruthfully; 'I couldn't, for thinking of you.'

'You darling liar.' She edged towards him. 'Dreams,' she said. 'Dreams.' After a while, she asked, lazily: 'What time is it?'

'I don't know and I don't care.' Palfrey ran his fingers through her hair. 'I've always heard it said that you shouldn't marry a woman until you've seen her first thing in the morning.'

'Will I do?'

He laughed. 'Do you remember in Berlin, when——'

The words broke the spell of their enchantment and reminded them of the morrow. It did not lessen their contentment, but it made them thoughtful for a few minutes then, and at intervals during the day.

. . . . . .

There was a final session with Brett the following morning. Drusilla was wearing a two-piece suit of severe cut and German material, and Palfrey wore good quality German flannels. Two light fibre cases, crammed full, were already at the airfield. Now and again, Drusilla fingered the platinum ring on her finger and smiled, but she looked steadily at Brett. Palfrey seemed to have forgotten that a dream had come true —as if it had really been a dream, and they were now facing reality. In a way, he felt like that.

'I'd like to clear up one or two misapprehensions first,' Brett was saying with a smile. 'I did not bargain for Drusilla going with you, but, all things considered, I think it wise. She would only eat her heart out if she were to stay at home, and you would find her on your mind, Sap.' He smiled.

'Now you will want to know exactly what has been prepared for you. Information has been sent through Orishu to Tokyo that Colonel Baron Karl von Klieb and his wife escaped from Germany three weeks ago, and are trying to reach Japan by air. We don't know the routes which the Germans would take and we don't know where they refuel—they have a string of refuelling stations on the route, and that's one of the things we hope you'll be able to find out. As you are von Klieb but masquerading as Palfrey, you won't need to know where those places are. On the strength of being Palfrey, you will get as far as Chunking in Allied aircraft—and you'll make your way from Chunking to Japan with Orishu's help—officially you'll meet him by accident outside Chunking, but actually you'll find him waiting for you at Delhi.'

'New Delhi?' asked Palfrey.

'No, the old city. Japanese in New Delhi would be too conspicuous. You'll find him at the shop of Amsa the Tailor, the best-known Indian tailor in Delhi. You'll ask Amsa to make you a copy of your suit, Sap, and under the collar of the suit you leave with him you'll put three stitches in green cotton. Can you manage that, 'Silla?'

'I'm taking some darning silks,' said Drusilla. 'I'll manage it all right.'

'Nicely melodramatic,' murmured Palfrey.

'You're the last man to scoff at melodrama.' Brett smiled again. 'By the time you get back you should have a remarkable story to tell me! Now listen carefully, because this is extremely important. Orishu will send a message telling you to meet him at Amsa's after dark, and the time will be 8.59. If the message gives a different time, don't go, but wait at your hotel—the airport hotel—until you get a message from Orishu quoting that time. If you don't get it within three days, come through to me by radio-telephone.'

'That's clear enough,' Palfrey nodded.

'I don't expect any trouble in Delhi,' said Brett, 'but we

want to make as sure as possible that nothing goes wrong. I will give you photographs of Orishu, profile and full-face. But as you're not familiar with the Japanese, it may not help you much—they look surprisingly alike, unless you're used to seeing them regularly. Orishu is a painstaking fellow and he has adopted two marks by which you can identify him. There will be a streak of grey in his hair, on the right—his right—side of the parting, about a quarter of an inch wide.'

'His right side,' murmured Palfrey.

'Yes. And the nails of his right hand will be trimmed short, those of his left hand long. He speaks good English, and he might address you as von Klieb.'

'Do I understand that from New Delhi onwards we're in Orishu's hands?' asked Palfrey, thoughtfully.

'No—we shall make the arrangements for you to get to Chunking, as I've told you,' said Brett. 'But Orishu might suggest different arrangements and you'll be wise to be guided by him. Now, about Stefan. I've been in touch with Moscow and suggested that he represents himself to be Hans Goetz, one time Gauleiter of Amsterdam—Moscow liked the suggestion, Sap.'

'Intelligent people, the Russians,' Palfrey murmured.

'So as to remove the risk of the three of you being suspected because you have travelled together, you won't go on to Japan from Chunking with Stefan. But you'll see him there,' said Brett, 'and make arrangements with him there about a rendezvous in Japan. Most Germans who reach Tokyo are housed in a building near the Shiba Temple, and you'll probably be sent there as soon as you arrive. Stefan should be there, too, but you're to meet as strangers—our research shows nothing to suggest that von Klieb and Hans Goetz ever met. All known details of the two men are in your papers, for you to read up. Von Klieb's wife is not well known, but there is some information about her. That's clear enough, isn't it?'

'Perfectly,' Palfrey assured him.

'If all goes well, it will take you about a fortnight to reach Tokyo,' said Brett. 'It wouldn't be wise to get there any quicker, in view of all the circumstances, and I'll use the intervening time to elaborate your impersonation as much as I can.' He smiled. 'I think that's about the lot, except for Drusilla's hair.'

'Hair?' exclaimed Drusilla.

'I know this is a blow,' said Brett, 'but you'll have to dye it—bleach it, rather!—as soon as you're in Tokyo. We haven't been able to get a photograph of von Klieb's wife, but we do know that her hair is fair. It'll be all right dark when you get there, but they'll look for light hair at the roots within a few days, so you'd better go the whole hog and bleach it, and say that you've washed the dye out. Orishu will look after that for you—a great deal will depend on Orishu.'

'I wish there weren't so much,' said Palfrey.

'I think you'll overcome your prejudice when you've worked with him for a few weeks,' smiled Brett. 'Well, that's about all. I've instructed Orishu to get you out of the country if it becomes apparent that you are known. I don't know how long you'll be there, but with luck you will spend a month or two and pick up a great deal of useful information.' He stood up, and as Drusilla was about to rise, smiled down at her, and then kissed her forehead. 'God be with you, my dear. When you come back you'll have that normal life you're longing for!' He shook hands with Palfrey. 'Good luck, Sap.'

'Thanks,' mumbled Palfrey. 'One thing is puzzling me, though. It's on my mind, rather.'

'What is it?'

'Uncomfortable kind of feeling,' Palfrey's words were hardly audible; but he looked frankly into Brett's eyes. 'I mean—why haven't you been wholly frank? It's hard. We're taking risks, you know.'

Brett said, quietly: 'I have been as frank as I can, Sap, and I've kept nothing back which will make any difference to you.'

'Oh,' said Palfrey, and smiled bleakly.

When they were outside, he looked back from their taxi. Brett was standing in the doorway of his house, and just behind him stood his white-haired butler, Christian. Brett had a hand raised in farewell; Christian's smile was set. The taxi moved off, with Drusilla waving out of one window and Palfrey the other. As they drew back, finally, Palfrey took Drusilla's hand. His fingers toyed with her wedding ring, but he did not smile. 'What made you think there was something else?' she asked him quietly.

'Instructions all too vague,' said Palfrey. 'It may be that they've a suspicion of something brewing and they don't want us to know, in case we elaborate it before we get there and have a theory in advance. Or it may simply be that the Marquis is afraid we might give something away.'

'It can't be that!'

'I hope not.' Palfrey squeezed her hand. 'I certainly hope not, my sweet. They do say that the Japs are past masters in forcing confessions, don't they? It may be that Brett, on instructions, has kept one vital thing back. However, it can't make any big difference to how we work.'

'I don't think I've ever known you so gloomy,' said Drusilla.

'Ah! I wasn't a married man before.' His face brightened and he slipped an arm about her shoulders. 'I am now, you know!'

They were used to air travel, and no sense of novelty relieved the boredom of the next two days. The aircraft stopped at Gibraltar to refuel, and they spent a night at Alexandria, but did not move outside the airport hotel. They had a different set of passengers on the second part of the journey, and another completely new passenger-load from Alexandria to New Delhi, the longest single flight so far. Beneath them on that route, even the hilly and mountainous country was monotonous after the first half-hour, although they had been stirred by a glimpse of the Nile delta and the fertile land on either side of it.

There was a curious sense of unreality about it all. Palfrey was more restless than Drusilla could remember. It was as if the fact that they were married had given him a greater sense of responsibility, although she found it difficult to believe that was the whole explanation. He was worried by what he thought Brett had kept back, and she wished for once that he did not possess a curious kind of perception, amounting almost to a sixth sense. Without it, however, he would never have been of such service to the Allies, and would certainly never have been sent out on this mission.

Towards evening on the second day, they were flying over dark countryside with occasional stretches of reddish brown rock. Central India was spread out like a relief map in front of them. In the distance were the hazy shapes of hills or mountains, but there was nothing near enough to be impressive, until suddenly the sun glinted on something ahead of them. Drusilla leaned towards the window.

New Delhi looked as if it were a model city built on gigantic lines. Green lawns in front of most of the buildings and flowers in riotous colouring were clearly visible. They could see the airfield and the block of buildings clustered at one side of it, the cylindrical balloon waving from the top of the control-tower.

They could see the old town as clearly as the new: a mass of dark buildings huddled together. It was almost impossible to see the streets criss-crossing it, and the mass was relieved only here and there by the white roofs and pinnacled towers of mosques and temples. There was a touch of the sinister about it, compared with New Delhi, and as they circled to land Palfrey looked at Drusilla with one eyebrow raised.

'We can call this the starting-place,' he said.

'Eight-fifty-nine,' murmured Drusilla. 'Tonight, I wonder?'

'I hope so!'

They landed smoothly. Everything was remarkably normal on the airfield, which had been vastly improved during the war, and stretched for miles in either direction.

A native boy came for their cases and led them to the small hotel attached to the airfield, one used mainly for passengers staying for one night. Everything was modern: there were showers and running water in all the rooms, and the smiling native servants almost fell over one another in their eagerness.

The manager came along as they entered the room, and said cheerfully:

'You've picked a warm night, even for this part of the world!' He was a tall, lean man dressed in formal evening dress, and looked surprisingly cool. 'If you take my advice you'll get into pyjamas and rest in a long-chair until the dinner-bell goes. You'll have half an hour to dress after the first bell. Is there anything you want?'

'No, thanks,' said Palfrey, and then, as the man was half-way to the door, said suddenly: 'Oh, there is one thing. I'm told there's a good tailor here, and I came away at short notice without much in the way of clothes.'

'You want to look Amsa up,' said the manager. 'He's an old rascal, but a first-class tailor provided he's got something to copy from.'

'This suit,' suggested Palfrey.

'Then that's all right. If you're going in the morning, I'll be glad to run you to the old town, and drop you at Amsa's.'

'I was thinking of popping out now,' said Palfrey.

'Oh. I can't get away tonight, I'm afraid, but I'll gladly put a car at your disposal.'

There was nothing remarkable about the brief journey into the old city. It was quaint, picturesque, extremely dirty, and gave off a malodorous stench which, for the first few minutes, made them keep a handkerchief at their noses. They grew used to it, however, by the time the native driver had pulled up outside a tiny shop in a narrow, long and straggling street.

The shop with a window had a facia board with the name '*Amsa the Tailor—Good Class*' printed in gilt letters, and on the window were the words: '*Excellent tailoring for Ladies and Gentlemen, warmly recommended by His Majesty's*

Army, etc. Also British Overseas Airways.'

'Happy thought,' said Palfrey.

The doorway was narrow, and inside the shop it seemed dark, although a single electric light was burning, and several natives were sitting cross-legged, stitching industriously. Partitions on either side of the centre shop were filled with bales of cloth.

As they stood waiting, their heads bent because of the low ceiling, a little old man shuffled from the back of the shop. He bowed low.

'Amsa the tailor, *sahib, memsahib.'* He gave Drusilla a bob rather than a bow. 'At your service night and day.' He gave a broad, toothless smile. 'The *sahib* requires a suit urgently?'

'Most urgently,' said Palfrey, smiling. 'I'm told that you are the best tailor in Delhi, Amsa.'

'Very kind,' said Amsa, beaming. 'Most kind. You will select the cloth, perhaps?' He clapped his hands, and two of the men who had been sewing put down their work and jumped to their feet. 'Linen, perhaps? Good Yorkshire serge? Tweed? Flannel?'

'Linen, I think,' said Palfrey.

Amsa snapped a few words in his own dialect, and as if in a frenzy his men pulled out bale after bale of linen and flung them on to a low bench. Amsa picked up the first, felt it between his thumb and forefinger, and nodded.

'Good,' he said. 'Finest Irish. Only a little we get today, *sahib,* but more is to come, they say. At the price, very cheap —*very* cheap. Belfast.' He beamed.

'How much?' asked Palfrey.

'Seven guineas,' said Amsa, promptly.

'It seems——' began Palfrey.

'Amsa, you old scoundrel, that's three guineas more than you'd charge me!' roared a deep voice, and into the shop strode a heavily-built man whom they had seen at the hotel. 'Don't let him swindle you, Palfrey!' he boomed. 'Skinner told me you were coming, fellow ought to have known better than to let you come alone to this old robber's den!'

Amsa, instead of being outraged, emitted a shrill cackle of laughter.

'Meester Smith so funny,' he said. 'Me no charge more than suit worth. Me charge Meester Smith low price for recommending me. Six guineas, lowest. Best Belfast linen.' He grew earnest. 'The *sahib* a large man. Require much cloth.' He held up a bale, unwound the cloth skilfully and let it fall to the ground at Palfrey's feet. 'You see! Six guineas, very good price, very cheap.'

'I——' began Palfrey.

'Don't you pay a penny more than five,' said Mr. Smith, a shadowy figure whose head was bent but who was smiling broadly. 'If you do you'll spoil the market for the rest of us.'

'No fear spoil market for Meester Smith,' declared Amsa. 'You wish pay only five guineas, *sahib*? Pleased to oblige. This cloth—good, English linen. *Very* fine special quality. Not Belfast.' He looked sadly at the first bale. 'Good, but not so good. Yes?'

'I'll have the Irish linen,' said Palfrey.

Amsa's face was almost split in two.

'*Sahib* is a wise man! Because of his wisdom, no guineas—six pounds.'

'When will the suit be ready?'

'Tomorrow,' said Amsa, promptly.

'As soon as that?'

'Work of the best and the fastest, on the recommendation of Meester Smith,' said Amsa. He bowed low, bobbed again in front of Drusilla, and ushered them to the door.

Daylight was already fading as, at Drusilla's suggestion, they walked along the narrow street, seeing countless shops without windows and an astonishing array of wares. Pottery, exquisite shawls and scarves, silver- and gold-work, imitation jewels, copperwork, woodcarvings which made Palfrey's eyes sparkle, food shops, stores and small warehouses of every description were crammed into the street.

Smith strolled along with them, and offered a belated apology.

'I hope you didn't mind me butting in like that, Palfrey. I know Amsa of old—he's a wily old rascal, and his prices go up by leaps and bounds when he sees a stranger unaccompanied. Never shop in the old town without someone who knows the ropes, that's my tip.'

'It was thoughtful of you to come,' Palfrey assured him.

'Nonsense! Something to do,' said Smith, airily. 'Any plans for tonight?'

'Eat and sleep.'

'Oh, never mind *sleep*. You won't be able to in this heat, anyhow. How about a rubber of bridge?'

'I'm not a great player,' said Palfrey.

'Who is these days?' demanded Smith. 'That's arranged, then. Splendid, splendid! My wife will make a fourth—why don't we eat together, anyhow? Eh?' His voice travelled along the street clearly. 'And afterwards,' he added, lowering his voice to a gigantic whisper, 'what about one or two stories, eh?'

'Stories?' asked Palfrey, startled.

'You know,' said Smith, digging him in the ribs. 'You can't hide away in Delhi, old or new!' He roared with laughter. 'We've seen the papers, you know; surprising how soon they get out here. That reminds me—congratulations! India, not Italy!' He laughed again. 'We'd give a fortune to know what things were *really* like in Europe, Palfrey, that's gospel truth. Mrs. Palfrey won't mind, I'm sure.'

'I think we ought to get an early night,' said Palfrey.

No message came from Orishu; soon after dinner they fell asleep, and it was well into the morning when they woke up.

Palfrey's feeling of disquiet was not quite gone. His suspicions of Smith were much stronger, and the only information he could get, without making the questions too pointed, was that Smith was a commercial traveller who often spent a few nights at the Delhi airport. He stuck to them during most of the day, escorting them to the old city again in the late afternoon—evenings and mornings, he said, were the only times when it was possible to breathe in the narrow, smelly streets. He fended off all persistent efforts to sell them trinkets and knick-knacks, and he was certainly good company.

When they got back, Palfrey looked at Drusilla with one eyebrow raised, and said thoughtfully:

'Careful attention, and we haven't been out of his sight for half an hour all day!'

'We haven't had a message from Orishu, either,' said Drusilla, uneasily. 'Sap, do you think anything's gone wrong?'

'How could it, yet?' asked Palfrey.

'The Marquis warned us that it could. Don't pretend to be satisfied. And darling, I'm thirsty!'

The waiter who answered their bell bowed and smiled, mixed the drinks they ordered, and bowing and smiling like an automaton, backed out of the room.

'Odd fish.' Palfrey picked up his glass. 'I—— Hal-*lo*!'

Drusilla saw him pick up a small piece of folded paper. They stared at it before Palfrey opened it, and Drusilla stepped to his side and read over his shoulder: *Tonight—8.59 —O'u.*

'Well, well!' said Palfrey. 'The time's all right, the little green cotton stitches did the trick! Now we've got to find a way of getting out of this place tonight without Smith following us. If we give him half a chance, he'll be on our heels.'

3 : Orishu

To THEIR surprise, Smith was not in the restaurant at dinner. Nor was his wife, a middle-aged, faded little woman who had said very little the previous evening. A larger aircraft had come in late in the afternoon and was due off again for Calcutta immediately after dinner, and although the service remained good, Palfrey was on edge in case he found it difficult to get away in good time. He had already arranged for a car, saying that he and Drusilla wanted a little jaunt at night to try to get cool. The manager had readily put one, a Buick, at their disposal; Palfrey was to drive.

The moon was almost full when, at half past eight, they left the hotel and walked towards the Buick, which glistened in the moonlight. No one appeared to take any interest in them, and Palfrey drove off the airfield towards the old city, feeling more cheerful than he had done all day.

He found Amsa's shop without difficulty.

The moonlight cast a shadow of the shop over them as they stepped out of the car. One side of the street was brilliantly lit, while the other was in shadow. Palfrey thought he saw a furtive movement a few yards along, and his heart was in his mouth as he raised a hand to knock at the door. Wooden shutters were up at the other shops, but the printing on the glass window of the main shop was just distinguishable.

He had not touched the door before it opened.

'I am glad to see you, *sahib,*' said Amsa the Tailor, in a hushed voice. 'And *memsahib.*' The shop seemed to be in utter darkness behind him, although there was enough light from the street to show his white robes. He stood aside for them to enter and then took Palfrey's arm and led him towards the back of the shop. 'You are a little early, I believe.'

'A few minutes,' Palfrey said.

'So. Wait here, please.'

They found themselves in a narrow, ill-lighted passage. A flight of stairs led up from it, and Amsa hurried along, pulling his robes high. His scraggy feet, in straw sandals, showed as he hurried up the stairs. They stood alone in the semi-darkness, looking at each other.

'I wish we could have met Orishu in less dramatic circumstances,' muttered Palfrey.

'You still don't trust him, do you?'

'I hope Brett's right,' said Palfrey, fervently.

'*Sahib*!' called Amsa, from upstairs.

'I'll lead the way,' said Palfrey.

He kept his right hand in his pocket as he went up, clutching a gun, but he felt foolish when he reached the head of the stairs and, in a better light, saw Amsa beaming at him by an open door.

'He arrives, *sahib,*' said Amsa.

They stepped into the room.

Standing by a chair in one corner of a room which was, surprisingly, furnished in European style, was a man who stood no higher than Palfrey's shoulder. He was dressed immaculately in European clothes, and his round, yellow face was set in a broad smile. There was something unreal about the fellow, just as there had been about the whole journey and their brief stay in India. He shone from his sleek head to his polished shoes, and when he extended his right hand the light shone on diamond rings.

His hand was hot, but his grip was firm.

'I am Orishu! I cannot say how delighted I am to meet such distinguished people,' he said, and bowed to Drusilla. 'Please be seated.' They sat down, and he turned to a cabinet by the wall. 'You will wish for something to drink, I have no doubt; it is the most thirsty of climates. Like that of Japan!' He grinned. 'Ice, Mrs. Palfrey?'

'Please.'

Ice chinked in tall glasses, whisky and water gurgled after it.

'I cannot tell you how greatly I am honoured to be entrusted with your safe keeping,' declared Orishu, his grin broadening. 'From the moment that the honourable nobleman advised me of my new charge I was delighted. The drink is to your liking?' He bowed towards Drusilla.

'Excellent,' she said.

'I am very glad. In my humble way I wish to do everything I can to be of assistance. I beg you, please, not to allow suspicions and distrust to take possession of your minds. I will do nothing—*nothing*—but play the game!'

There was something boyish and also rather touching about his earnestness. Palfrey felt his suspicions fading, and yet at the same time was embarrassed because Orishu had obviously divined them; that suggested that Orishu was a man to be reckoned with. Palfrey saw the little streak of white on the right side of his parting, and noticed that Orishu spread out his hands; the nails of the left were longer than those of the right.

'I am sure you won't,' said Palfrey.

'Please! Forgive me for talking in such a way; my desire is

only to be helpful! We must, of course, leave here now.'

'Leave?' asked Palfrey, startled.

'My dear sir, all the inhabitants of Delhi know that you are here! We can be overheard. Amsa is a good and trustworthy fellow, but there are people who are greatly interested in me and it would not be wise to stay too long. I assure you of safe conduct, you need have no fears. Fear, if we are to experience it, will not come yet.'

'But——' began Palfrey.

'Permit me,' said the Japanese.

He opened the door, and stood bowing low before it. Palfrey, again feeling a little uneasy although admitting that there was no apparent cause for it, stepped past him into the passage. He and Drusilla stood waiting while Orishu closed and locked the door, and then turned towards the stairs.

'Follow, please,' he said. 'A word of warning—you will need to keep your heads low, the passages and the doorways are not made for Europeans!' He bowed again before going steadily down the stairs.

'We can't do anything else,' said Palfrey. 'I——'

Suddenly Orishu slipped.

He had reached the foot of the stairs, and was half-turning towards them. Perhaps that unbalanced him. Whatever the cause, he fell heavily, and Palfrey uttered an exclamation of alarm and hurried down. As he drew near the Japanese he realised that the man was curiously still. Then he saw the little pool of blood on the floor, near Orishu's head.

Drusilla said, sharply: 'Sap, is he——'

'No accident,' said Palfrey, 'but I didn't hear a thing.' He went down on one knee and felt for the man's pulse; even before that, however, he thought Orishu was dead, for the wound was in the middle of his forehead. The ill-lit, smelly passage seemed to be filled with shadowy, threatening creatures. Palfrey did not even raise his voice to summon Amsa; he stood up slowly, staring at Drusilla—and then he heard footsteps.

A man came from the front of the shop and appeared on the threshold. He was dressed like Amsa, but even in the poor light they could see that he was a Japanese. His face was sombre and he looked at Palfrey steadily. Palfrey's hand tightened about his gun, although this man's hands were in sight.

Drusilla drew a step nearer to Palfrey.

'Who . . .' Palfrey began, and then realised the folly of a question, and waited, warily. There was another doorway on the right; if needs be he could make a dash for that, telling

Drusilla to precede him. He thought that he could injure the man before any harm could befall either of them, although he felt uneasy about the silence of the shot which had killed Orishu.

The Japanese spoke at last.

'I am—greatly sorry, Dr. Palfrey. I did not wish that to happen. There was no other way.'

His English was excellent, with only a slight accent. He was a very different man from the fellow on the floor, but *there was a streak of white on the right side of his parting, and he was holding out his hands, not too obviously, but enough for Palfrey to see the difference in the length of the nails.*

'It is a serious matter,' he said, slowly. 'I do not quite know how to deal with it, Doctor. I, of course, am Orishu. This man represented himself to be me, I imagine?'

'He did,' said Palfrey.

'I feared it. He has followed me for some time. It is possible that I am suspected. On the other hand, it may be that he alone believed that I am helping you, and that he wished to make a triumphant report to Tokyo.' The newcomer rubbed his hands together and added softly: 'You will find it hard to believe me, now. I think I can satisfy you about that, in good time. The problem now is what to do with him and what to do with Amsa. I am afraid that Amsa allowed himself to be bribed.'

Palfrey asked: 'Where is he now?'

'I have dealt with him for the time being,' said the Japanese. 'He lives here alone, and there is no great difficulty for the moment. It would appear that we shall have to send him away, but that will be a great nuisance. I——'

He broke off, for there was a light tap at the front door of the shop.

Palfrey saw him start. Then he turned and, without a word, disappeared into the shop itself. Palfrey turned to Drusilla, and said:

'He'd hardly give me a target like that if he weren't genuine.' He stared at the dead man, and his hand strayed to his hair. moist with sweat, and began to coil a few strands about his forefinger. 'I hope——'

A vast whisper, immediately recognisable, floated in from the shop. The door closed, and Palfrey stared towards the door, recognising Smith's voice. He stood quite still until Smith came into sight and grinned at him cheerfully.

'You're a lucky man, Doc! They nearly got you that time!'

'They?' echoed Palfrey.

'Our friends the enemy,' said Smith. 'It wasn't a bad trick, was it, but Orishu here is up to most of them. Anyhow, you needen't worry about it. I'll look after the corpse, and you and Orishu can get on with your chinwag.'

'Ah,' said Palfrey. 'Corpses are your speciality, perhaps?'

Smith grinned.

'I've seen a few in my time.' He put his hand to his pocket, and Palfrey was wary until he drew out a small envelope and held it towards him. 'That'll satisfy you, I think. I do a bit for Brett from time to time, and I was here as an unofficial bodyguard. I hoped there'd be no trouble, Doc, but you can never be sure with these perishing Japs. Can you, Orry?'

Palfrey stared at the man who claimed to be Orishu; he could imagine nothing less suitable than 'Orry' as a nickname, but a faint smile flickered over the yellow man's features, and he appeared to take no umbrage.

'So you are fond of telling me, Mr. Smith. I am much more troubled by how to deal with Amsa.'

'I'll talk to him,' said Smith. 'I think you'll find that this customer paid him a fiver, and that's all he knows. If we frightened him good and proper, we won't have any more trouble with Amsa the Tailor.' He bent down and lifted the dead Japanese. 'I'm on my way to the river,' he said, and with a grin he ducked beneath the doorway. The dead man's head banged against it with a thud.

Palfrey opened the envelope and took out a thin slip of paper. The sight of it cheered him, for on such paper the Marquis of Brett sent messages in code. It was of a peculiar pinkish colour, as thin as Indian rice paper, and it always took a lot of unfolding. Smith had been so confident that he had not troubled to wait until Palfrey read the message. Orishu, if this was indeed the man, looked on expressionlessly.

Palfrey was familiar enough with the code to translate as he read:

Arnold Smith, who will give you this, Sap, is reliable. You will only receive it if there are difficulties in India. Smith knows Orishu.

The expression on Palfrey's face was enough to make Drusilla relax, and even Orishu's set face took on a faint smile.

'It is satisfactory, I hope?'

'Quite,' said Palfrey. 'Where do we talk?'

'Upstairs,' said Orishu.

His English was as good as the man's who had impersonated him, and far less flowery. As he led the way upstairs he told them that the room was rented by Smith, as a convenient rendezvous, but that as Amsa was not reliable it would probably not be used again. He still seemed preoccupied by the problem of what to do with the tailor. He made a visible effort to shake off the preoccupation, and smiled grimly when he saw the drinks.

'You do not, I trust, feel tired?' he said.

'Tired?' echoed Palfrey, and then whistled. 'By George, that's a bad thought! He might——'

'Had he intended to drug you I think he would have used a drug which acts quickly,' said Orishu. 'Please sit down, Mrs. Palfrey—I beg your pardon, Frau von Klieb!'

Drusilla sat down, and Orishu spoke, worriedly.

'I shall have to advise you to stay here for a few more days. Before I let you go nearer to Japan I must find out all I can about Matsu—the dead man. I can explain a little more about him,' he added. 'We worked together in Berlin and have always worked in the same places. I have been transferred to Delhi, because there are hopes that an organisation among the Indians, sympathetic to the Japanese, can be maintained. I am, in fact'—he gave another faint smile—'trying to help such an organisation, and you will be relieved to hear that I find very few adherents! Those who show willingness are dealt with by the excellent Mr. Smith and the authorities. Matsu, as I believe I have said, may have become suspicious of my true loyalties, and been watching so that he could betray me and be rewarded. On the other hand, I must make sure that he was not ordered to watch me by Tokyo.'

'Supposing that's the case, what happens?' asked Palfrey.

'I shall be most reluctant to set foot in Japan,' said Orishu, 'and shall try to find someone else who is not suspected and who will prove an adequate guide. It is to be hoped that I obtain reassuring news, because few of my fellow-countrymen can be trusted—except by the Emperor.' The faint smile played at his lips again. 'Now, of course, your trust has been shaken.'

'It's getting stronger,' Palfrey told him.

'I am glad,' said Orishu, simply. 'Will you be happy enough to stay here for, perhaps, a week?'

'Yes,' said Palfrey, promptly. 'In fact it wouldn't be a bad idea to stay here in any case. We can get used to the heat.'

'Your friend the Russian Andromovitch, is now in Chungking. He will wait there until you arrive.'

Palfrey's eyes brightened. 'Is he well?'

'I imagine so,' said Orishu, dryly. 'Another thing is of equal interest. When in Japan, I was able to get in touch with three of my friends. All of them are trustworthy, all of them will help you. I have given their names and addresses to Andromovitch. You had better have them also—I will write them down for you before you go, and thus there will be less risk of their being lost. And that is all.' Orishu sounded troubled, still. 'I wish I could have sent you on your journey immediately, but I assure you that it would be unsafe. Will you stay at the airport hotel?'

'I think so,' said Palfrey.

'It will serve excellently. As the truth has now been divulged, I will send word to you through Mr. Smith, who will stay in New Delhi until you have left. Understand,' added Orishu, earnestly, 'I do not for one moment think that you and Mrs. Palfrey are under suspicion. I think that Matsu knew that I had an assignation, and determined to keep it for me. Unless, perhaps, he gave you to understand differently.'

'He made it clear that he knew who we were, and that he was supposed to be working for the Marquis,' said Palfrey.

Orishu's hands clenched, and his eyes opened wide for the first time.

'He knew as much as that! I confess, Doctor, I am even more alarmed. It could not have been worse,' he added, and repeated with obvious disquiet: 'No, it could not have been worse.'

4 : Mr. Ho Sun

'ORISHU may be a clever fellow,' said Palfrey, lazily, 'but he isn't always right. To wit—it could have been much worse. Remember how he scared us that night?'

'I do,' said Drusilla, feelingly.

'Since when we have had a peaceful week.' Palfrey was lying on his back in a long-chair, with the fan stirring his fair hair. 'And I, for one, asked for nothing better. That trip into the hills was glorious! Enjoyed yourself, darling?'

'It's been grand!'

'Unanimous,' said Palfrey. 'However, it can't go on like this. If we don't get news from Orishu pretty soon I shall try to contact the Marquis. He'll be expecting word from us, I fancy.'

'Orishu's probably sent it to him.'

'I didn't think of that. Hallo, I hear a gangantuan bellow.' He straightened up. 'There's one thing, you always know when Smith is around and about; he must be the most conspicuous fellow in Delhi. Yes, I mean you,' he added, as Smith opened the door and caught the last sentence.

Smith chortled. 'Oh, everyone knows me! Or they think they do! Catch!'

He was carrying a parcel under his arm, and he tossed it gently through the air. Palfrey caught it neatly; it contained something soft.

'A present from Amsa the Taylor,' said Smith. 'Your suit old boy, and I made him make you a present of it as a kind of peace-offering. May I help myself to a drink? I see you've become civilised,' he added, 'and keep the stuff in your room.' He poured out a generous peg of whisky and added a splash of soda.

'What have you done to Amsa?' Drusilla asked.

'Put the fear of death into him,' Smith grinned. 'I don't think he knew Matsu was up to serious mischief—I think he thought it was a confidence trick of some kind, and that he would get a big rake-off. I also think he will know better than to try the funny stuff again, although I don't intend to use the room much.'

'I see,' Palfrey remarked.

Smith looked at him curiously.

'You're a funny customer,' he said. 'I'd heard so much about you that I expected a—that is, someone very different,' he amended, in some confusion.

Palfrey smiled.

'You expected a man with a presence. That only shows you how foolish it is to believe all you hear. Have you heard anything from Orishu?'

'Oh yes,' said Smith. 'I knew there was something I had to tell you!' He laughed when Drusilla sat up hastily and Palfrey stiffened. 'I'm damned if I would be so anxious to be on my way to the Land of the Rising Sun! It's all clear. Chungking next stop. A long-distance transport bus will drop in for you this evening, and you'll have dinner in the air.'

. . . . . .

The transport carried mostly cargo, and there were only two other passengers, both Chinese. They wore European clothes and spoke excellent English, but had little to say on the early part of the journey. The crew consisted of the commander and four assistants, laconic yet genial men who took the flight as a matter of course. The aircraft was fitted out comfortably, having bunks as well as easy chairs, and soon after they took off Palfrey dozed and Drusilla slept.

When they woke up the sun was streaming into the cabin and the steward was walking along the gangway with a tea-tray.

Palfrey sat up and smoothed his hair.

'Not bad service.' He smiled at the steward. 'Thanks. How are we going?'

'Well on time and course, sir.'

They peered out, and saw the rugged peaks of the mountains of North Burma seeming, in their majestic grandeur, completely remote from men and machines.

Palfrey poured out tea.

'Quite a tour,' he said.

'Yes.' Drusilla was still peering out. 'It's so hard to realise that there are men fighting down there.'

It was almost impossible to realise it. From the air the lower slopes of the foothills looked like a smooth, bubbly green mass; vegetation spread unchecked over vast stretches of the country. It was impossible to see roads or clearings, and, with the mountains behind them, there seemed nothing but the jungle on all sides.

The first officer came out of the pilot's cabin, as immaculate as if he were on board a luxury liner.

'The captain's compliments,' he said, 'and we'll be in Rangoon in an hour's time. We're only a few minutes late. Breakfast on board or in Rangoon, as you prefer.'

'On board, I think,' said Palfrey.

'How long will we be at Rangoon?' asked Drusilla.

'Only about an hour,' said the first officer.

The Chinese, still keeping themselves to themselves, decided to have breakfast on the airfield, and Drusilla and Palfrey enjoyed crisply fried bacon and eggs, excellent coffee, and rolls which seemed new. As the machine flew south-west the scene beneath them changed. Now they were flying over great clearings, and the pilot, coming out of his cabin, chatted pleasantly.

He went back to his cabin to put the aircraft down. Not until they were out on the great airfield did he say that Rangoon was always a tricky place on which to land—the airfield was on a slope, and not all the efforts of Japanese, Americans and English had succeeded in making it level.

They were there for exactly one hour, and had time only to stretch their legs, no opportunity at all to go into Rangoon itself. They took on one more passenger, a little Burmese with a bright blue robe, a turban and—incongruously—a furled umbrella. He bowed politely to them as he passed to his seat, and then kept in the background, in exactly the same way as the Chinese had done. Palfrey felt a little uncomfortable, wondering if he should make an advance.

As they became airborne again he strolled along the cabin, seeing the Chinese looking over the mighty harbour crammed with shipping of every conceivable kind.

'China is beginning its industrial revolution,' said one of the passengers. 'It is like a new birth!' He fell silent, and Palfrey wondered what was passing through his mind.

Villages, small towns, large towns and great tracts of country which looked unravaged by war passed unendingly beneath them. The aircraft seemed to fly on a straight course, and the pilot and first officer kept coming into the cabin for a chat. The pilot was a tall, lean man with a wide smile and a pair of warm grey eyes—a comforting type of fellow, eager to be friendly.

'How far to go?' Palfrey asked when he came out towards evening.

'Not long,' he said, regarding Palfrey thoughtfully.

Palfrey sensed some sort of change in his attitude—it was a little more formal and polite. He was puzzled, but said nothing to Drusilla, who would declare him a worse Jonah than ever. Yet when the first officer came out next the same change appeared to have come over him—he stopped for a few words, but his gaiety seemed forced, and he searched Palfrey's face more carefully than he had done before.

'What the devil *is* the matter?' wondered Palfrey, testily.

There seemed no difference in the attitude of the crew towards the Chinese, but he was quite sure that they had changed towards him and Drusilla. He leaned back, with his eyes half-closed, and then saw the door between the two cabins open slowly. He did not sit up. The door opened a few inches, and he caught a glimpse of a man's face—it was one of the junior members of the crew, and he held something in his hand. He looked down at it, then at Palfrey; then he closed the door.

'Stay here, sweet,' said Palfrey.

He rested a hand on Drusilla's knee and went forward. He had been in the pilot's cabin twice, each time by invitation. Now he opened the door and saw the backs of three men, the pilot at the controls, the wireless operator at a small bench, the second officer poring over a photograph. Palfrey stood on tiptoe, to try to see the photograph. It was of a man, and if the first officer would move an inch or two to one side he would see who it was.

A voice from behind him made him jump.

'Excuse *me,* sir!'

It was the steward, who had come out of his cabin in the tail of the aircraft. The three officers looked round quickly. If there had been any doubt before, there was now none at all that they they regarded him with suspicion. The pilot was not smiling as he said abruptly:

'Return to the cabin, please!'

'Oh.' Palfrey raised puzzled brows. 'No longer friends?'

'Passengers are not allowed forward,' said the pilot.

He made an unexpected movement, putting his right hand to his pocket—the kind of gesture which Palfrey always associated with a man who carried a gun—and kept it there. The expression on his face was wary and hostile The steward laid a hand on Palfrey's arm, so he turned back and rejoined Drusilla.

She looked puzzled as she asked: 'What has happened?'

'I don't quite know,' said Palfrey, 'but they've a bee in their bonnet about me. Curious business.' He tried to be flippant, but was not successful. He thought that the Chinese were looking at him curiously, and they showed no further inclination to talk. The Burmese was asleep, his head nodding, his hands clasped to the handle of his umbrella.

A long way off Palfrey could see the sprawling mass of a large town. The first officer, quite formal now, walked up the passage.

'We are about to land,' he said. 'Get ready, please.'

He stood by, watching Palfrey closely; no such precaution had been taken at Rangoon or anywhere else *en route.*

The airfield looked like any other—a little collection of buildings about the control-tower, mechanics waiting to get to work on the machine as soon as the engines stopped, a small party of men waiting by the side of several private cars, two jeeps, and a string of empty lorries to take the cargo.

'Well, here we go,' Palfrey said, with forced heartiness.

They touched down.

In bright sunshine which seemed to strike back off the sun-baked earth Palfrey stepped on to Chinese soil for the first time in his life, and helped Drusilla down.

He stood a few feet away from the aircraft, blinking in the dazzling light. As his eyes grew accustomed to it, however, he could see more clearly.

There were Chinese in uniform—khaki shirts and shorts—with guns slung over their shoulders. Two or three British and American officers were also there, and some Chinese and American military policemen. The first officer hurried past

Palfrey towards a Chinese captain who spoke in an undertone, and then looked round at Palfrey.

'My sweet, something's gone seriously wrong,' murmured Palfrey. 'I——'

The captain came forward. He was a young, loose-limbed individual, his yellow face expressionless. Two of his men kept close behind him. He stopped in front of Palfrey.

'You are Dr. Palfrey—is that right?' He had a strong American accent.

'Yes,' said Palfrey.

'You are under arrest,' said the Chinese, laconically.

As they walked across the airfield towards one of the cars, Palfrey was too incensed to speak. The captain led the way, two men followed with Palfrey and Drusilla, and two others brought up the rear. A curious crowd had collected, and Palfrey saw a man standing with a camera in front of him. He turned hastily, but not until he had heard the click of the camera. He coloured. Drusilla, looking towards the man, was taken full-face. She averted her head hastily, and her cheeks flamed.

They were led to a small building by the side of the airfield. The captain led the way into a long, low-ceilinged office, where there were maps spread over all the walls and on several trestle tables. A colonel looked up from the only desk.

'Dr. and Mrs. Palfrey, sir,' the captain announced.

'Is that so?' said the colonel.

He was a middle-aged man, with deep yellow skin, grey hair and a pair of curiously light blue eyes, and his English was good. He looked extremely sceptical.

'So it's Dr. and Mrs. Palfrey, is it?' The thought seemed to amuse him. 'Have you ever heard of Colonel Baron Karl von Klieb, Doctor?'

'I . . .' began Palfrey.

Then understanding dawned. Drusilla, looking towards him, saw the expression of annoyance fade and a broad smile replace it. Even the colonel looked taken aback. Palfrey's smile became a set grin, until suddenly he drew his heels together and clicked them smartly, then shot out his right hand and barked:

'Heil Hitler!'

'So that is how you feel about it, is it?' The colonel regarded him with distaste. 'Your journey's over, von Klieb.'

'I am honoured,' said Palfrey.

'But——' began Drusilla.

'It is all right, my beautiful.' Palfrey turned to her and smiled. 'The amazing Chinese have discovered our guilty secret!'

They were taken to a much smaller room, furnished only with two chairs and a small table, and the door was locked on them. The room was hot. There was only one window, and that was closed and too high in the ceiling for Palfrey to reach it. He was mopping his forehead when the door opened and the captain came in again, with two men and a woman in uniform. She led Drusilla through another door, while Palfrey submitted himself to being searched with a fatuous smile on his face. The one thing he hoped was that he would not be kept away from Drusilla.

She returned after ten minutes, and the others withdrew.

'Well!' she exclaimed. 'Of all the——!'

'My sweet, it's quite obvious what's been arranged,' said Palfrey. 'I wish I hadn't talked so freely, someone might have overheard me. The colonel and his men obviously don't know the truth.'

'I could have smacked that pert young woman's face,' said Drusilla. 'There isn't much she doesn't know about searching a suspect! You really think the Marquis arranged this?'

'There isn't any doubt.' Palfrey grinned. 'We've been arrested as the Baron and Baroness von Klieb, my sweet—travelling as the Palfreys. There isn't much doubt that someone who saw the arrest will carry news of it to Tokyo. In an hour or two we'll "escape"—whether they'll just let us go or whether there will really be a prison break to make the whole thing seem more realistic is a moot point.' He lit a cigarette. 'Sit down, my sweet! It's exactly what we wanted. I wish they'd bring us a drink,' he added, plaintively; 'this isn't how we treat our prisoners-of-war!'

'Is it all necessary?' Drusilla asked, obviously still put out.

'It's a good idea and I've no complaint to make,' said Palfrey. 'I was a mutt not to have realised what they were up to on the aircraft. Obviously they had a radio message.'

They were held in the little room for nearly an hour. Then the captain came for them, and led them outside, where a gleaming Packard was waiting. Three motor-cyclists were astride their machines near the car. The crowd had grown, and there were several camera-men among it. Most of the people were natives, but a few Europeans pressed towards the car, only kept away by military police.

'I hope we aren't going to die of thirst,' Palfrey complained on a note of acerbity.

'You will be given food and drink,' said the young captain, formally.

In different circumstances, Palfrey would have been fascinated during the short drive through the outskirts of Chungking. The masses of wooden buildings, many of them new and some looking as if they would fall to pieces at the slightest puff of wind, were close together on either side of the wide, well-made road. By-streets led off the main road at frequent intervals. As they drew nearer the heart of the city the shops were more pretentious and the buildings, although mostly of wood, looked more substantial.

Soon they saw tall, concrete buildings. Here and there were familiar-looking bombed-out buildings, steel girders twisted and broken and blackened by fire, but there was surprisingly little evidence of bomb damage; it was some time since Chungking had been heavily raided.

They went through the centre of the town and, in the outskirts, drew up outside a concrete building over which the Stars and Stripes and the Union Jack flew side by side with the flag of Free China. There were sentries—English and Chinese—posted outside the main doors. The car and motorcyclists pulled up, and the captain said:

'Do not try to escape, please.'

Palfrey made himself look solemn as he walked from the car to the building. Drusilla was sufficiently agitated to look troubled without having to try.

They were led along interminable passages until at last the captain opened a door and stood aside for them to enter. They were left in a cool, low-ceilinged room which had ample window space. It was pleasantly furnished with wicker long-chairs and wicker tables. Outside there was a gaily coloured awning to shade the room. They were alone for a few minutes before a Chinese 'boy', wearing a white coat and white shorts, entered with a tray, glasses, lager and water, on the top of which ice floated enticingly.

'This is more like it,' Palfrey teased. 'Drink up and cheer up, my sweet. We're not going to face an execution squad.'

'Good afternoon, Doctor,' said a man from the door.

Palfrey turned—and the door closed behind Orishu, dressed now in European clothes. There was the familiar, rather enigmatic smile on his round face, and he looked sleek. It was like seeing an old friend.

'Hallo, hallo!' said Palfrey cheerfully. 'You've come to put us out of our misery, I hope.'

'I trust you will forgive this little trick,' said Orishu. 'It was not until a spy from Tokyo boarded your aircraft at

Rangoon that it was decided to do this.' His smile broadened. 'You did not know there was a spy, of course?'

'The Chinese?' asked Palfrey, startled.

'No, Doctor—the Burmese gentleman with his umbrella! He is foolish enough to think that he escaped notice, and of course he will hasten to report your arrest!' Orishu rubbed his hands together softly. 'It was fortunate, and gave us an excellent opportunity to hoodwink Tokyo completely. Chungking, of course, teems with Japanese agents, some of them renegade Chinese, most of them half-castes. That will interest you less than what is going to happen now,' he added.

'You're quite right,' said Palfrey.

'We will leave you here, in great comfort, until tomorrow night,' said Orishu. 'After dark, you will be allowed to escape. You need have no fear—the ammunition used to fire at you will be blank, and you will be in no danger. I shall not come again, so I will go into some details now. You will be taken out of the side door, and a little way along the street, rickshaw boys will be waiting to take you away. You may trust them implicitly—as Baron von Klieb and his wife. You understand?'

'Yes,' Palfrey nodded.

'They will take you to the residence of Wu Ling, a Chinese merchant who, like me, works both for Tokyo and for the Allies. When you are there, I shall visit you and we will make plans for your safe transport to Japan. Meanwhile, please, sleep peacefully—you are in no danger, although you must be careful what you do. Until the last moment, the officials here will not know the truth.'

'Make sure about that blank ammunition!' said Palfrey.

That evening and the following day passed uneventfully. Most of the time Palfrey studied the dossier on von Klieb and Drusilla made a point of familiarising herself with it. They had ample food, highly seasoned but otherwise just as they might have received at home, and iced drinks were always available. Their bedroom opened out from the main room and but for the fact that they could not go outside, it was a pleasant, restful spell.

They finished dinner in silence. It was nine o'clock before the boy came in to take the trolley away, and Palfrey looked anxiously towards the door, hoping that someone else would come in. No one did. The boy bowed again and pushed the trolley out, and it was not until half an hour after he had gone that Palfrey, looking towards the door, saw the handle turning. 'Zero hour,' he said, softly.

The door opened. A tall Chinese stood on the threshold, dressed in European clothes. He smiled and beckoned them. They picked up their bags and went to the door.

It was all disappointingly normal.

Obviously the staff had been warned, for there were no alarms, and in a few minutes they reached an open door which led to the street. They did not expect any shooting now; the arrangements were perfect. The first cause of disquiet came when Palfrey saw a car standing a few yards along the street. The Chinese led them towards it.

'But——' began Palfrey.

'Silent, please!'

Suddenly the quiet was broken by a high-pitched American voice. A searchlight from the building was switched on, and it blinded Palfrey. The Chinese bundled him into the car, and he heard the engine start up. Drusilla was pushed inside roughly after him—and all the time the whole street was bathed in that bright, unnatural light. The car moved forward slowly, the Chinese running alongside, obviously about to jump on board. Then Palfrey heard a machine-gun.

There was no mistaking the *bup-bup-bup,* nor the sharp noise as bullets hit the back of the car. The Chinese gasped suddenly, and dropped away. Palfrey looked out of the window and saw him sprawling, face downwards, in the road. He also saw two motor-cyclists start off in the wake of the car, which gathered speed and swung round a corner. As they disappeared in the light of the searchlight, he saw men crouching near a little house—and he saw a speckle of light from the guns they held. A crash followed, and the last thing he saw at that corner was one of the motor-cyclists sliding along the road with his machine on top of him.

Drusilla had not spoken, but the pressure of her hand on his was very tight.

The road along which they went was a broad one, gaily lighted with lanterns on either side, open shops thronged with people, and sidewalks equally crowded. People turned and stared towards the car, their startled faces disappearing swiftly. Then it turned another corner, into a dark street. It travelled even faster, its engine roaring.

'What—what has happened?' asked Drusilla at last.

Palfrey sounded remarkably casual.

'I don't know. But I rather think we've been rescued by the wrong people. I mean, this isn't a rickshaw is it?'

There was nothing they could do.

Sounds of pursuit had faded. Palfrey could not bring himself to believe this great car could go unhindered through the streets, but the driver went round corner after corner without mishap, and they were obviously approaching the outskirts of the city. They crossed a bridge, and could see the lights on either side reflected on the water. They had reached another built-up part of the town.

Then the car slid to a standstill.

The lights were switched off, and Palfrey started as the door opened. He could not see the man who stood there, but heard a soft voice: '*Quickly please!*'

'Sap——' began Drusilla.

He nudged her, and spoke in German.

'It is all right, Hilde!'

She realised her slip, and did not speak again while Palfrey climbed out of the car and helped her down. They grew more accustomed to the darkness, and could see the figure of the man who had opened the door. Other figures and some square shapes were a little away ahead of them.

'*Quickly!*' repeated the Chinese.

In front of them were rickshaws; Palfrey identified them now, and for the first time he wondered whether after all he had made a mistake. Even if he had not, obedience was the only wise course. If they had been the von Klieb's they would be only too glad to be rescued by anyone—but there were bleak thoughts in his mind as he allowed himself to be hustled forward.

A man shone a torch.

'One here—one there!' said their guide, in English.

Drusilla climbed into a rickshaw; it was not easy, but the man helped her. Palfrey wished they could have travelled together, but got into the chair in front. In a moment it was lifted and the rickshaw boy began to run. The motion was surprisingly smooth and easy.

Palfrey felt keenly aware of being on his own.

Drusilla's rickshaw was behind him, and he could not see out. Curtains were drawn round the rickshaw, obviously for that purpose. He could just hear the padding of the boy's feet, but that was all.

The journey was a long one, but Palfrey was taken by surprise when it stopped. He sat up with a jerk as the curtains were pulled aside, and the little door opened.

'Quickly, please,' said the man who had spoken before.

It was still dark, but Palfrey could see the outline of the

other rickshaw and saw Drusilla climbing out. As he joined her he noted that there were three men besides the rickshaw boys, and that several more of the little carriages stood in the road. He saw a high wall surrounding a house, only the roof of which was visible; a dark, flat shape against the star-lit sky. There were other houses nearby, but he saw none of them clearly as a door in the wall was opened and he was hustled through.

The door clanged behind them; a man stood on guard by it.

'Quickly, please,' said their escort.

He led the way towards the house, from the front door of which a light was glowing. There were lights at the windows, too, coming from behind bead curtains. A verandah appeared to run the whole breadth of the house, and was approached by a short flight of wooden steps. The front door was open. They were led into a square hall, which was furnished plainly with bamboo furniture and richly-coloured carpets. Two great lacquered vases stood on either side of a wide doorway, which opened into a large room. Their guide remained outside it.

'Welcome, Baron von Klieb.' The man who spoke spread out his plump hand and bowed to Drusilla. He was tall and stout, a Chinese dressed in quasi-European clothes. 'You will forgive me, I know little German. I speak in English, which you also speak well.'

'Excellently,' said Palfrey.

There was a barely perceptible change in his manner. He held himself upright, without the faintest suggestion of a stoop. He looked squarely into the Chinaman's face, and there was a haughty, even a supercilious expression in his eyes, which took on a glassy look. He bowed stiffly from the waist.

'Your most humble servant, Colonel—Ho Sun.'

The man smiled again, and seemed delighted with himself. 'A foolish word was allowed to slip from the mouth of a garrulous servant of an acquaintance of mine. I knew that you were to be rescued from your plight. I decided, Baron, to make sure you were rescued by someone who could be relied on not to return you, for a reward, to the Allied authorities. There are so few who can be trusted,' he added, shaking his head sadly, 'so very few.'

His English was excellent, and he had only a slight accent. He wore a white linen coat and long, wide trousers, which hid his feet. His thin hair was brushed smoothly across his head, and his little slanting eyes twinkled. There was something likeable about the man, whom Palfrey felt sure was a great rogue.

'I knew nothing of any rescue attempt,' he said stiffly. 'I was most pleased, as you can imagine.'

'I was told that you had been arrested at the airfield, and my heart bled for you. Here, I told myself, was an opportunity of repaying some of the debt which I owe your country.' His smile was bright, and his voice smooth. 'So, here you are—the Baron von Klieb and his wife, safe and, I trust, happy!'

'I do not understand you.' Palfrey's voice was chilly.

'I will explain a little further,' said Ho Sun. 'I am fully aware, Baron von Klieb, that you hope to get to Japan, where you will find friends. I do not know,' he added, very gently, 'whether you are wise to wish to go to Japan. However—do I understand that you wish to continue your journey?'

'Is there an alternative?'

Ho Sun waved his hands.

'There are several! You could be returned to the Allied authorities, who doubtless are extremely angry at having been outwitted! Or you could be exchanged for a friend of mine who is in the hands of of a well-known merchant who is at once my friend and rival—one Wu Ling.' He paused, and the gaze of his narrowed and thoughtful eyes did not move from Palfrey's face.

Palfrey repeated uncertainly: 'Wu Ling?'

'You do not know him?'

'I know no one in Chungking.'

'The other alternative,' Ho Sun closed his eyes and pressed the tips of his fingers together, 'is for you to stay in China. It is a large country. Much of it is unexplored. There are hiding-places, where you and your friends can live in comfort and in peace—a little colony, where the new Reich can be born. The cost, for such a wealthy man as you, Baron, is trifling. For one thousand pounds in English money, or five thousand American dollars, I will obtain safe transport for you.'

'I go to Tokyo!' snapped Palfrey.

'That is a *much* more difficult matter,' said Ho Sun, gently. 'Remember that there is the sea to cross. Either a boat, or else an aeroplane is needed, and both are very expensive. I have shipped Germans to Japan,' he added, pressing the tips of his fingers together again, 'and I endeavour to make the expense as low as possible, but it could not be arranged for less than two thousand pounds—or ten thousand dollars. For a wealthy man such as you, of course——'

'You are ill-informed. I have only a little money.'

'Indeed,' said Ho Sun. 'Indeed. But you have jewels, Baron?'

'They are well hidden.' Palfrey paused. 'Herr Ho Sun, I regret the cost of going to Japan is so high. If it is necessary, however, I will pay it.'

'Oh, it is necessary,' said Ho Sun. 'You are a remarkable man, Baron—but then, so are all your countrymen! You do not realise, perhaps, that if you were dealing with a man less honest than I, you would not have any jewels left with which to deal with—er—your contacts in Japan.'

Palfrey flushed. 'You use threats, Herr Ho Sun?'

'My dear Baron, I beg you not to think so harshly of me. I simply marvel at your honesty. Come! I will value the jewels which you have brought with you.'

He held out his hand.

Palfrey hesitated only a few seconds before he stood up, took his brief-case, and pressed at the sides of the handle. They seemed to be of solid leather, but the ends came away from the case and two lengths of leather tubing were in his hand. He pulled at a stuffing of cotton wool at either end, and let the contents roll out on to the desk. The bright light shone on them and they gave off brilliant shoots of fire—all were small but exquisite diamonds. There were a dozen in each of the handles.

'A *most* ingenious idea!' Ho Sun picked up one diamond, and beamed at Palfrey. 'You call yourself a poor man, Baron!'

'Those diamonds belong to the Reich!'

'Then I call you an honest man,' said Ho Sun. 'One of these is worth much in English or American currency. One, I think, will be enough to take you to Japan. Hide the others, Baron, lest I become too eager!'

'It is necessary for me to trust you,' said Palfrey.

He hoped that he was not acting the part of an unimaginative Prussian too exaggeratedly. Ho Sun had probably dealt with others of the kind, would be quick to judge whether he were genuine or not. It was impossible to guess what was going on behind those smiling eyes, although the man seemed to handle the single diamond which he retained with loving fingers He held it up again, and the fire seemed to spring from it.

Palfrey replaced the others.

'I advise you to be extremely careful with that precious briefcase,' said Ho Sun. 'Not all men are as honest as I!' His smile broadened. 'Now, Baron—I ask you once again. Do you still wish to go to Tokyo?'

'That is my destination.'

'So much trouble.' Ho Sun heaved a sigh. 'I will, then, arrange for transport to Japan. You understand that there are dangers and that some delay may be necessary.'

'Not, I trust, excessive,' said Palfrey.

'No more than it must be for your safety,' said Ho Sun. 'You will not, of course, stay here. Tonight you will remain, but tomorrow you will leave Chungking. I will arrange it. You will go to the foothills, to a village where you will be quite safe with good friends of mine. Do not, I beg of you, display your wealth to them, or they may become bad friends of yours!'

'You wish to alarm me!' snapped Palfrey.

'I do not, Baron, I wish to warn you! These people, however, will feed and guard you. In a few days you will be told whether you are going to Japan by sea or air. If by air, then it will be much simpler, but there is the danger of being shot down by both the Americans and the Japanese. By sea, I think, you have more chance. Have you a preference?'

'The safer way is better, Herr Ho Sun.'

'I congratulate you on your wisdom! But if I can obtain a fast aeroplane, I will do so. Meanwhile rest in peace, Herr Baron! You will be in no danger here!' He pushed his chair back and stood up, then clapped his hands.

A servant entered, clad in a long robe, his hands pushed inside the wide sleeves. Ho Sun spoke in Chinese. The servant bowed, spreading his hands in front of him, and then turned to the door. Palfrey and Drusilla followed him, with Ho Sun's voice ringing in their ears.

'I trust you will sleep well, Baron!'

5 : The Village in the Foothills

THE next day was very much like the one before. No one came to see them except the boy who served their food, and he did not open his mouth. All they could see from the window was a bare yard. Two men were standing by a gate, which was just in view and both carried rifles. The house seemed to be on the outskirts of the city and away from a main road, for there was little sound of traffic. No one came in through the gate, and the only sound they heard inside the house was the occasional ringing of a bell.

'I suppose the police and military are searching the city

high and low,' said Palfrey. 'When the colonel knows the truth and knows also that Orishu was outwitted, he'll be the sorest soldier in Chungking! The Americans and the Chinese won't be idle,' he added. Then, with a grimace: 'What are we in for, I wonder?'

He took the precaution of removing the jewels from their hiding place, and put them, wrapped in a handkerchief, in his pocket.

For that day, at least, they were in for nothing. Even when Ho Sun came into their room, after dark, he had little to say and was intent on getting them out of the house. Rickshaw boys were waiting outside, but there were no incidents. They were carried a mile or two outside the town, and then transferred from the rickshaws to an open lorry already crowded with men and women, mostly in European clothes.

For the most part, they were a silent crowd; Palfrey thought they were frightened. The lorry jogged along at a fair pace, over a good road, but after an hour—when he judged that they were fifteen miles away from the starting-point—it left the road and lurched and bumped over uneven ground. A woman began to wail. A harsh voice bade her stop, and they went on in silence. Suddenly the lorry pulled up. Men came from a low-walled building and hustled them all off the lorry. Only Palfrey and Drusilla were left near it; the others were herded through a gate in the wall, and the gate closed with a clang.

A man came up to them, and he had a familiar request.

'Quickly, please!' he said.

They stumbled after him over the stony, uneven ground. They skirted the wall and now and again, from a rise, they could see the big buildings which it surrounded.

Then a low-pitched voice came out of the darkness, speaking Chinese. Their guide answered. A torch was shone on his face, and then on to Palfrey and Drusilla. Apparently the inspection was satisfactory, for the guard grunted and let them pass; the barrel of his rifle was pointing towards the sky. They continued to climb up a path which twisted and turned through an expanse of shrub-covered rock.

Suddenly they came upon a clearing.

There was a small fire and about it a large crowd of men was squatting. There was an appetising smell of stewing meat. Horses were stamping near by. Their guide went straight to the fire, and in its red light they saw a man get to his feet. When he was standing at his full height he proved to be a veritable giant. He had a bandolier across his chest and a rifle slung over his shoulder. He wore a steel helmet of American pattern, and they could see his long, drooping moustache.

After a small interchange of words with their guide, he spat towards the fire, then put his hand under Palfrey's chin and stared into his eyes. What he saw seemed to satisfy him.

The wraith-like figure of their guide appeared again.

'Quickly, please!'

Palfrey felt on the point of laughing—but that mood passed as he was led away by the guide and two other men, while Drusilla stayed by the fire. He tried to turn back, but the men hustled him on. He heard an outburst of laughter, and a cold shiver ran up and down his spine. In that moment he could have wrenched himself from his escort and rushed back, but he forced himself to go on. The cold shivers came one after the other. He felt utterly desperate, and yet he let them drag him on until they reached what appeared to be the entrance to a small cave.

'Quickly, please!'

'Haven't you *any* other words?' demanded Palfrey absurdly. 'I——'

He stopped himself, realising that in his alarm he was speaking in English when he should have used German. His heart beat uncomfortably fast, but no one appeared to have noticed anything. He could no longer hear the laughing from the party by the fire, but he felt something thrust towards him. His fingers clutched cloth. Then a burning brand from a fire he had not noticed, for it was behind some trees, was brought to the cave. In its light he saw his guide gesticulating wildly, and one of the other men pulled at his coat. He realised what they wanted, and began to undress, to the accompaniment of several urgent reminders from his guide.

He retained his underwear and slipped the handkerchief containing the jewels into the front of his singlet. The man did not seem to notice, and helped him on with the gown. It smelt badly, and he felt unbearably hot as it dropped from his shoulders and he was muffled up under his chin. Then one of the men pushed his head forward and the other began to wind a scarf about his head, turban fashion.

Soon he was with the party by the fire again; they were no longer sitting idly, but eating voraciously from a gigantic stew-pot. In the red firelight he searched the faces of the people about him, but saw no sign of Drusilla.

He asked in German: 'Where is my wife?'

No one heeded him. They went on eating, the only noise

came from clicking teeth and busy lips. He moved away, and no one followed him, not even his guide, who had found a way to the stew-pot and was interested in nothing else. He was working himself up into a frenzy when, suddenly, two people came from a path nearby. They were Chinese, dressed in long robes, and shuffling forward. Only the fact that they held hands made Palfrey took at them closely; then he saw that one was leading the other.

His voice cracked. ' 'Silla!'

'Karl!' exclaimed Drusilla.

'Great Scott!' thought Palfrey. 'She's cooler than I!' He hurried forward. In the poor light he could not recognise her face. Her head was covered with a turban placed at a rakish angle. He thought her robe was whiter than his, and as he searched her face he saw her smile.

They were left alone, a few yards from the edge of the scrum round the stew-pot. Palfrey was perspiring freely as he gripped her hand.

The dinner-party broke up, and their guide came hurrying for them, crying his accustomed words. They were hustled a little way down the hillside, and suddenly found themselves surrounded by mounted men—the mounts were mules. For a wild moment Palfrey thought that he and Drusilla would have to ride them, but a cart rumbled towards them, drawn by a team of three of the beasts. They were helped aboard and sat on a rough wooden bench at the side of the cart. Two or three men joined them, and then with riders on either side they rode into the night.

At dawn next morning the caravan stopped in a clearing in a range of hills. Their guide, whom they saw in daylight for the first time, was a little wizened man with an anxious expression. He led them to a spot beneath a large rock, where long grass had been gathered and put down to make a bed. His concern for them was touching, and when he had gone Palfrey said:

'I think I shall take to "Quickly".'

'He's a dear,' agreed Drusilla. 'I—Sap! What did you do with the diamonds?'

'They're all right,' said Palfrey. 'It's a queer business, my sweet. One moment I forget that our native tongue is German, the next moment you do, and I don't suppose there's one among the bunch of brigands here who can tell the difference between English and German. We'd better stick to

German, though; it will be good practice for later on.'

They travelled on after dark, rested the next day, and started off again on the third night. They stopped frequently, for obviously there was a system of patrols, thrown out well ahead of the main party, and when one of these patrols came riding back they stopped in the nearest clearing, sometimes for a few minutes, sometimes for more than an hour. The men seemed cheerful and light-hearted, cautious but not afraid. Now that they had been seen by daylight, Palfrey discovered that only half of them were Chinese; some, he felt sure, were Asiatic Russians, and there were even a few Europeans among them.

They ate rice, hard biscuits, cold meat and eggs—which they viewed with a suspicion which was never justified—and had only water to drink. It was never really cold. Each night Quickly prepared a bed of grass, and then left them to themselves. They felt assured now; all the nervousness of the first few hours had gone. Then towards dawn on the eighth day, they came to the village.

It was a straggling collection of wooden and mud huts, completely primitive. It nestled at the foot of hills higher than any they had crossed, and there were sandstone humps and hillocks all about them.

Quickly hurried to Palfrey and Drusilla as soon as they were out of the cart. He had given up using his pet phrase, and now just beckoned them. This time he led them to what seemed likely to be the largest house in the village. By the time they arrived, the ferocious-looking leader of the band was already there, talking to a very old man who sat on a low stool on the verandah in front of his house and smoked a long-stemmed pipe with a huge bowl.

It was obvious that he was bargaining, and just as obvious that the old man was not greatly impressed. The leader gesticulated wildly, his voice rose and fell, his words grew more excited. Then he took a wad of dollar bills from one of the pockets of his bandolier and waved them in the air. He shook his fists, eyed the notes longingly, growled beneath his breath, and then pushed the whole wad into the old man's hand.

The old one took his pipe away, nodded, and started to talk freely. The leader stopped scowling and began to smile.

Quickly touched Palfrey's sleeve.

'Okay,' he said, and led them to the back of the little house and into a room which was pleasantly cool.

In the middle of the morning, Quickly came to the room,

and stood on the threshold, smiling broadly. When Palfrey smiled back at him, he went to the narrow window, which had no glass, and pointed towards the distant hills. Then he touched his chest and pointed again.

'So you're going back,' Palfrey interpreted.

Quickly went through the pantomime again, and then edged towards the door. He bowed low, three times, and then disappeared; the last they saw of him was his broad smile.

'So we've lost a friend,' said Palfrey slowly.

Soon they heard someone approaching with shuffling steps, to the accompaniment of a thumping noise. The house quivered beneath each thump. The shuffling drew nearer, and then stopped. After a pause the door opened and an old man stood on the threshold.

His lined face was tanned a deep brown, and a wispy grey moustache drooped almost to his chest. He wore the now familiar drab white coat, which reached almost to his knees and wide trousers; his thin, knuckly fingers were clasped about the head of the stick on which he was leaning. He stood staring at them for a long time, and Palfrey stared back, not sure what to expect.

Laboriously, the old man spoke in English.

'I Tsui Lin.' He nodded. 'You my guests.' He nodded again. 'You wish stay here—two-three days?'

Drusilla said: 'Yes, please.'

'Welcome,' said Tsui Lin. 'My home most poor. You meet all. I chief man village. I wish no trouble.'

'We will cause none,' Palfrey assured him.

'I wish no trouble,' repeated Tsui Lin. 'Much trouble already. To all the gods we pray for rain. No rain come. Crops, very bad.' He uttered each word with great care, and seemed to smile with relief when he finished. 'I learn noble language English from humble, clever daughter.'

He advanced into the room, and grunting, lowered himself on one of the low stools, supporting himself by pushing his stick against the wall as he did so. 'I tell you, please, about my family. Three daughters, three sons. Some die in battle against Japanese.' He spoke quite unemotionally, but Palfrey's heart missed a beat, and Drusilla moved towards another stool and sat down, as if her legs would not support her. 'Two daughters, three daughter-laws, in house. Very good. Very hard work. One daughter, very clever. Live in big town, Chunking. One time fight the Japanese. Please, do not cause trouble.'

'Have some of your guests caused trouble?' Palfrey asked.

'Some. Not my guests. Guests my brothers, my uncles. Not this village, other villages. You stay long?'

'Not very long,' said Palfrey.

'Welcome,' said Tsui Lin. 'Please.' He pressed his stick against the wall and began to rise to his feet laboriously. 'My wife, she visit clever daughter, Chunking. Along come Japanese, make big noise. My wife, she not come back. Please, make no trouble.'

They spent most of the next few days in that room, except at night, when they were taken to another room in the house. It was a bedroom with two camp-beds, a jug and a bowl, and other oddments which they had not expected to find in this remote village.

'Obviously they often have birds of passage to stay,' Palfrey said. 'What do you think of them now, my sweet?'

'I love them,' said Drusilla. 'All of them! I would like to see the clever daughter, all of them seem to worship her. What do they call her?' She answered herself; 'Laughing Fragrance. Laughing Fragrance!' She laughed lightly. 'Yes, I'd like to see her.'

By day, they were taken to the gardens and fields. The effect of the drought was evident on every hand.

The village, a small one, was surrounded by cultivated land, and during the day the daughters of Tsui Lin worked in them, with wooden tools, sometimes accompanied by the old man himself. It was obvious that he was the leader of the little community, for all day visitors came and spent some time with him, often under the eyes of Palfrey and Drusilla, who listened to the soft Chinese and wished they knew what was being said. Nearly every man who came seemed happier when he went away, and after each visitor had gone Tsui Lin began to fill his pipe and tamped the tobacco down; it was always a long time before he lighted it.

Then one day he shuffled to their bedroom, when they had gone there after breakfast. There was something different about him. He was not smiling, and seemed no longer to be friendly. He waited on the threshold for some time, and Palfrey said: 'Please come in.'

Laboriously, Tsui Lin came in and sat down.

'You German?' he asked abruptly.

'Yes,' said Palfrey, awkwardly.

'German friends Japanese,' declared Tsui Lin.

'Not all of them.' Palfrey's mouth felt dry.

Tsui Lin considered this for some time, and then asked:

'You good German?'

'Yes!' said Palfrey, fervently.

There was another short pause, then the old man announced: 'No good German!' He seemed a different creature. 'All German bad. Like Japanese. All bad. You stay here. Do not try go away. Stay here. You understand?'

'Yes,' said Palfrey, in a strangled voice.

'Remember.' Tsui Lin began to get up, and Palfrey went forward to help him but was waved aside imperiously. Grunting and obviously in pain, their host got to his feet, bowed to Drusilla and went out.

'I didn't expect that,' said Palfrey, after a long, tense silence. 'At least he's got the right idea.'

'I wonder how long we will have to stay here.' Drusilla was miserable. 'We don't seem to make any progress at all. If we are sent back to Chunking——'

'We'll perform another escape act,' said Palfrey, brightly. 'After all, Orishu is our guardian angel. Cheer up, my darling!' He slipped his arm about her waist and kissed her cheek. 'We ought to know that time isn't important out here.'

'It's important for us,' said Drusilla. 'All we do is to go from one place to another, wait for a few days, and then move on to somewhere else for another wait. It's——' She broke off, staring out of the window, and Palfrey, seeing the change in her expression, stared in the direction of her gaze.

Two men were coming along the village street, one a huge fellow walking slowly, one a little man walking quickly. The giant was clean-shaven, otherwise he might have been taken at a distance for the chieftain who had escorted them to the village. The other man was undoubtedly 'Quickly Please'.

'Do you see Qui——' began Palfrey.

'Sap!' gasped Drusilla. 'Sap, that's *Stefan*!'

Palfrey said stupidly: 'Darling, you're seeing things, it can't be!'

'It is! His face is dark brown and his hair's been shaved off, but it's Stefan. Sap, we're all right!'

Suddenly the huge man turned and looked towards the house. Palfrey eagerly raised a hand. The giant stopped in his tracks, stared, and then gave them a broad, heartening smile. Quickly began to talk swiftly, the other nodded, while Palfrey felt weak with relief; it *was* Stefan Andromovitch. They were no longer alone.

The two men disappeared near the front of the house. Palfrey heard Tsui Lin's stick thumping on the floor, followed by voices, but he could not understand a word that was said.

The door opened. Tsui Lin came in again, and Stefan followed him, pushed past him and strode to Drusilla's side. He gripped her wrists and hauled her to her feet.

'Drusilla, how glad I am to see you! And you, Sap!' He gripped Palfrey's hand in a crushing grip. 'I was afraid that you would never get here safely—you have to thank Sing!'

'Sing?'

'Your guide,' said Stefan, 'but we can talk about that later.' He turned to Tsui Lin and spoke swiftly, in Chinese. The old man nodded from time to time, and then he looked at Palfrey; on his lips there was a faint smile.

'All Germans bad,' he said. 'Some English—good!'

Palfrey laughed. 'I am good English!'

'So my friend declares. You are quite free. You still wish join Germans?'

Palfrey said: 'What Germans?'

Stefan spoke swiftly in Chinese, motioning Palfrey to silence. There was a quick interchange of words, and after them Tsui Lin seemed satisfied. He bowed to Drusilla, backed away, then turned and went out. As the door closed behind him Stefan threw open the dirty white robe he was wearing, and fanned himself with a bright red handkerchief. His smile was so broad that it seemed inane.

'Stop grinning,' said Palfrey, 'and talk!'

It was not, after all, a very complicated story. Stefan had spent some time in a village near this one, and he knew the old man well. He had, in fact, known that Tsui Lin was often approached to give sanctuary to fugitive Germans, and most of those left to his care had found themselves, sooner or later, back in Chungking. It was largely through him that the Chinese authorities had learned that there was a regular traffic of Nazi fugitives; he also knew that there were others who gave them sanctuary and did not send them back to Chungking. There were rumours which said that as many as a hundred Germans had passed through these hills in the past three months—rumours which had undoubtedly reached Brett in London.

Stefan did not know where they went.

Nor did Tsui Lin. His task was to keep his particular charges at the village until someone came to fetch them away. Those who came for the men, it appeared, did not know the eventual destination, but took them to another village hundreds of miles away to the north, from where they went to a third. As Stefan talked, Palfrey got a deeper impression of the unimportance of time and distance in this vast country.

The one fact which emerged was that somewhere much further north there *was* a colony of Germans. So far, all the efforts of the Allied authorities in Chungking had failed to find out where it was.

'So much, then, for the general situation.' Stefan was sitting cross-legged on the bare boards. He smiled from time to time, and his delight at being with them was a pleasure to behold. 'Now for your part, Sap! You were to have been rescued by Wu Ling's men——'

'Who *is* this Wu Ling?' demanded Palfrey.

'Didn't Orishu tell you? He is a Chinese merchant with business connections with the Japanese. He has traded with them for a long time and they regard him as a trusted collaborator. Actually he works for the Chinese Government and does a very good job, my friend! Unfortunately there was a spy among his staff. He has a business rival, Ho Sun. Did you meet Ho Sun in person?'

'We did!'

'I am told that he is a most engaging rascal,' said Stefan, and added with a smile: 'It is useless to try to apply the codes by which you live in England to those that rule out here. As far as Ho Sun is concerned, traffic in German fugitives is legitimate trade—he gets paid for it, he sends those whom he gets out to here or to one of the other villages through which the traffic passes, and that is the end of it as far as he is concerned. So much for Ho Sun! As I have told you, he had a spy in Wu Ling's ranks, and Wu Ling had a spy in his—none other than Sing! Sing knew who you were, that is why he came with you. He left his party a few miles from the village and came to tell me where you were. While you're in China, he will be your personal servant.'

'Quickly, please!' said Palfrey, and he laughed with deep satisfaction. 'No wonder he was so helpful!'

'But how long have you been out here?' asked Drusilla.

'I first came here four months ago,' said Stefan. 'It was my first mission after we had finished the work in Africa. I have been back to Moscow once or twice and reported what I have found —and that is now general knowledge in China. The Germans have a powerful colony somewhere in the northern mountains.'

'What I want to know is, what we are going to do now,' said Drusilla.

'There are two alternatives,' said Stefan. 'One is to go to the

German colony, as the old man half suggested. The other is to make our way to Japan independently. I have been thinking of the best course, Sap, and decided—as I decide so often here—to wait until Orishu comes to give advice.'

'So you also fall back on the little Jap,' mused Palfrey.

'He is—what you say?—a wizard,' declared Stefan, emphatically. 'One never knows where he will appear next. One moment, he is in Chungking, the next he is in Hankow, the next he comes, perhaps, to this village and reports that he has just returned from Japan! How he does it I do not know. I do know that he left for Japan three days ago and that he promised me he would come to see me here. So it is a matter of waiting for a little while longer.'

'I don't mind so much now,' Drusilla told him, 'but I *must* have a bath.'

Stefan turned smiling eyes towards her.

'I have often gone without a bath for months.'

'Brute!' Drusilla pulled a face at him.

'But here the amenities are admirable,' Stefan assured her. 'Within two miles of the village there is a stream, and half a mile further on the stream widens into a pool. Sometimes I bathe there. How would you like'—he frowned, seeking the right word—'to picnic there, Drusilla?'

'Are you serious?'

'Perfectly! I can borrow mules, I think—have you ever ridden a mule?'

'No, but——'

'Contrary to all reports, they are docile creatures,' Stefan stood up. 'I will go and make arrangements. Unless Drusilla has her bath and changes into proper clothes for a little while, she will be completely demoralised.' He winked at Sap, and then grew serious. 'One thing is most important. In the village you must wear these native clothes—nomads always wear robes and turbans. In the hills, if you like to change, we can take your others with us. Sing—what is it you call him?'

'Sing Quickly.' Palfrey smiled.

'He will bring them,' said Stefan; 'he made sure that they were not stolen. I will be back soon,' he added, and went out.

Later, riding bareback and with their feet nearly touching the rocky ground of the trail which led through the hills, Sing Quickly leading the way, Stefan following and Drusilla and Palfrey bringing up the rear, Palfrey pondered deeply over the situation. The change for the better was miraculous, and yet, like so many other incredible things, the new situation was quickly accepted; he was already wondering what the next move would be.

Japan still seemed an illimitable distance away.

He watched Stefan, who had to poke his legs out in front of him, and who was far too large for the sturdy mule which was carrying him. Clad in a robe with the sun shining pitilessly on his shaven head, he looked very different from the dark-haired, well-dressed Stefan Andromovitch who had taken so important a part in their earlier adventures. Palfrey had come to regard him as a touchstone. In the four years of their friendship he had never known the Russian to lose his temper, make an unwise decision or be anything but his natural, unruffled and good-natured self.

There was greatness in Stefan, and although he was fiercely loyal to the Soviets there were few men who could more justly claim to be cosmopolitan. The great men of the Kremlin trusted him implicitly, and from the time that the Marquis of Brett had conceived the idea of a small band of men with representatives from the major Allied Powers working together on important espionage tasks, Stefan had been a corner-stone of that organisation. He had married eighteen months before, and his wife was working in Moscow, on the staff of the Russian section of the War Crimes Commission. Stefan rarely talked of her, and no one would have dreamed that he hated every day that he was forced to spend away from her.

They came upon the stream, left the mules to feed, and walked through the shade of the rocks towards the pool. It was not large, but the water was crystal clear, making Drusilla's eyes glisten when she saw it. They stood looking at it, feeling cooler than they had for days.

'What wouldn't I give for a swim-suit!' said Drusilla. 'Will Sing Quickly be shocked if——'

'I shall be,' declared Stefan, with mock severity. 'I have a present for you, Drusilla. I am of course, not unacquainted with your husband's Puritan mind, and so . . .' He took a small parcel from the sleeve of his robe and handed it to her with a bow. She unfastened the string, and as a woollen swim-suit unfolded, she looked at Stefan with real affection.

'You're incredible!' she told him, and meant it.

'It is surprising what one can buy in Chungking,' said Stefan. 'Also, this pool, being well protected by rocks and . . .' He laughed as Drusilla turned and climbed towards a little crevice between boulders, and then stripped off his outer clothes. Palfrey followed suit.

Later, they had lunch of rice and pork, and a small slab of chocolate apiece. Time seemed to stand still in that wild, rugged spot. Nothing seemed to matter, past, present or future.

Palfrey was drying himself in the shade, watching Drusilla, who had found that it was just possible to swim in the centre of the pool, when he saw Stefan's expression alter. He glanced in the direction of the Russian's gaze. Sing Quickly was standing on a rock and waving.

'What does that mean?' he asked idly.

'I will go and see,' said Stefan. 'I think perhaps you had better persuade Drusilla to get dressed, Sap—in the native clothes, please. It is perhaps Orishu,' he added, and strode swiftly towards the rock, putting on his robe as he walked.

Drusilla came out at once. She sat for a few minutes, with the water glistening like pearls on her arms and shoulders, and Palfrey almost forgot Stefan and Sing Quickly as he watched her. She leaned forward suddenly and kissed him. Then:

'I suppose I must change?'

'Holiday over for today,' Palfrey nodded. 'I—hal-*lo*. Look at Stefan!'

Stefan was racing down the path towards them, beckoning urgently. Drusilla dried herself on one end of her robe, and disappeared as Stefan came up. He looked upset, and spoke as soon as he was in earshot.

'It looks like trouble at the village, Sap.'

'Trouble?'

'Yes, it is being attacked.'

6 : In the Trail of Death

THEY stood looking down on the village.

It was a scene which Palfrey had often seen before, the terrible spectacle of refugees rushing away from their burning homes; but here it seemed far worse than it had done elsewhere. That little, isolated place, so peaceful and serene, was reduced to a seething burning mass.

Around the village were men on horseback, all of them with rifles at their shoulders. They seemed to ignore the villagers who were fleeing for safety, and watched the burning houses for someone else to come out. Suddenly a man staggered out of the smoke; there was the crack of a shot, and he fell in his tracks.

Stefan said: 'They want Tsui Lin.'

Palfrey said: 'And there isn't a thing we can do.'

'There may be,' said Stefan, softly. 'There is such a thing as vengeance.'

'We've no weapons.'

'There are enough and to spare not far from here', said Stefan. He looked a different man, as if the fire had burned and shrivelled something within him. 'Will you come?'

'Of course!'

'Sing!' exclaimed Stefan, but the little Chinese was already leading the mules towards the rock.

They were out of sight of the refugees as they mounted. For the first time the smell of burning came to their nostrils. They heard more shots, and the cordon of horsemen had not moved except to put the finishing touch to their work of destruction.

'Come,' said Stefan.

Sing Quickly led the way. His face was expressionless as he urged his mule forward, going between rocks where there was barely room for Stefan to pass, and climbing higher up the hills. They left the stream well behind them, and the country grew more wild and barren. For some time no one spoke, but at last the Chinese stopped and climbed off his mount. He spoke to Stefan, in Chinese, who answered quickly.

'We were not unprepared for this,' he added. 'Raids have been made on other villages where the head men have failed the Huns.' He stopped by Sing Quickly's side and began to pull at a rock which moved away from the hillside and disclosed a small cave. He stood outside while Sing Quickly ducked and went in, and then pushed out automatic rifles, a sub-machine-gun, ordinary rifles and boxes of ammunition. Stefan and Palfrey loaded the automatic rifles. Palfrey was not quite sure what was intended, but had implicit faith in Stefan.

'If they are going north, and that is likely, they will pass near here,' said Stefan. His bleak face was turned towards Drusilla, whose eyes reflected the horror of what she had seen. Then he led the way along the path, which seemed to end abruptly. Actually it turned a sharp bend, and for a few hundred feet it ran beneath a towering hillside, with a sheer drop of several hundred feet on the other side.

'We could use hand grenades,' Palfrey murmured.

'The hillside here is not safe for them,' said Stefan 'We are safe ourselves. They would have to return through the village to get here, and they are not likely to do that. Drusilla, must you stay?'

'Yes.' Drusilla picked up one of the rifles, and weighed it in her hands, then put it to her shoulder. Sing Quickly watched her closely, and after a few seconds he brought her some ammunition. They took up positions on the edge of the path, where they looked almost straight down on to the trail.

Palfrey saw the first riders enter the defile.

Stefan said: 'I will fire when they reach the first large rock. Drusilla, you fire when they reach the second. Sap, you and Sing Quickly when they are nearing the end of the defile.' He spoke in Chinese to the little wizened man, who nodded vigorously. The riders seemed a long way off, but were rapidly drawing nearer. They rode two abreast, and there were twenty of them altogether.

Stefan waited until the last of the men had passed the rock he had mentioned—and then the automatic rifle began to speak. That first attack, completely unexpected, had a terrible effect. It was almost possible to feel the consternation among the riders. Some rode forward more swiftly, three fell from the saddles; those nearer the rear turned and raced for the safety beyond the rocks. Stefan began to fire single shots. Drusilla and Sing Quickly fired after him, and two more riders fell. Most of the others, riding single file now, were approaching Palfrey's target. He watched coolly as they drew nearer, and wished that he were a hundred yards closer to them. He saw two of the men staring upwards at the cliff. A few shots were loosed off towards them, but none came near.

Then the first riders came into his sights.

He felt a savage satisfaction as one man fell. A second and a third went down, and he heard the squealing of a wounded horse. Tight-lipped, he kept on firing, but now those who remained unhurt were near to safety. One after the other they disappeared, and the defile echoed to the thunder of the horses' hoofs.

'Good,' said Stefan. 'Two men have gone back, Sap. They may try to get through again. Watch them, Sing!'

The little man scrambled to his feet. He was not smiling, yet there was satisfaction in his expression as he went with Stefan to the mules, and they mounted swiftly.

'Where——' began Drusilla.

'They're after prisoners,' said Palfrey. 'We'll be all right here.'

It was more than an hour before they heard a sound behind them.

'Stay here,' said Palfrey.

He got to his feet and went back along the trail leading to the stream. He stood behind a rock, peering downwards until he saw Stefan walking by the side of his mule, over the back of which was a man whose head was bandaged. Not until they got much closer did Palfrey see that the wounded man was tied to the mule. It suddenly struck Palfrey that this prisoner might be able to give them vital information about the German colony.

He stepped forward, and Stefan smiled grimly.

'You see, we have one.'

'Nice work,' said Palfrey. 'All right, 'Silla!' She came from behind the rock and they approached the others, meeting them near a clearing. Palfrey watched as the prisoner was untied from the mule. He was a big fellow, wearing khaki drill shirt and shorts, and there was blood on his right leg as well as on the bandage about his head. None of those things attracted Palfrey as much as his face, *for he was a white man*!

'Well, well!' said Palfrey. 'A capture indeed, Stefan!'

'Yes. He swore most colourfully in German.' Stefan lifted the man bodily and put him on the ground, with his back against a rock. The fellow looked up, frightened yet defiant.

Stefan spoke in German.

'From where do you come?'

The man did not answer.

Stefan repeated in a harsher voice:

'From where do you come?'

In the silence that followed Sing Quickly advanced slowly on the man. From his dress he took a knife, and the blade glinted in the sun. He ran his thumb along it in such a way that Palfrey shivered, and the German seemed to shudder. Sing Quickly went nearer to him, and Stefan repeated:

'From where do you come?'

The German gasped: 'From near the village of Hunsa! Do not allow him——'

'That is not enough,' said Stefan.

The man drew back, and naked fear drove defiance from his eyes.

'I had my orders!' he gasped. 'I had my orders!'

'We have heard that excuse before,' said Stefan. 'From whom did you obtain your orders?'

'From—from Herr Oberst.'

'So you consider yourself on active service?' said Stefan.

'Yes, yes! I am a prisoner of war; I demand——'

'You will never again be in a position to demand anything,' said Stefan, slowly. 'You will receive far worse punishment if you do not tell us quickly why you came to the village.'

There was a long pause; in it, Sing Quickly whetted the

blade of his knife again, and the sight of it in the hand of the mild-looking little man was as incongruous as the sight of the German who considered himself to be on active service. Then the German broke the silence with an explosive gasp, and he began to talk freely. He spoke with a Bavarian accent—Palfrey and Drusilla understood every word.

He was one of a small group of Germans who had been in the neighbourhood of the village of Hunsa for some months. It was a regular fighting unit, with a Major, two junior officers and forty men. Now and again such expeditions as this were arranged, but usually they were sent out to bring in men named by the Colonel—their duty was that of escorts.

'For whom did you come to this village?' asked Stefan, sounding ridiculously formal.

'For Baron von Klieb and his wife.' The man glanced at Drusilla, then at Palfrey, and his lips quivered. 'They were to be taken to the village, that was known. Others have been taken there and have disappeared. The old man of the village was a traitor. We went there to find the Baron—the Baron,' he faltered, with another glance at Palfrey. 'The old man said that he had gone away. It was his last chance. We—we were under orders, I tell you, under orders!'

Stefan said: 'Where were you to have taken the Baron?'

'To Hunsa.'

'Where would he be taken from there?'

'I—I do not know. I do not know! Not all of us are allowed to know, but'—there was a cunning glint in his eyes as he went on—'I think perhaps I could lead you there! I believe that I know where the others are hiding. I have heard stories of it, it is a wonderful fortress; there we shall be able to live for years!'

'I see,' said Stefan. 'I do not think you will live for years.' He glanced at Palfrey. 'Sap?'

As they returned to the village, Palfrey spoke in German; the man aswered swiftly, volunteering much more information. As far as he knew, his was the only unit operating in this part of China. It ranged for several hundreds of miles in each direction from Hunsa. The men usually travelled on horseback, although there were several motor-cyclists, and the Colonel often travelled in a stolen jeep. The Major's name was Spenn, the junior officers, both *oberleutnants,* were named Weiner and Spatz. There was a Colonel Barlack, who rode with them sometimes. They had two field-guns near Hunsa, but these had never been in use, and they had plenty of small arms and ammunition, including grenades and ample supplies of high explosives. There were one or two Chinese who worked with them, and occasionally a Japanese visited headquarters. He had, he said, been in China for nearly a year, but operations had only been started four months ago.

When he had finished, he looked at Palfrey as if to seek some sign of relenting, and then said harshly:

'You are an Englishman! I am a prisoner of war!'

They were in sight of the village. Most of the people were standing near it, staring at the smoking ruins. The acrid smell of burning was heavy on the air, and a few of the little houses were still ablaze; little brands of fire flew about the fields, smuts and burnt cloth floated like black snow in a gusty wind. Palfrey pointed towards the scene and said:

'That is not war.'

All they found in the ruins of the big house were the charred bodies of Tsui Lin, who had not believed in good Germans, and his family. Palfrey looked at the wreckage of what had been a pleasant room, and then looked back along the street towards the prisoner, who was now surrounded by the villagers, all of them silent and staring at the man, who was trembling violently. After a long time an old man came from the crowd towards Palfrey and Stefan, bowed, and spoke in an undertone. Stefan looked at Sing Quickly, who translated into a dialect with which Stefan was familiar.

Stefan said, in English:

'They want to deal with the prisoner themselves.'

'What does it mean?' asked Palfrey, uneasily.

Stefan smiled. 'Not torture, if that is what you are imagining. They are not uncivilised, Sap, you know that. They will doubtless hang him. They would like the satisfaction of doing that themselves. Eleven men, five women and three children perished.'

'I'm not a bit sure that we should not hand him over to the authorities in Chungking,' said Palfrey, still a little uneasily.

'It will only postpone his fate,' said Stefan, with a touch of impatience.

The four of them left the village half an hour afterwards to gather the horses of their dead attackers; when they looked back from the foothills they saw the body of a man swinging from a tree at one end of the village, his legs kicking. Palfrey said nothing, but urged the mule on, and soon they were in the foothills. Stefan seemed to be familiar with the path, and this time he rode ahead. Sing Quickly rode behind them.

carrying a rifle on his shoulder. Palfrey glanced round at him from time to time, always finding him peering this way or that, as if expecting an attack at any moment. His watchfulness put Palfrey a little on edge, and he hoped Drusilla had not noticed it. She seemed absorbed in her own thoughts, and rarely looked away from the trail ahead of them.

Stefan stopped at last.

'We must go carefully here,' he said, 'in case any of those who escaped have returned.' He climbed off the mule, which stood only as high as his waist, and walked forward cautiously, keeping close to a rock which rose sheer for several hundred feet. The others pressed forward. Soon they were in a narrow cutting through the rock, which would debouch into the defile where retribution had at long last overtaken some members of this last outpost of the Third Reich.

Stefan stood at the entrance to the defile. There was something curious about his stillness, and Palfrey pushed past him and stared at the bare rocks and boulders lining the trail. There were no bodies; there were no horses and no wounded. On the ground there were patches of blood, dry and brown in the sun, and covered with flies. That was all.

All four of them stood very still. There was no sound in the defile; the silence was oppressive, and the sun burned down. At last Palfrey mopped his forehead with his wide sleeve and looked up from the defile.

Drusilla broke the silence.

'So they came back for the dead.'

'And may still be here,' said Palfrey. 'What's the best thing to do, I wonder?'

'We'd better get back to the village,' Stefan decided. 'It is just possible that they will return for further vengeance.' He was looking at the bleak hillside, as if trying to see signs of movement, but after a while he turned round and they headed back.

It was a slow, trying journey.

Not one of them would have been surprised had an attack been launched from either side. The German had given his party's strength as forty men, and they had seen only a score or so; the others might be near.

Palfrey was turning the situation over in his mind. Even if the villagers were armed, it might be difficult to stave off another attack, and probably only a few of the men knew how to handle firearms. He spoke his thought, and Stefan said:

'All of them can handle firearms, Sap. This countryside has been occupied by the Japanese, and that made them learn the arts of war. I think I shall advise them to make for the hills, arm some of them, and wait there for Orishu. It will mean there is little chance for bathing, 'Silla!'

'Bathing!' choked Drusilla.

Incredible though it seemed, the villagers had managed to salvage oddments from the ruins. They were searching among the hot embers, even the youngest children were helping, and carts and mules were carrying heavy loads. Through it all the corpse of the prisoner swung in the breeze, ignored by everyone. The man who had asked to deal with the prisoner came forward again, and with Sing Quickly acting as interpreter, Stefan told him what he advised. There was no argument. Within an hour about two hundred people were walking towards the stream, and as Palfrey watched them plodding on, silent but for the children, apparently placid, as patient as beasts of burden and yet carrying themselves with a great dignity, tears welled up in his eyes.

'The chief trouble will be food,' said Stefan. 'They have already sent a messenger to the nearest big town, but it will probably be several days before help can arrive.'

Palfrey frowned. 'But surely there's food nearer than Chungking?'

'The nearest village is over thirty miles away,' said Stefan, 'and there is not likely to be any great reserve of food. At least there is plenty of water here,' he added, and looked towards the stream, while the people plodded onwards, then scattered among the rocks and hollows in the ground where they could settle for the night.

They waited for five days.

No one visited them; no one came with food; they were hungry most of the time, for the little store of rice was carefully husbanded, and equally shared. As a reserve, Stefan had a few small blocks of chocolate which on no account would he add to the general store.

The patience of the people was remarkable. By day some of the men, all of them old, went down to the fields to work, but they returned before nightfall. All the time, the camp was guarded by armed men, but there were no alarms. Each day, after dark, a man left to carry word of their plight southwards, for they were afraid that the first messengers had been waylaid.

On the fifth evening Palfrey was drowsily looking up at the stars, painfuly aware of the gnawing emptiness of his stomach. He was listening to Drusilla's heavy breathing when he heard a different sound. Stefan was a little way down the hill, and Palfrey stood up and walked towards him. The sound drew nearer; it was a motor-engine, some distance off.

'Can you hear that?' he asked.

'Yes. I am going to the village.'

'Is it a relief lorry?'

'The engine does not sound heavy enough,' said Stefan, and broke into Chinese. Out of the gloom the figure of Sing Quickly emerged, and they made their way towards the village. Not far down the trail they passed an armed guard and told him to wait there. Then they saw the lights from the vehicle shining on the blackened ruins. Three men made silhouettes against the light, all standing by the side of a small private car.

'I think it is Orishu,' said Stefan, and spoke to Sing Quickly, who broke into a run.

They saw him speak to the three men, who turned towards them. The light from the headlamps was good enough to show the figure of a man who might be Orishu, and in a few minutes they saw that it was the Japanese, with two Chinese companions. They met him in the eerie darkness, and not far from the rotting corpse still swinging from the tree.

Within five minutes the two Chinese were in the car and on the way back along the dusty road. By Stefan's side was a small bag, containing provisions which Orishu had brought for them, and they carried it back to the stream, glad that there was now every hope of saving the villagers from starvation; these provisions were an earnest of what would come later. It was obvious that none of the messengers had got through, and that puzzled Palfrey. If the road from the village was being watched by the men of the German unit, why had Orishu been allowed to pass? What was more important—would the car be allowed to go through?

'It will take a longer road than the men on foot,' said Orishu, in his quiet voice. 'I should not worry about that, Dr. Palfrey.' He seemed quite unaffected by what he had discovered. 'So you have definite news of the Germans near Hunsa?'

'Did you know about them?' asked Palfrey.

'It is rumoured that some have been seen near the village,' said Orishu. 'Perhaps you do not understand the difficulties of sending information through a country as vast as this. Hunsa is four hundred miles from this spot. It is as isolated as the village here, and in mountains, not in low hills. It is our next objective, I think.'

'Not Tokyo,' said Palfrey, half-regretfully.

'Not Tokyo yet,' Orishu corrected, softly. 'I have just come from there, Doctor——'

Squatting by the side of a rock, with Palfrey propped up on one elbow, Drusilla lying at full length, and Stefan sitting upright against the rock, he talked for a long time. It did not occur to Palfrey to doubt what he said; he believed the man implicitly.

It was known in Tokyo that Baron and Baroness von Klieb were in China, and spies had been ordered to tell them to go to a meeting-place on the mainland, where they would receive instructions. This, said Orishu, he had learned from the Legation near the Shiba Temple. He did not go into details, and they had to accept his bald statements, so unsatisfying to their curiosity. The German authorities in Tokyo wanted them to stay on the mainland for a while, and to disobey would be foolish.

Palfrey raised an objection.

'How will they know that we've received the message?'

'Everyone who could help you to get to Japan knows of it,' said Orishu, simply. 'Do not allow yourself to make the mistake of under-estimating Tokyo's system, Doctor. The spy system in this part of China is perfect. Disobedience would be fatal. In any case, why should you wish to disobey? When you reach Hunsa, you will doubtless be led to this German colony, and that is a good thing. Your danger will start after you have left there, or perhaps while you are with your new compatriots.' His voice did not alter its monotonous tone. 'You are prepared to go, I hope?'

'Whenever you like,' said Palfrey, quietly.

'Is Stefan coming?' Drusilla asked.

'He will travel by a different road,' said Orishu. 'It will be better for you not to meet, officially, until you are at Hunsa. You understand that you will be largely on your own at Hunsa, Doctor? Sing will be unable to stay with you there, perhaps will not come with you. I shall have one man on whom you can rely, but I have fewer here than in Japan. There are, of course, Chinese who can be relied upon implicitly, and I have arranged with the Chinese in Chungking to compile a list of them. I hope it will reach you before you enter the village.'

'How shall we enter?' asked Palfrey.

'You will go with a nomad family,' said Orishu, 'accompanied by a Chinese guide. You will be known to the wanderers as foreigners, and will have nothing to do with them. You understand?'

'Yes,' Palfrey nodded. 'There'll be a chance to talk about it more fully in the morning, won't there?'

'Yes, an hour or two,' said Orishu. 'You are wise if you are about to suggest that we rest, Doctor. I have not slept for forty-eight hours.'

Palfrey was awakened by a roaring noise which made him sit bolt upright. Drusilla started and clutched at his hand. He saw several men and women rushing for the hillside, as if seeking cover, while the roaring increased; this time there was no doubt that it was an aeroplane. He saw it swoop over the hills and fly towards them. He saw the fear on the faces of the people, and he knew that they had been bombed and were afraid.

The aircraft had Chinese markings, but that was no guarantee that it was friendly.

Something fell from its belly.

'Down!' cried Palfrey, but Stefan let out a joyous shout, and Palfrey looked up again and saw a parachute opening; soon two more came floating down. The people rushed towards the spots where the parachutes, with great containers attached to them, hit the ground and were dragged along for a hundred yards before they came to rest.

'I had the wind up properly,' Palfrey said, sheepishly. 'So they've discovered us at last!'

Orishu, who had not moved from the pile of dry grass on which he had slept, spoke quietly.

'The car reached a radio station, I imagine.'

Palfrey was surprised to find that tins of European food had been dropped for them in one of the canisters. They breakfasted off rice, tinned ham and coffee; it was the first coffee they had tasted for nearly a fortnight, and drinking it was turned into a ceremony. Only Drusilla spoiled the occasion by wishing aloud for tea.

The change in the attitude of the villagers was remarkable, also. Gone was the patient, weary plodding and the set faces; they were smiling and talking freely, looking towards the little party of Europeans in obvious gratitude; and the children seemed to be affected by the same high spirits. More people set off for the fields that morning, including women and children, than had gone before. Some even started to clear up the mess in the village, and Stefan said:

'They will rebuild, I think, on the exact spot where the old village was. Perhaps it was a good thing for those who remain alive, Sap, for it was a *very* dirty village.'

Palfrey smiled, without amusement. 'Have it your own way. When do we start for Hunsa?'

'Later in the morning,' said Stefan. 'I shall come only a

short way with you, Sing Quickly will not, after all, remain. Orishu is afraid that he is suspect.'

The fact that they were going off without friends made them more silent than usual. Sing Quickly hung about them, darting forward to perform a little service whenever he could, and Palfrey wondered if he could plead for the company of the little man for part of the journey. He decided that it would be wiser to let Orishu have his own way. So soon, they would be on their own except for another wandering tribe. . . .

They went off before midday, riding mules. Before four o'clock they came to cross-roads in the lower foothills, and there they left Stefan and Sing Quickly; only Orishu accompanied them across the bare rocks. The country seemed the same, a vista of monotonous hills, crags and boulders, with little growth of any kind. From the brow of the hill they looked down and saw Stefan standing by the side of the little Chinese; both raised their hands in farewell.

'We will be met here,' said Orishu.

It was nearly dark, and they could see only a few dozen yards about them. They were still in those interminable hills, but for a little while they had ridden over green fields, where workers had been bent over the soil and little huts had dotted the landscape like an English allotment on a vast scale.

'I have not told you this before,' said Orishu, 'because it seemed better for me to tell you now, Doctor. When you are questioned by the Germans, you will say that you went to a village where an old man sent you, under escort, to the people who will deliver you to Hunsa. That is all. You do not know the name of the village. All you know is that one of your guides was named Sing. You may describe Sing. It may be possible, at a later date, to use him again. The Germans will think that they made a mistake, after all, in destroying that village. You do not, of course, know that it was destroyed—it was done after you had left. You have met no one except your companions. Is all that clear?'

'Yes,' said Palfrey.

Orishu loked from him to Drusilla, and then asked slowly:

'You are both intent on continuing?'

'Yes,' said Drusilla, promptly.

'Much may come of your great venture.' The Japanese was weighing every word, 'and whether it is good or bad, success or failure, I shall always carry with me the memory of two very brave people.' The faint smile curved his lips, and then he turned away and pointed northwards. 'I see a cloud of dust. Your new escort is approaching.'

'How shall we ride?' asked Palfrey.

'On horseback, which I understand you would prefer. You will remember, please, that there is no need to pretend that you are Chinese.'

An hour afterwards, in the saddle, they set off in the middle of a party of eight horsemen, fierce, wild-looking fellows whose belts bristled with guns and knives, all of whom wore bandoliers, khaki shirts and shorts, and yet rode barefoot. The horses were small, wiry beasts, so spirited that for the first hour of the journey both of them had to concentrate on obtaining mastery.

On the third day, after riding through open country, they came upon a small wood, and once they were in the middle of it they discovered dozens of tents, some of them only single pieces of canvas or hessian stretched over stakes pushed into the ground to make a roof. People were moving through the undergrowth, and children were standing and staring at the riders who had just appeared. Palfrey likened it to a large gypsy encampment in the Balkans.

They stayed there for one night, and next morning the whole camp broke up. No one came to speak to them. They discovered that during the night the horsemen had ridden off, but two horses were left for them; when they mounted no one stopped them. There were at least three hundred people in that travelling family, all heavily burdened. There were two other horsemen, and several people on mules. But the majority were on foot, pushing tiny two-wheeled carts piled so high with goods that the contents seemed to touch the ground on either side. A dozen oxen, pairs of them drawing great carts, seemed to be owned communally.

Off they went, the horsemen at a slow walk, and soon they reached different country. There were few cultivated fields. Great forests were on either side, but they were moving through a tract of open land. Most of the time they were on the bank of a dried-up river. Its sandy bed showed great cracks where the mud had dried out in the sun.

The sense of unreality had never been greater. There were moments when Palfrey felt like laughing at the incongruity of it all, and others when he was in the grip of an acute depression. He did not share either mood with Drusilla, who was surprisingly contented, and took great interest in all that went on around her.

He judged that they had travelled a great deal more than four hundred miles from the burned village when they came to the brow of a hill and, looking down into a shallow valley, they saw a village. For the first time they were addressed—the first time for many days and nights. It was one of the other riders who came up, stood looking at them expressionlessly, and then said with great care, as if he had rehearsed it often:

'This Hunsa.'

He drew his hand from the pocket of his coat. There was a small package, which he handed to Drusilla, who took it with a ready smile.

'Hunsa,' repeated their informant, and turned and rode off.

Drusilla looked at the packet. Palfrey frowned when he saw her expression, and then was startled when she threw back her head and laughed. Helplessly she handed the packet to Palfrey; it was about the size of a small packet of cigarettes, with a bright label, which read: *'Hair dye—peroxide'*.

Palfrey read it, looked at Drusilla—and then his laughter merged with hers.

They were taken to the village a little later, to a wooden house on the outskirts, where obviously they were expected. It was primitive enough, but no more so than that of the burned-out village, and there were some amenities, for there was a bowl on a wooden table, a jug of cold water, and a towel. They had not been in the room for long before a girl came shuffling in, carrying another jug of water, steaming hot. She bowed nervously and went out, while Drusilla said: 'I suppose that's for my hair.'

'I'll lend you a hand,' said Palfrey.

In the morning Drusilla's hair was inspected with great care; between them they had done a good job, and for a few days no one would suspect that she was really dark. There was plenty of the peroxide left, Drusilla said, and provided she was able to have an hour or two to herself from time to time she would not have much trouble with carrying off that little deception. It seemed so trivial, compared with everything else, that Palfrey found it hard to believe that Orishu had really left that peroxide with their escort, and that Brett's words would come true so far away from England.

Soon after breakfast was finished footsteps sounded in the passage outside their room—not the quiet, regular footsteps of a Chinese, but clear and sharp. They stopped outside the door, and there was a tap.

Palfrey called in German: 'Come in.'

The door opened and a man came in, wearing khaki shirt and shorts, his fair hair clipped close and his wide shoulders squared. He clicked his heels and bowed first to Drusilla, then to Palfrey, and said in his native German:

'Have I the honour to address the Baron and Baroness von Klieb?'

'Yes,' said Palfrey, stiffly.

The set young face broke into a smile. He was little more than a boy, and there was an eager light in his pale blue eyes.

'Allow me to present myself—Oberleutnant Wilhelm Spatz.' He clicked his heels and saluted again. 'You are to be warmly congratulated in reaching Hunsa! Only one in five who attempts it succeeds.'

'Indeed,' said Palfrey.

'Herr Oberst wishes to see you at the earliest possible moment. You know that Colonel Barlack is in command perhaps?'

'I was told that I might meet him,' said Palfrey.

Spatz led them out of the house, across a narrow street into a wood which grew close to the village. The path through the woods led upwards, until suddenly it ran into a little clearing where a single tent was pitched. Half a dozen men, clad in khaki drill, were working at tables in the open. All cast curious glances towards them as they were led to the tent. Before they reached it the flap opened and a short, stocky man, clad in full field uniform of the German Army, appeared and saluted them.

Palfrey drew himself up.

'*Heil Hitler!*'

Colonel Barlack looked at him thoughtfully. His square face was bronzed, his eyes were narrowed against the sun. He pursed his full lips and gave a little sardonic smile.

'We no longer serve Hitler, but the Reich,' he said. 'Good morning, Herr Baron. Or should I call you Dr. Palfrey?'

7 : The Colony of the Fourth Reich

PALFREY nearly betrayed himself. Only the fact that he had been affecting annoyance at the rebuke after the Hitler salute saved him. He could not see Drusilla's face, but she did not move. His own lips relaxed in a smile.

'As you wish, Herr Oberst! I have been Palfrey for so long that I answer to both names!'

'So I understand,' said Barlack, and he smiled broadly, making Palfrey's heart thump with relief. 'I congratulate you on your success. True, we have helped a little, but you made your own way to China—a remarkable feat.' Palfrey did not think there was a double meaning to the words. 'We are glad you are here, Herr Baron, we are in need of officers like yourself.'

Palfrey clicked his heels and bowed.

'And we shall be delighted to receive the Baroness,' said Barlack, smiling at Drusilla. 'We have very few ladies with us. You have found the journey wearying, of course?'

'Very,' said Drusilla.

'You shall have rest, I assure you, and clothes which will be a delight for you!' Barlack was establishing himself as a genial fellow. 'You are tired of living as natives, I have no doubt. I can sympathise, although I came here so long ago that I have never had to resort to the disguise. Seven years,' went on Barlack, narrowing his eyes. 'Most of them waiting with little to do except prepare for what might never happen. It is a long time, Herr Baron, a very long time.'

'But not, I trust, wasted,' said Palfrey, with a touch of acerbity.

Barlack stiffened slightly.

'Not wasted at all,' he agreed. 'It is fortunate that some of our leaders had sufficient foresight to realise that the day might come when in Europe things would go against us.' He looked at Palfrey steadily, his eyes still narrowed. 'It is a fortunate thing for you also, Herr Baron, for this is a most dangerous country. Only last night——'

He broke off and looked away, as if he were suddenly conscious of the fact that he was talking too freely. Palfrey wished he had completed what he was about to say. There was an uneasy feeling at the back of his mind that the men who had moved the corpses and the horses from the defile near Tsui Lin's village might have seen either him or Drusilla, and brought in a report Barlack might be waiting to verify before giving them his full trust.

'How long are we to be kept here, without food or rest?' he asked sharply, and Barlack apologised at once.

'I am sorry, Herr Baron. Please be seated. I am waiting for instructions before you can go further.' He waited for them to sit, before seating himself. 'You understand that it is most necessary to be careful of everyone—extremely careful. It would be disastrous if anyone hostile to us were to find where we have made our headquarters.' He raised his voice: 'Orderly!' When a man appeared at the flap, he ordered iced drinks and fruit, and soon Palfrey and Drusilla were regaling themselves on peaches and iced lager. They accepted it without showing any surprise. 'We do, of course, take every precaution,' Barlack went on, 'and——'

'It occurs to me,' said Palfrey, 'that further precautions might be taken in this village, Herr Colonel. It would be easy for a spy to reach this clearing.'

'It would be impossible for anyone to approach within half a mile without being seen,' said Barlack, 'and in two minutes all trace of our presence here could be removed. *All* trace,' he added, with a faint smile. 'While we are waiting, perhaps you would like to see a demonstration.'

'It is of no account.'

'Herr Baron is very trusting.' Barlack was obviously annoyed, and showed it with mild sarcasm. 'In seven years, however, I can assure him that we have become accustomed to danger, and have taken all precautions. I——'

A shrill whistle, which might have been the call of a bird, interrupted him. He stood up so abruptly that Palfrey backed away and spilled his drink.

'Come!' said Barlack. 'Strangers are approaching.'

He ducked beneath the flap of the tent, and they followed him quickly, putting their glasses down but each carrying a peach. As they reached the clearing an astonishing sight met their eyes; the officers were standing by the tables, some of which were already being folded, and orderlies were sweeping papers into tin boxes. The scene presented a paradox, for the confusion was almost methodical, but they did not stay long enough to see it through. Barlack and two other men led the way through the trees, until suddenly one of them stopped in front of a wall of rock. He stretched up and pulled at a branch of a small oak tree; a little patch of ground, with small trees growing in it, moved round and revealed an opening in the rock; it was not unlike a revolving stage.

'This way!' snapped Barlack.

By then others were following them, and Drusilla and Palfrey stepped gingerly forward into the darkness. It was soon relieved by the glow of electric light, however, and they had no trouble in going down a flight of steps carved in the rock. They hurried along a high-roofed passage, with the sounds of the men behind them echoing loudly. Then they went through a doorway and Barlack turned into a room on the right; all the others passed on.

The room in which they stood was a fantastic place; obviously it was a natural cave, but the walls had been faced with cement or concrete; it was odd-shaped, but the walls were decorated with maps and diagrams, in much the same way as an advance headquarters in the field. The most fantastic thing, however, was the roof; in parts it was not much more than ten feet high, but in others it stretched up for forty or fifty feet, and the rock was in its natural state. The colours in the rock were wonderful, thrown up by the light, glittering enough to dazzle them.

Against the wall beneath one of the highest places was a wooden ladder, like a fire-escape, with a small platform at the top.

Barlack put a hand on Palfrey's arm.

'Come with me,' he said. 'The Baroness will excuse us.' He led the way to the ladder and began to climb. Palfrey followed. By the time he reached the platform and looked down, Drusilla seemed a great distance away; she was standing in the middle of the room, looking up at him, her eyes narrowed because of the brilliant colours.

'Look!' said Barlack.

Palfrey stared at what he thought was the face of the wall, but he saw a patch of grassland, fringed by trees. There was no sign of tables or tent, nothing to indicate that men had been there, as far as he could see from that point of vantage. Barlack was smiling in satisfaction. Suddenly a man came into sight and was followed by several others; they wore the hip-length coats and drab trousers of Chinese infantry, and were heavily armed. They walked across the clearing, looking right and left—and then one of them suddenly went down on his knees.

Palfrey said: 'You cannot hide footprints!'

'It is a clearing often used by wandering families,' said Barlack, now smiling superciliously. 'All who work there with me wear straw sandals, or else their boots are soled with straw. Smoking is not permitted. It is necessary sometimes to work in the open air, for the sake of our health, but we can stay in here, if necessary, for weeks. The caves are air-conditioned. I trust you are satisfied, Herr Baron.'

Palfrey did not answer until he saw the Chinese get up and gesticulate as if he were giving word that he had found nothing of interest. The patrol was soon lost to sight, and Palfrey turned to Barlack.

'The arrangements appear to work perfectly,' he admitted.

'We have scouts outside,' said Barlack, 'and we shall be advised as soon as the area is cleared.'

'Yet I was led here from the village by Oberleutnant Spatz,' Palfrey said. 'He did not appear to take great precautions. Is it wise to trust the villagers?'

'The old man of the village can be trusted,' said Barlack, and grinned. 'His two daughters and three sons work for us, and if anything should go wrong, much will go wrong with them! The house where you stayed is out of sight of most of the village. Spatz came to you and returned with you only when we knew that no one was watching. Do not allow yourself to be alarmed, Herr Baron *every* precaution is taken. Shall we go down?'

Palfrey went backwards down the ladder, making heavy going of it. Barlack followed him briskly.

'Do not imagine,' he said, when he reached the floor, 'that you have yet approached the headquarters—very few are allowed to do that, and only those who undergo the most stringent tests, Herr Baron.'

'That is as it should be,' Palfrey approved.

He started when a bell rang.

Barlack smiled. 'We are civilised here,' he said. He went to a desk and answered a telephone. 'The office of the *Oberst* . . . Yes . . . Yes, at once.' He replaced the receiver and looked up at Palfrey with a broad smile. 'Your very good friend, General von Klowitz, is coming to see you,' he declared. 'Sit down, Herr Baron, please! Make yourself comfortable.'

'Ah,' said Palfrey. 'Yes!'

He sat down, thankful that Barlack had told him the name of the man who was coming. Now all that he had read and learned of von Klieb passed through his mind. Von Klowitz was a Junker of the old school, and von Klieb had been trained by him at Potsdam in the early days of the war. Von Klieb, in fact, had been described as one of the General's most promising junior officers and according to the reports which Brett had gathered only the hostility of the Nazi party to favourites of von Klowitz had prevented him from becoming a General before the collapse of the German armies. The most significant thing, apart from the testing encounter which was coming, was that von Klowitz had been banished from Hitler's councils before the invasion of Normandy; Brett had not been able to trace him thereafter.

He glanced at Drusilla, who smiled back, trying to appear unconcerned. Barlack was attending to some papers, but he looked up covertly, as if he half expected to see them trying to exchange a message. Outwardly they looked calm enough, and Palfrey felt much easier than he had when the unknown had faced him. What ensued was entirely up to him; von Klieb had only been married for eighteen months, and there was no evidence that von Klowitz had ever met his wife.

The General was a tall, thin man with a hard, lumpy face, a close-clipped moustache and a heavy scar beneath his right eye, in which he held a monocle. Everything about him cried *Junker*! He stood on the threshold, with a hand at his monocle, looking at Drusilla. He completely ignored Palfrey. After what seemed a long time, he advanced with a broad smile, and as Drusilla stood up he extended a hand.

'Welcome, my dear Baroness! I always knew that Karl would have exemplary taste!'

He bowed low over her hand and turned to face Palfrey. For a moment his keen gaze rested on him. Palfrey, aware of his ungainly appearance in native clothes, felt as if he were stripped naked, and was thankful that he had not resorted to any disguise.

The keen gaze faded, and von Klowitz advanced with his hands outstretched.

'Karl, my dear fellow! What a fine Chinaman you make!' They shook hands, and then Palfrey drew back and saluted. 'Pooh, my friend, you need not stand on ceremony here,' declared von Klowitz. 'I have been greatly troubled from the moment that I heard you were on your way here. It is a marvellous feat of endurance—I congratulate you and your most charming wife! Let me see, now, her name . . .' He hesitated.

'Hilde,' said Palfrey, smiling.

'Hilde, yes! I deplore the fact that I was unable to come to your wedding.' He smiled roguishly at Drusilla. 'Come, now, you have been here long enough! Has Barlack looked after you well?'

'Very well,' said Palfrey.

'Excellent! Come, my dear!' He took Drusilla's hand and tucked her arm under his, folding his free hand over hers. The orderly opened the door, and Palfrey bowed to Barlack, whose face was set and expressionless. They went into the passage, where Palfrey was startled at seeing three sedan chairs, with boys standing back and front, lined up in the passage. 'It was fortunate that I was visiting this part of our new domain,' said von Klowitz, with heavy humour, 'or you would have had to wait for some hours, Karl! True, I knew that there was a hope that you would reach us during the next day or two, and accordingly timed my visit to try to make sure that I would welcome you. We shall not be long in these chairs,' he added, 'but it is quicker than walking.'

He helped Drusilla into one, and in a few minutes they were off.

They were carried for about half an hour.

Then the chairs were stopped and lowered. Palfrey climbed out. Von Klowitz had already reached Drusilla and was helping her. They appeared to be at the end of a passage, and a single electric light was burning. Palfrey could see a corner and a dark void beyond it. He heard a sound which was like running water, but except for that patch of darkness there were only cement-faced walls about them.

Again von Klowitz took charge of Drusilla.

'You see how admirable are our arrangements,' he said, and led the way to the dark patch. He waited for Palfrey to join them.

There was just room for them to walk abreast. In front of them, some distance off, was a mellow light. The sound of running water grew more distinct. They walked for perhaps a dozen yards and then found themselves on the bank of a river which flowed sluggishly beneath a great high cavern. Quays of concrete were built on the banks on either side, and there were several sampans moored to iron rings. Further along was a launch and two motor-boats. Immediately in front of them was a large sampan with a boy at the oars and another standing to help them aboard.

'It is unlikely that any part of our headquarters will be discovered,' said von Klowitz, 'but if Barlack's section should be in danger, a long section of the passage along which we have come will be blown up—it is heavily mined, of course. Only a mass of carth would be found, and no way could be found to pass it. There are, naturally, several ways out of this place, so we should be quite safe. Ingenious, you will agree?'

'Very,' said Palfrey, sounding properly impressed.

As soon as they were aboard the sampan, the boys began to row. The eeriness increased. The loud noise of the oars, the heavy breathing of the boys, the smile on von Klowitz's face as he sat in front of Palfrey with Drusilla's arm tucked under his, made absurd contrasts. The river was surprisingly wide, and there was a strong current, for they had to go some way downstream before they reached the middle and then went on, more swiftly, towards the opposite bank. The bare, natural wall of the cliff was broken in several places by doorways with doors standing open like those of large garages. Out of one of them backed a small, electrically-driven car.

Von Klowitz slapped his thighs.

'Your face, Karl! You are astonished! Oh, we have harnessed Nature very well here. Not far away there is a waterfall which we have used to great advantage, and there is no shortage of electricity. If this surprises you, however—wait!'

'How far do we drive?' asked Palfrey.

'It will take over an hour,' said von Klowitz, airily. 'It is a little over fifty miles from here!' He chuckled again. 'You had no idea that our preparations were on such a grand scale, had you?'

'No,' said Palfrey. 'No idea at all.'

'It is a fortunate thing that *some* of us had foresight,' said von Klowitz, and a different note crept into his voice. 'It was long apparent that the Nazi fools might blunder often enough to lose the war.'

They got into the car.

Palfrey kept a discreet silence until von Klowitz began to talk again as they drove along a good road which had room for two lines of traffic. He was trying to make himself believe that such a road could stretch for fifty miles through the mountains when suddenly they turned a corner and he was blinded by the sunlight as they broke into open country.

Von Klowitz's and Barlack's confidence was not surprising. Obviously they were at a considerable height, for on either side there was rock-strewn land, where patches of pine trees and jungle growth grew in abundance. Sometimes great dark stretches of primeval forest disappeared in a misty darkness towards the heart of a great mountain; and slowly it dawned on him that they were in the middle of a mountain range, and that probably the country through which they were driving had not been explored until the Germans came.

They were in the Inshan Gargan Mountains, said the General. The spot had been discovered many years before and surveyed for such an emergency as had arisen. They had been helped by the Japanese, of course, and by one of the war lords who had not been prepared to sink his differences with Chiang Kai-shek. Even if it were known that they were sheltering in these mountains, the range stretched over such vast distances that no expeditionary force was ever likely to find them. The road along which they were travelling was not noticeable from the air, because it was well camouflaged; if Karl cared to look at the surface . . .

Palfrey studied it for the first time.

He saw the patches of paint daubed on it, and saw also the many rocks and boulders which lined the route. From the air, even if a thousand photographs were taken, it was extremely unlikely that the road would appear. He should not have been surprised by this fresh evidence of Teutonic thoroughness, but it appalled him.

Von Klowitz went on:

'Even if the road should be discovered, my dear Karl, it would serve little purpose. It can be blown up in several places and there are by-roads, built intentionally to take any curious people to the wrong place. Oh, it is a tremendous conception! Soon you will see much more.'

'Indeed,' Palfrey murmured. He knew that they were climbing. Ahead of them was a vast mountain, its peak so high that he could not see it. Great forests grew on its lower slopes, and then thinned out to bare, bleak rocks. The contrast between the wild nature about them and the electrically-driven car, which did not slacken speed, had a numbing effect on his mind.

'We are about to enter a tunnel,' announced von Klowitz.

The words were hardly out of his mouth before the road took a sharp turn on a steep gradient, and then they entered the yawning mouth of the tunnel. It was dark except where the headlights shone on the rocks on either side and the smooth surface of the road. Occasionally green eyes stared at them from the road and sides, but the driver did not slacken speed. They drove on for perhaps ten minutes, which meant that they covered at least seven miles before they broke into the countryside again—and for all that the unpractised eye could tell, they might have been in the same wild region.

They were still climbing.

'One more tunnel,' said von Klowitz, 'and then you will see what we have prepared for the Fourth Reich!'

Palfrey nodded, but he was thinking: 'We can't possibly get out of here on our own.'

Drusilla seemed to be giving all her attention to the General; Drusilla could always be trusted to do the right thing. Von Klowitz spoke to her most of the time, calling her Hilde and patting her hand affectionately.

'One more tunnel,' he repeated, 'and then you will see the eighth wonder of the world! Here we can work, if needs be, for generations. In some ways it is similar to the Nazi fortifications in Nordia,[1] but we have different plans here, you

[1] See *Dangerous Quest*.

understand.'

'Different?' said Drusilla, hopefully.

'*Very* different,' said von Klowitz.

They entered the next tunnel without warning, and it stretched for seven or eight miles before they saw daylight ahead of them. The car slowed down for the first time since leaving the river, and when it emerged into the light of day again it stopped.

'The eighth wonder of the world,' said von Klowitz, softly.

Palfrey sent him one swift glance, and saw the expression in his eyes. It was one of exultation—and there was justification for it. Palfrey looked down at a scene of almost incredible beauty.

Beneath them, thousands of feet from the ledge on which they had stopped, was a green valley which seemed to stretch for hundreds of miles. There was bleak mountainside about them, and some hundreds of yards of the same barren, rocky slopes immediately beneath them; then there was a belt of forest, probably a mile thick—and then fields, which looked cultivated, and the shallow valley with its soft pastures and great copses. Through the centre ran a small river, which looked like beaten gold.

There were no signs of habitation.

'One would think,' said von Klowitz, softly, 'that we had found Shangri-La. But there is no secret of everlasting life here, Karl! Have you seen enough?'

'I can never see enough,' said Palfrey.

Von Klowitz laughed. 'You were always an artist at heart. I was surprised that you became such an adept at war.' He leaned forward and touched the driver's shoulder, and the car started off again, down a steep slope and then, always losing height, through the forest which closed about them as if they were in a land of perpetual night. Soon they passed through woods where oak and birch and beech grew in abundance, and beneath which the grass was luxuriant and soothing.

Palfrey said: 'Surely this can be seen from the air.'

'Yes,' said von Klowitz, 'but there are similar valleys. Few people know whether they can be entered—I do not think they have been explored before. I first became aware of their existence when I read an old Chinese book about the mysterious lands beyond the Tibetan mountains. I nursed the memory for a long time, and some years ago broached the subject to my friends.' He spoke very softly, as if his thoughts were of the past. 'The Japanese held much of the country near here at the time, and parties were organised to explore the valleys. Few of the parties ever returned, but two did—one from this valley.'

'Was it—was it inhabited?' Palfrey asked, his mouth dry.

'We found no lost tribe,' said von Klowitz. 'I believe that some of the valleys are very sparsely inhabited. All the work here was done by imported labour from Manchukuo and from Japan—our engineers, of course, directed it. Have you yet seen any sign of habitation?'

'No,' said Palfrey.

'There are five hundred people living here,' said von Klowitz, softly. 'They live in small houses built in the woods, which give full protection during the summer and autumn. In the spring and winter we live in the mountainside, Karl—the weather would make it impossible to live in the open, even if there was not a danger of being seen. Such weather! A Russian winter is a pleasant experience compared with what is suffered here. The first winters, when we were taken by surprise, were deadly.'

'How often have you been here?' Palfrey asked.

'I have visited the valley each year since 1939,' said von Klowitz, 'and for eighteen months I have been here all the time—since I was dismissed by that lunatic who brought us to disaster.' His face was set, and Palfrey made no attempt to interrupt. 'At least those days are past,' went on von Klowitz. 'We can rebuild—we can rebuild.'

Palfrey said: 'It is so far from the Reich.'

'It is near Japan,' said von Klowitz, cryptically.

He fell silent again, and they drove through a wood fresh with new grass and young saplings, where squirrels and rabbits gambolled and the birds swooped gracefully, lines of bright colour at first dazzling to the eye. They were travelling slowly now, and after they had gone across a clearing they entered another wood—and for the first time Palfrey saw signs of habitation.

There were small wooden houses—like the shacks of backwoodsmen in Canada and Newfoundland. Some were covered with wistaria and ramblers. None was neglected. It was an idyllic spot, so quiet and peaceful, as if they had come upon an undiscovered village in a forgotten world. They passed cross-roads, where there were several larger buildings—shops where customers were being served. One long, low building had photographs outside it, and they were travelling so slowly that Palfrey saw the pictures of a film and realised with a sense of shock that it was a cinema.

'We have looked after everything,' said von Klowitz. 'It was decided, after an experiment in communal living, that it would be better for each family to have its own house, and where families were large, several houses. Single men and women, of course, are housed in hostels—but we do not encourage single women!' He shot a lewd glance at Drusilla. 'Our birth-rate is extremely high!'

'Indeed,' said Drusilla, but she laughed.

'Our headquarters, of course, are below ground,' said von Klowitz, more soberly. 'We are approaching them. Field-Marshal von Runst is most anxious to see you, Karl, and to hear of the latest events in Europe.'

'Von Runst,' exclaimed Palfrey.

'Oh, he is here,' said von Klowitz, airily. 'You have the real explanation of the disappearance of our most efficient generals, Karl! Churchill and Roosevelt probably believe that they were murdered by the Nazis—it is better that way. *We* know better!'

He laughed as the car pulled up outside a small wooden building. The ground beyond it was raised, as it might be for an efficient air-raid shelter, and there were several ventilation shafts. The little building looked like the others which they had passed, and Palfrey was wondering what new miracle they would discover when suddenly the door opened and a man stepped out. He was small, dressed in a bright green robe, a scanty turban, and—a thing Palfrey could hardly believe—carrying an umbrella. It was only when he looked up and stared at the car that Palfrey recognised him.

It was the Burmese who had flown with them from New Delhi.

8 : The Von Kliebs at Home

PALFREY was taking a bath.

Drusilla sat by the open window of their four-roomed bungalow, which overlooked a small lawn, trim and bright, and where there was a border of bush roses, azaleas and, in little beds of their own, mulberry, almond and orange trees, already laden with unripe fruit. It was evening, and a cool wind blew from the mountains, which she could not see.

She wore a suit of white linen, a gift from von Klowitz, and she had bathed in perfume water. So far she had met no other women, and had seen very few of the men. Those whom she had seen had shown no surprise at her presence; she realised that there was nothing unusual in the arrival of strangers.

A gurgle of water told her that Palfrey was nearly finished. She stood up and went into the tiny kitchen, where a meal was laid on an enamel-topped table. There was white bread, lettuce, tomatoes and cold ham; it was all so fantastically unexpected.

They would not have a full-time domestic servant, von Klowitz told them, but a woman would come for two hours night and morning, and there would be no need for Drusilla to spend her time in doing housework. She wondered, a little anxiously, how she would be expected to spend her time; if she were to laze and loll about, it would be too much for her nerves.

She recalled the shock she had received when she had seen the little Burmese, who had bowed politely and then gone off —where, she did not know.

Palfrey appeared on the threshold. His hair was damp and brushed down, making his face look thin. He wore white shorts and a cellular shirt, short socks and sandals with straw soles; and he looked gloriously cool.

'Hungry?' she asked.

'Famished!' said Palfrey, and added: 'This is my idea of setting up a home, Hilde!'

'Is it?' asked Drusilla. She was acutely conscious of the danger with which they would constantly be surrounded. She thought in English, but it would be dangerous to utter a word except in German. She started to eat, cheered up by his apparent confidence. He was in his brightest mood since leaving London.

'We'd be fools not to believe the best,' he said. 'We've a chance in a million. True, we aren't exactly surrounded by friends, but Stefan knows that Hunsa is the village to start looking for.'

'After what we've seen, they'll never let us out.'

Palfrey smiled. 'Stefan and Orishu got us in; Stefan and Orishu will get us out, or will have a damned good try. On the whole I prefer it to Tokyo.'

'Are you really as confident as you pretend?'

'Yes and no,' said Palfrey. 'I wouldn't like to gamble on getting out alive, but I think there's a good chance. Orishu knows a lot more than he's let on, and the Junker gentlemen who litter the valley are in for some rude shocks. The little Burmese gave me a turn, but he shouldn't have done. Von Runst told us that the gentleman had just reported very categorically on our arrest in Chungking. That was a touch of genius on Orishu's part, and our passport to the valley. All we have to do now is to take a cue from the Chinese, and watch and wait.' He laughed. 'So far, all for nothing. I've still got the sparklers close to my skin.'

'I hope that's all we need worry about,' said Drusilla. 'What did you think of Barlack?'

'An efficient creature, who didn't like it when I implied that he might have been exposing himself to undue danger,' said Palfrey. 'I—— Hallo, visitors!'

There was a knock at the front door, and he went to open it, wiping his fingers on a linen table-napkin. He saw a stranger, dressed as he was; the man came in, smiled and shook hands.

'You will doubtless remember me,' he said, smiling broadly. 'I was delighted to know you were here, von Klieb—delighted! You have not changed much, my friend!'

'I'm a bit thinner,' said Palfrey.

Alarm flared up within him. This was how danger would come—suddenly and without the slightest warning, leaving them with no protection. This man's face was slightly familiar, he had probably seen a photograph, but he could not remember who he was. On his cheeks were duelling scars, souvenirs of Heidelberg, perhaps; von Klieb had been to Heidelberg. He offered cigarettes and tried to appear self-possessed and gay.

'I would not say that you are much thinner,' said the stranger, who seemed unimpressed by the lack of warmth in his welcome. 'You are dazed, perhaps? It was a week before I recovered from what I saw on my way here. It is real, my friend—as real as the Heidelberg days, and Professor Schwartz and Mitzi——' He stopped, and put a hand to his lips. 'Your pardon! I had forgotten that you had taken a wife! I am told she is of great charm.'

'Very great,' said Palfrey. 'I——'

The man startled him by springing to his feet and clicking his heels; surely only a Prussian officer could succeed in clicking his heels in straw-soled sandals! Then he advanced towards the door, where Drusilla was standing. He took her hand and bowed low over it, while Palfrey stared past him to Drusilla and tried to make her understand his plight. Probably she had sensed it, which was why she had come.

'Your husband was just singing your praises, Baroness,' said the stranger, gaily. 'I do not wonder! From this very moment the heart of Fritz von Marritz is yours!' He kissed her hand lightly. 'Karl, you are a lucky dog!'

'Don't I know it!' said Palfrey, breathing more easily. The knowledge that this was Fritz von Marritz, who had been with von Klieb at Heidelberg, was enough to enable him to skate over the most difficult moments.

'Karl, of course, has never told you that he has such a handsome friend!' declared von Marritz.

'He has——' began Drusilla.

Something clicked in Palfrey's mind. There was no record that this man had ever been a close friend of von Klieb's; there were several others of whom the records had spoken, but von Marritz was no more than an acquaintance, they had never been confidants. He broke in swiftly:

'I have so many handsome friends, Fritz. Are any more of our year here? Bülow, Arne or Hugo von Otten?' His memory was clear now. 'I heard that Hugo had also disappeared.'

He thought that the expression in von Marritz's eyes was one almost of disappointment, but the man's voice was friendly enough.

'He did not get here, Karl. He tried, but he was caught and executed in Chungking, after a farcical trial.' His face clouded. 'That happens to too many of those who start out. You have been fortunate.'

'At one time it did not seem possible that we would ever arrive,' said Palfrey. 'We always seemed to be travelling. Well, Fritz, tell me about yourself. What have you been doing?'

Von Marritz shrugged his shoulders.

'What is there different from that of anyone else? Russia, Italy and Normandy—and then disgrace because I favoured an earlier surrender. I was nearly caught after July 20th. If the lunatics had listened to us, we would never have been forced into this plight.' He looked savage—just as von Klowitz had looked when he had talked of Hitler's men without naming them. 'Well, we are safely here!' he went on more cheerfully. 'I am at fault, Karl—I should have told you at first. There is a little reception about to be held. You will come as the guests of the evening, I hope. I warned the others that you might be too tired, but judging from the Baroness——'

'Hilde,' Drusilla encouraged with a beaming smile.

Von Marritz bowed and clicked his heels again.

'I am greatly honoured! I was about to say that no one could look less travel-worn. You will come?'

'Thank you, yes,' said Drusilla.

'I will send a messenger for you in half an hour,' he told her.

Then, as Palfrey reached the front door with him, he added in a low-pitched voice: 'Give me a moment in private, Karl.'

'I will walk to the gate with you,' said Palfrey.

'Your wife will not follow?'

'Why should she follow?' asked Palfrey, with a frown.

Von Marritz grimaced.

'I forget that you have only just arrived. I warn you, Karl, that it is not as perfect here as it might appear. The women are, naturally, very jealous. All von Runst worries about is increasing the birth-rate!' His grimace became a scowl. 'There is no nonsense about pure Aryan blood with him, I warn you!' He lowered his voice, and sounded a little sheepish. 'I thought you should warn your wife that there will be Chinese women at the reception—they mix freely with us. I myself . . .' he coloured furiously. 'There was a time when it would have been inconceivable!'

'I understand.' Palfrey smiled. 'I do not think it will shock Hilde!'

'I am relieved,' said von Marritz. 'There are five men to each German woman, and that is unwise. It will be corrected, of course, as soon as possible.' Again he grew more cheerful. 'I will admit, Karl, that the Chinese women are remarkable! One has only to forget their looks—although,' he added, a little dreamily, 'they have complexions and physical grace which would make even your wife envious! My own . . . wife . . .' He hesitated.

'Yes?' Palfrey prompted.

'She comes from one of the oldest families in China,' von Marritz said. 'In Chinese eyes, she is beautiful. She is not, I think, unattractive in any way. The names they have! Milk names, they call them,' he added. 'Can you conceive, Karl, a woman who calls herself Laughing Fragrance?'

'Laughing—Fragrance!' exclaimed Palfrey.

'You see? It is absurd,' said von Marritz.

Palfrey's heart was thumping uncomfortably. The surprise in his voice had nothing to do with the name itself, only with the fact that it was one which he would never forget. *Laughing Fragrance*: the voice of Tsui Lin seemed to speak in his ears. '*I have clever, humble daughter in the big city*'; Laughing Fragrance!

He did not need to keep up appearances, for von Marritz hurried away and disappeared among the trees. Slowly Palfrey returned to the house. Drusilla had been watching from a front window, and she saw from his expression that something had affected him. She asked no questions as he sat in a small easy chair, and stretched out his long legs.

'Laughing Fragrance,' he said, with a sigh. 'Remember?'

'Tsui Lin's daughter?' Drusilla caught her breath.

'A Chinese woman of that name is here,' said Palfrey. 'I gather that there is a form of marriage, and that von Marritz calls her his wife. I suppose it is a common enough name,' he added, with an effort. 'A coincidence, no more.'

'It—it must be,' Drusilla faltered, dismayed.

'Let's call it that. Anyhow, she doesn't know us,' went on Palfrey, lighting a cigarette. 'I suppose we shall see her to-night,' he added. 'He didn't say whether we should change.'

'They wouldn't go to those lengths,' said Drusilla.

It was not the custom to change for the informal receptions given in a long, low-roofed wooden building near the cinema, to the new arrivals from the world outside. The room was crowded. There was a gramophone and a radio, a small orchestra of Chinese, who played flutes and violins, a little spasmodic dancing, abundant drinks and white-coated servants.

Men outnumbered women by at least three to one. Palfrey saw von Marritz and tried to catch a glimpse of the woman who was named Laughing Fragrance, but he could not be sure that he knew which of the Chinese it was; he could not tell them apart with any certainty, although one, taller than most, and more good-looking in European eyes, attracted his attention. She was the centre of a laughing group in which von Marritz always figured.

He sensed something else.

There was a tension in this room, as if the people were on edge. Being confined had worn their nerves and it showed in little outbursts of bad temper. The beauty of the settlement, the charm of the setting, were but a cover to hide the tension, the taut nerves and those sudden outbursts. He had one cause for satisfaction: no one else claimed to know him. Drusilla was in some difficulty when women tried to find out her background; it appeared that in spite of the acceptance of mixed 'marriages', caste was still important. Drusilla parried the attacks skilfully.

'Herr Baron,' came a gentle voice beside him. He looked round and saw a small man with a humped back, white-haired, and with sad-looking eyes and a noble face.

'Good evening.' Palfrey bowed formally.

'I am glad to welcome you,' said the white-haired man, in his gentle voice, 'but I wish also to give you a word of advice.

You are young, my friend, and you have been here but a few hours. Already, you have enemies. The husband of such a woman as your wife must have enemies,' he added, softly.

'You are talking nonsense!' snapped Palfrey.

'I understand your anger,' said the old man, 'but I have no reason to interfere, except that I wish to save you from harm. You are a man of perception. I have watched you closely. Through your mind there runs a single refrain: "They are a group of people living on their nerves." Is that not so?'

In spite of himself, Palfrey made a grudging admission.

'They do appear excitable.'

'They are like creatures whose bodies are constantly shaken by powerful electric currents,' said the old man, softly. 'Their nerves are those currents. They are liable to outbursts of hysteria, even to madness. I should not like to stand by and watch you and your beautiful wife become a prey to such unnatural emotions as possess most of the people here.'

'I do not think we are acquainted,' Palfrey said coldly.

The old man said: 'I am a doctor, Herr Baron. A psychiatrist. I am not unknown in Europe, Professor Kriess.'

'Kriess!' exclaimed Palfrey. 'I...'

His voice trailed off.

In that moment he knew that he had done a fatal thing. The name of Kriess was not well known except among the medical profession. There was no reason why von Klieb should have heard of him, but there was every reason why Dr. Palfrey should know his name.

'I have a close friend with the name Kriess,' Palfrey added stiffly. 'I——'

'It is warm in here,' said Professor Kriess. 'Come outside, where it is cooler. You will not be missed, I assure you.'

He kept a hand on Palfrey's arm as they went out of a side door. A wide lawn, hedged about by rose bushes in full bloom, faced them. Palfrey walked slowly, mechanically, without looking at his companion. Desperate thoughts were running through his mind. Better by far to find a way of killing the man than to allow his suspicions, almost certainly aroused, to be voiced. Kriess led the way to a corner, where almond trees in a wide cluster stood clear in the light of a full moon, stopped and said, still softly: 'Dr. Palfrey, you are a brave and foolish man.'

'I am the Baron von Klieb!' snapped Palfrey. 'I——'

'We have been at conferences together, you and I,' said Kriess. 'I do not mistake faces, Doctor. I have had you pointed out to me by many people. Your fame reached even Germany before the war, you understand. Shall we drop pretences?'

'There is no pretence!' said Palfrey, angrily, but his heart was beating so fast that he hardly heard his own voice.

'If you insist, I will aid your little deception,' said Kriess. 'I give you my assurance, Doctor, that you have nothing to fear from me. Have you noticed my nose, Doctor?'

'Please! I am not a doctor!'

Kriess sighed. 'I beg your pardon. Have you noticed my nose, Herr Baron?'

'No,' said Palfrey, staring at the man's nose.

'You have now,' said Kriess, ironically. 'It is large, is it not? And convex. The nose of a Jew. I am a Jew, Herr Baron. I am not a Nazi, nor a Prussian, nor a German—I am a Jew. It is said that I am the greatest living specialist in nervous disorders. I do not claim that, I tell you so because it explains why I am alive. Certain gentlemen in the Nazi party were subject to serious nervous disorders, Herr Baron. I was required to treat them until von Runst brought me away. That was when he had discovered that some of the people who had lived here for a few years were already suffering from those same disorders. Am I making myself clear, Herr Baron?'

'Admirably,' said Palfrey, stiffly.

There was no point in walking away; he must make no admissions, but this man guessed the truth and would not easily be persuaded that he was wrong.

'I am glad,' said Kriess, simply. 'I am here to help the men and women to recover from their illness, sometimes from their madness. You understand why I am sad, Herr Baron?'

'If this is true——'

'My friend, we cannot be overheard,' said Kriess, gently. 'I can tell you this, and I think it will set your mind at rest. No one else suspects you as yet. However, there are men here who have already cast lustful glances at your wife, and they are your enemies. I have known three murdered in their beds because they brought their wives with them, Herr Baron.'

Palfrey was faced with a decision which had to be made soon—whether to admit the truth to this old man or whether to insist that he was von Klieb.

He badly needed a friend in the valley.

Kriess went on, with a gentle smile: 'I am quite prepared to call you "Baron" and to help you, but I must give you my advice.'

'You are kind,' said Palfrey, stiffly.

'I am a man, Herr Baron. My advice is this: *get out of the valley*. I would advise you exactly the same even if you were von Klieb—except, of course, that I would not dare, for you would tell von Runst of it and I would not be left in peace. *Get out of the valley,* quickly!'

Palfrey said: 'I know neither the way in nor the way out.'

'Such a resourceful man as you will find a way out,' said Kriess. 'I might, perhaps, be able to help you.' He studied Palfrey's face in the bright moonlight, and suddenly he smiled. 'I know that I am wasting my time,' he went on. 'You are here for a purpose. You will try to achieve it. I do not think you will succeed, Herr Baron. Now I will not foist myself upon you any further.' He inclined his head gravely. 'I shall look forward to the pleasure of calling on you and the Baroness tomorrow.' Then he turned and walked back towards the hall.

Palfrey stood in the shade of the mulberry trees, watching him. He did not once look back. As he disappeared, Palfrey became aware of several other people in the grounds—there was nothing odd about the *tête-à-tête;* that was one relief.

A man and a woman passed within a few yards of him. The woman was German and younger than most of the others, attractive in her plump, blonde fashion. She was leaning heavily on the arm of a man whom Palfrey had seen at von Runst's headquarters. He watched them idly, trying to concentrate on what Kriess had said.

A shout from nearby made him start and look towards the hall. He saw a man burst from the doorway and rush across the lawn towards the couple, now near him again. Even in the moonlight the madness on the man's face was apparent; his lips were turned back, his eyes looked wild, and he carried a knife in his hand, the blade bare and glittering in the moon.

The woman gasped, 'Hans! . . . Hans! . . .' and then her voice trailed off. Her companion made a curious noise in his throat and turned away—and then Palfrey realised that the fellow was unable to run, his right leg was stiff. The man with the knife, silent now, was coming at great speed, making little noise on the turf. The knife was raised.

'Here!' exclaimed Palfrey, and moved forward. He was between the man with the knife and his quarry, and he shot out his foot; the crazed fellow fell over it, taken completely unawares. As he fell, Palfrey bent down and grabbed his wrist; the knife dropped from his fingers. Palfrey picked it up, and then backed away. The man lay on the ground, panting for breath, while the other couple stood watching, as if too frightened to approach.

'It is the heat,' said Palfrey, quickly.

'The heat,' cried the man with the stiff leg. 'Fetch Professor Kriess, please!'

Palfrey said: 'He is in the hall. Go for him.'

As he waited with the woman, who stared at the man on the ground, wide-eyed and trembling, several men came from the hall. Kriess was not among them. Two picked the prostrate man from the ground and, carrying him between them, took him by the side of the hall towards the main street. By the time Kriess appeared they had gone. A few words of explanation from the third man were enough to send Kriess hurrying in the wake of the little party, while someone took the woman's arm and led her away.

Palfrey went back to the hall. In a corner von Marritz was talking earnestly to Drusilla. The tall Chinese woman with the superb complexion was standing near them, smiling faintly—that smile which had now become so familiar, the smile of Tsui Lin, Ho Sun and many others, which made Palfrey feel so insignificant. She looked at Palfrey invitingly. He ignored her, and joined Drusilla.

Von Marritz spoke hurriedly.

'Karl, you should not interfere—do you understand? You *must* not interfere. Such things do not happen. They are not noticed. It is a necessary pretence. Von Runst will be angry if he learns that you interfered.'

'I begin to understand,' said Palfrey, and added briefly: 'I thought the man was going to attack me. Is there any objection to interfering in such circumstances?'

'No, no!' said von Marritz. 'I did not know that, it makes a great difference.' He looked immeasurably relieved. 'I shall report that before anyone else can put in a different report. You understand, Karl, that not everyone gets used to the heat quickly here. You will excuse me?'

'I think we will go . . .' Palfrey hesitated over the word, and then added: 'home.'

'That is wise,' said von Marritz. 'Perhaps . . .' he hesitated. 'My wife . . .'

The tall Chinese woman approached, moving with a grace which would have made her noticeable anywhere.

Von Marritz introduced her swiftly, and added:

'My wife will also go home; it is near your house, she will like your company.' He bowed stiffly and hurried off, while Laughing Fragrance looked into Drusilla's eyes, and said in excellent English: 'The Baroness has only to tell me to leave her.'

'Why should I?' asked Drusilla, as if puzzled.

'It is too hot in here,' said Palfrey. 'Come along.' He took each of them by the arm and led them out, glad to be in the fresh air again. He walked quickly at first, then slackened his pace. 'We are tired after the journey,' said Palfrey, 'and so much is strange.'

'It will grow stranger,' said Laughing Fragrance. She seemed to hide laughter in her eyes and voice. 'I think, Herr Baron, that you will enjoy it more than most. And you, Baroness, tonight you were a great success. I beg of you not to allow too many men to pay court to you, their wives are jealous. How absurd!' She raised her hands. 'This is my house. Good night.'

She walked towards a small house and, like Kriess, she did not look back.

Bright moonlight shone through the open window into their bedroom. Outside, the leaves of almond, mulberry, orange, peach and pear trees held a whispered conversation which seemed to magnify the silence. In her small bed, Drusilla slept soundly.

Palfrey was on the point of falling asleep when a faint sound disturbed him. He opened his eyes and stared at the window, but when the sound was repeated it came from the door. He looked towards it, going rigid. Nothing happened for what seemed a long time, and then it began to open. He started to get out of bed, but before his foot touched the floor, a voice came softly.

'Do not make the slightest sound.'

The voice was familiar, but he could not place it. The whisper made Drusilla stir again, but she did not wake up. The words held no threat; there was no hint of menace, only caution.

They came again. 'Do not make the slightest sound.'

Palfrey thought: 'That's Laughing Fragrance!'

She left the door open and advanced towards him, holding out a hand as if enjoining silence. Drusilla stared. Palfrey turned and saw her eyes open wide.

'It's all right,' he whispered. 'Don't make a sound.'

The Chinese woman came and stood by the side of his bed.

'I come as a friend,' she said. 'I am afraid that I was followed. Be very careful, please.'

'I do not understand,' said Palfrey, stiffly.

'There is no need for pretence with me. Orishu warned me that you would be coming, Doctor.'

'Orishu!' exclaimed Drusilla.

'Please, not so loud!' urged Laughing Fragrance. 'You have tried very hard, Dr. Palfrey, but I am afraid you have been followed. The truth is suspected. I know that von Runst and von Klowitz have been told that you are Palfrey and not von Klieb. Do not ask me how they know, nor how I discovered it. Be warned, and get away.'

Palfrey said: 'This is nonsense! I am the Baron von Klieb!'

'Please!' she entreated, raising a hand. She stood staring at him, as if trying to probe his thoughts. Drusilla sat up and watched her, and the room was very quiet.

'I have come here at great risk to warn you,' said Laughing Fragrance. 'Risk to myself and risk to my country. I am not suspected, but I will be if I am seen here.'

Palfrey said: 'I can convince Field-Marshal von Runst of the truth at any time.'

He spoke softly, looking into her eyes. He would not make a direct admission yet, for he believed it possible that this was yet another attempt to trap him—first von Marritz, then Kriess, now Laughing Fragrance. In spite of the possibility, he was not convinced of it, however. They had acted too quickly, Kriess and this woman seemed filled with a deep sincerity; yet he clung to the hope that he could serve some purpose here.

'You are a foolish man,' said Laughing Fragrance. She stared at Drusilla again, and added in a whispering voice: 'Von Klowitz admires you very much—*very* much. He is a beast of a man. His lumpy face and his glass eye—and his hands.' She seemed to shiver. 'Please, be warned by me.'

Drusilla said nothing.

Palfrey glanced at her, saw her strained expression; she was also frightened lest this prove a trick.

'If you doubt me,' said Laughing Fragrance, 'let me tell you that I received a message from Orishu telling me that you were on the way from London, that in Delhi he was impersonated by his second cousin, Matsu, that Orishu has a white streak on the right side of his parting and trims the nails of his right hand much shorter than his left. You *must* believe me!'

Drusilla said, 'Sap——' and the fact that she used his nickname told Palfrey how closely her nerves were approaching breaking point, and that she was finally convinced of the

Chinese woman's sincerity. Palfrey hitched himself further up in the bed, and smiled for the first time.

'I am beginning to believe you,' he said, 'but if you know the truth, you must see that we cannot run away now.'

'I tell you that they know you!'

'At the most they only suspect me,' said Palfrey, 'and if they suspect, they will not be surprised if I try to get information!' His mind was working much more freely, as if something had suddenly woken him up. 'If I get some I can pass it on to you—presumably you are not suspected. We must work like that. You had better go, or——'

'You will not succeed,' said Laughing Fragrance, 'but I believe that you will try. I will pray for you. If you wish to send word to me, give a message to Professor Kriess, he is the one man here who can be trusted. He might, also, provide you with some opium tablets, to secure a quick death if it becomes necessary.' The calmness of her words made their effect more telling. 'I have tried,' she said, and turned and went away.

Palfrey moved to Drusilla's bed and took her hand in his. 'Say the word and we'll try to follow their advice, but I'm not convinced that it would be wise. If we ran away and they caught us, that would put paid to everything, and it wouldn't make the situation any easier for you. If we stay, I suppose we've still half a chance.'

'Without weapons?' Drusilla protested with a catch in her voice. 'Sap, I——'

'If we're going,' said Palfrey, 'we'd better go now.'

She did not stir, but the pressure of her fingers tightened. They sat quite still for what seemed a long time. Then she relaxed, although he felt her shiver.

'You're probably right,' she conceded, at last.

'If von Runst is prepared to play cat-and-mouse with us for a few days we might get something worth passing on to Laughing Fragrance,' Palfrey said. 'At least, we can try. As a last resort, we can use the Professor's opium pills—I've no doubt he will let us have them.' From the beginning he had known that the odds were against them returning to England; there was nothing shocking about the possibility of death. He knew that he was warming to the thought of having a poison pill; it offered a solution to the worst problem—and it would help Drusilla to stand the strain.

In his mind's eye he saw a picture of von Klowitz, leering at her and saying: *'Our birth-rate is extremely high.'*

When Palfrey woke up next morning, Drusilla was dressing.

He grunted, and she looked round quickly, smiling at him so brightly that for a moment his thoughts were confused; the incident during the night seemed vague and far away. Drusilla came over to him and ruffled his hair.

'You look dreadful!' she said.

'I feel it.' Palfrey stifled a yawn. 'I had a pretty poor night. As for you—can't *any*thing keep you awake?'

'If you hadn't come in with me I think I would have been awake all night,' said Drusilla. They spoke in undertones, as if fearful that the walls had ears. 'You were right to stay, Sap.'

'I wonder if that's true.'

'While you've any chance at all to get information, you must take it,' said Drusilla. 'If she'd come in daylight it wouldn't have affected me so much. You will see Kriess, won't you?'

'He promised to call. My hat, what a place this is!'

Palfrey smoked and lounged in a long-chair after breakfast. Every time more than one man approached along the road his heart began to beat fast, but they always passed. Then von Marritz came out of his house, looking heavy-eyed, and approached them slowly. He yawned as he came up, and apologised.

'I must have had more to drink last night that I thought,' he said. 'I have a terrible headache! My wife tells me that I laid like a log all night!' He yawned again; doubtless Laughing Fragrance had drugged him to make sure that he did not see her leave. 'I shall rest, I think,' he added, 'but I came to tell you that for luncheon we shall eat in the central hall. That is the usual practice.'

'Thank you,' said Palfrey. 'Where is the hall?'

'Where we danced last night,' said von Marritz. 'Karl, I did as I promised and explained to His Excellency the Field-Marshal the reason for your interference last night. I did not think he was pleased about you. If he sends for you, I should be very humble and apologetic.'

'I will be,' Palfrey assured him.

'On the other hand, he may not send for you, but may make a speech at luncheon,' said von Marritz. 'He adopts that method sometimes, when he thinks that there is need for all of us to be reminded that we must not allow the—the heat to affect us.' He smiled sheepishly. 'You will remember how to behave if he sends for you? And now I must go back.'

He turned away, yawning.

Hardly had he gone than three men, in uniform, appeared along the road. Palfrey watched them closely. Drusilla stood up, as if she could not stand the strain—and then exclaimed beneath her breath, for the three men were entering their gate.

9 : Visitors from the Sky

THERE were two men and a lieutenant, none of whom was familiar to Palfrey. He stood up slowly, and told Drusilla to go inside. The men stood a few yards away and the lieutenant approached stiffly and saluted.

'Good morning Herr Baron. You will come with me, please.'

Palfrey frowned. 'At whose wish?'

'At the command of His Excellency the Field-Marshal,' said the lieutenant. 'At once, please!'

'Is it necessary to send an escort?' demanded Palfrey. 'I will be ready in a few minutes.'

'At once, please.'

Palfrey glared at the man, who coloured. Palfrey turned into the house, putting his hands in his pockets; he did not want Drusilla to see that they were unsteady. She was standing just inside the living-room; he kissed her cheek and smiled, and surprised himself by controlling his voice.

'It's probably a formality,' he said. 'If Kriess comes, ask him for what we want.'

'Yes.' Drusilla nodded, unable to say more.

Palfrey looked at her for an appreciable time—and then turned and hurried away. To buoy himself up, he walked very smartly.

They reached the headquarters, where a guard was on duty, and went downstairs. The place was solidly built, with concrete passages, heavy concrete roofs and concrete steps—it was as if it had been built as a protection against bombing, although surely none of them expected bombers to find them here. There was an atmosphere of hustle. Some of the men who had been at the hall passed him, but none paid him any attention. He was familiar with the way, and stopped outside the dark, wooden door of von Runst's room.

'Not in here yet,' said the lieutenant.

He led the way to a room a little further along, a cold, bleak place with a few chairs and a small table. He bowed and went out; Palfrey heard the key turn in the lock.

He sat there for at least another half an hour; then the door opened and the lieutenant stood on the threshold.

'His Excellency can see you, Herr Baron. This way, please.'

He was gratified when he saw how clearly he had remembered the details of the doors and passages from von Runst's office to the room where he had waited. He felt more confident, too—certainly that was the reverse effect of what they had intended. He saw the door of the Field-Marshal's room standing ajar—and then he heard hurried footsteps, and, running along the passage towards the door, came a Japanese.

For a single wild moment he thought it was Orishu; and then he saw that the man was older and plumper, that he was nearly bald, and had only one hand. His face was twisted with alarm, and Palfrey reflected again on the wrong impression he had received of the inscrutability of Asiatics. The Japanese disappeared into von Runst's room, and spoke rapidly in German.

'It is understood that no steps be taken——'

'Hold your tongue!' roared von Runst. Palfrey caught a glimpse of him as he strode towards the door and slammed it. The next words were inaudible, and Palfrey stared blankly at the closed door.

'His Excellency is not quite ready,' said the lieutenant, hastily. 'This way, Herr Baron.'

'I am tired of waiting,' said Palfrey, with a touch of hauteur.

'Please, Herr Baron! It would not do for you to be seen here,' said the lieutenant, who looked harassed. 'Come with me.' He led the way back to the waiting-room, Palfrey now with his head in the air and showing his annoyance. 'You understand that he was not expected to return,' said the youngster. 'I beg of you not to disclose the fact that you saw him, Herr Baron.'

'Why should I not see a Japanese?' demanded Palfrey.

'It is forbidden. It would perhaps be most difficult if it were known that I had allowed you—if it were known that you had seen him,' said the lieutenant, hastily.

'I do not see why I should cover up your errors,' snapped Palfrey. 'Did you or did you not tell me that His Excellency would see me? Am I to be marched up and down like a convict?'

'I am sorry, Herr Baron.' The man looked thoroughly miserable, and there was a pleading expression in his eyes. 'I did not know——'

'Ach! It shall be forgotten,' said Palfrey, grandly.

It was nearly half an hour before he was summoned again, and this time led without incident to von Runst's room.

Von Runst signed a paper with a flourish, blotted it, held it up and barked: 'Come nearer, von Klieb!'

Palfrey advanced smartly.

'Read that!' said von Runst.

Palfrey took the paper. It was a certificate of some kind, and when he saw the heading his heart contracted. He was conscious of von Runst's gaze, and tried to prevent himself from showing his feelings, but his heart was thumping as he read on, for the paper was a death-warrant. '*It is decreed by the Court of the Fourth Reich that SENTENCE OF DEATH be carried out . . .*'

Palfrey clenched his hands to prevent them from shaking, and then he saw two things at the same time: the smile on the Field-Marshal's face and the name 'Otto Lieber' on the warrant.

He handed the warrant back, and bowed.

'Thank you, Excellency.'

'Did you not think it was intended for you, von Klieb?' asked Runst. He had a deceptively pleasant voice in which even the gutturals lost their harshness. He was a handsome man, too, clean-shaven, with more hair than most Prussians were in the habit of growing, and a pair of gold-rimmed glasses gave him a mild expression; he was very different from von Klowitz.

'Why should I have done?' asked Palfrey. 'I know of no reason why I should be sentenced to death, Excellency. On the contrary—I have escaped death to come here to help.'

'To come here to help,' said von Runst slowly. 'Yes, that is the intention, von Klieb. I regret that you have made an extremely bad beginning. General von Klowitz told me that he had noticed a change in you, a hardening of your sensibilities, perhaps.' He paused, as if to allow the words to sink in, and Palfrey, forcing himself to show no reaction, felt sure that his real name was known, that this was part of the cat-and-mouse game which Laughing Fragrance had forecast. 'I can use strong-willed men, von Klieb, but only if their wills are subject to mine.'

'My only wish is to serve,' said Palfrey, stiffly.

'Excellent! Then understand that you will not serve me or yourself by interfering with matters of a private nature. It may interest you to know that the sentence of death which I have signed is on the man whom you prevented from—er—assaulting you, as I understand you thought to be the case.'

'I did,' said Palfrey.

'I see. Had you been here a day longer I should call you a liar,' said von Runst, unpleasantly. 'I will, on this occasion, assume that you acted under a misapprehension. You will not interfere again in my circumstances, not matter what you *think* is happening. This colony is admirably organised and very well run, von Klieb. It has been flourishing for some time. We do not need guidance on how to run it. Only, of course, if you have some special qualification—medical qualifications, perhaps?'

'Medical?' asked Palfrey, frowning. 'I——' He broke off and smiled bleakly. 'Your Excellency jokes! I adopted only the name of Dr. Palfrey, not his degrees.'

'You are *very* quick-witted,' said von Runst, heavily. 'I think I shall find you very useful, always assuming that you submit to my orders without question. I will overlook your folly of last night, von Klieb, but I want you to understand that you are on sufferance until you have proved yourself. Your actions will be watched and your manner carefully assessed. There is no room in the colony for rebels.'

'I am no rebel,' declared Palfrey.

'At the moment you look extremely rebellious,' said von Runst. 'Now, let us forget that. You have been warned.' He smiled again. 'What work do you expect to do here?'

'I am at your command,' said Palfrey.

'Most gracious of you! I will give you instructions now. I have reason to believe that one of the recent arrivals is *not* a loyal adherent to the Fourth Reich. I wish to find out who it is. There have been indications—trifling robberies, unauthorised visits to these headquarters and to other parts of the valley, which suggest that someone is endeavouring to find information. I wish you to report on anything and anyone you consider suspicious. You need not be greatly alarmed,' went on von Runst, 'for there is no possibility, *no possibility at all,* of a traitor leaving the settlement. It is, however, disturbing. You understand?'

'I will, of course, do my best,' said Palfrey, without enthusiasm. 'It would be misleading to pretend that it is the task for which I hoped.' He bowed stiffly, and as he looked at the man's beastly smile, it occurred to him that von Runst *wanted* the exiles to be set one against the other; the ragged nerves and outburst of uncontrollable rage not only amused but gratified him. 'Have you any further special instructions, Excellency?' he asked.

'None other than those I have given you,' said von Runst.

He nodded dismissal. 'You will report daily.'

Outside, in the bright sunlight and a warmth which was far greater than that in von Runst's office, Palfrey drew a deep breath of relief, and looked about him. He was left to find his own way back. He saw the first of the houses, a few hundred yards away, and strolled towards them.

Von Runst was not convinced of the allegations against him and was giving him every opportunity to pry, so that everything he did could be carefully checked.

Suddenly the quiet of the settlement was broken by a harsh droning sound—so like a raid-warning siren that he stood stock still. People in the middle of the road suddenly moved to the right and left and, to put the finishing touch to the similarity, *looked upwards*. He stared up, and as the wailing note faded he heard another sound, that of a motor-engine. Suddenly there was a loud roar, and through the trees he saw a small fighter aircraft take off. It rose swiftly, climbing steeply. He watched it, fascinated.

'You are startled, Baron,' said a man close behind him, and he started and turned round, to see Professor Kriess. He had not seen the man before, nor noticed his approach.

'Yes. Is it——'

'We take all precautions here,' said Kriess. 'It is an air-raid warning. It happens most weeks when an aircraft flies near. Now and again it comes too near—it is a passenger aircraft, you understand.'

'What happens if it flies too near?' asked Palfrey, in a harsh voice.

'It is shot down,' said Kriess, simply. 'No risks are taken. There is nothing surprising about aircraft being lost in such a region as this. Two have been brought down since I have been here, Baron, and each crashed in flames.' He touched Palfrey's arm. 'I have seen your wife. I will, of course, oblige her.'

'Thank you.' Palfrey felt a constriction in his throat.

'And I am very glad that you are so sensible,' said Kriess.

He went on his way.

Drusilla was standing by the door of the little house.

'What was that?' she asked. 'I thought I saw an aeroplane.'

'You did,' said Palfrey, and explained.

'I——Sap! What's that?'

'Karl, you sap! Gunfire, I think,' said Palfrey.

The barking noise which came from high above their heads was unmistakable. He wished that he could get to a clearing and watch. He saw a little group standing by a tree staring upwards; taking Drusilla's arm, he went to join them. They could just see a clear patch of sky and an aeroplane cavorting —and then they saw a larger one, flying slowly with smoke pouring from its tail.

The tension was on everyone. They heard the *pup-pup-pup* of the guns and the larger aircraft coming down more quickly. The fighter flew about it like an angry wasp; the shooting stopped. Then suddenly little black dots appeared against the sky, and Palfrey's hands clenched.

'They're jumping,' he said. 'Three . . . four . . . five of them, and the parachutes are opening!'

Palfrey stood watching, his eyes bright. Drusilla moved a little, to get a better view. There was silence among the watching crowd for what seemed a long time. The little white circles in the sky seemed incredibly tiny at first, but soon it was possible to see the men dangling from them, tiny dark marks against the pale blue sky. The stricken aircraft, flames and smoke now belching from its belly and its tail, went downwards towards the mountains, with the fighter circling it; the parachutists were over the valley itself, and Palfrey did not think that they would fall more than three or four miles from the settlement.

The high-pitched whine of an electrically-driven car broke the silence, and was followed by several others. Small cars with three men in each tore along the road and branched off on a side road, towards the spot where the parachutes were likely to land. Palfrey recognised von Marritz and the lieutenant from Headquarters.

'Let's get a grandstand view,' he said eagerly.

As he led Drusilla away from the crowd, the 'raiders passed' signal went; it was an odd reminder of days which they had thought were over. Palfrey hurried across his own garden and through another to a rise in the land where several of the residents were already standing. Their set faces and glittering eyes gave them away: they were frightened. Here, there could be little danger, yet the thought of danger was uppermost. They stared, fascinated, as the first parachute collapsed and a car moved forward, its three occupants bristling with guns. One after the other the others collapsed, dragging the men along the ground before they came to rest.

Soon the five men were herded together.

Palfrey felt Drusilla's fingers clutch his arm.

He watched with an increasing sense of excitement, for one thing stood out clearly: four of the men were short compared with the fifth, a giant who towered over them. When von

Marritz, who was six feet tall, stood by him, the man was still a head above him. The pressure of Drusilla's fingers tightened, but she did not speak.

The prisoners were hustled towards the cars, the tall man apart from the rest—and with von Marritz, as if he were privileged. He was the only one in Western clothes. It was too far away from them to see his features, but hope was rising in Palfrey's heart. Soon the cars moved towards the village; they had to pass within a few hundred feet of Palfrey, and as they drew nearer he found himself gritting his teeth, and he heard Drusilla's heavy breathing.

The four men in uniform came in the first cars; two were Chinese, two were probably English. Then the third car came, and they knew, without any doubt, that the fifth parachutist was Stefan.

Speculation was simply a waste of time, and Palfrey and Drusilla walked back to their house. The fact that there was nothing they could do wore their nerves.

They went along to the hall for lunch. Everyone seemed to have an abstracted air, and there was little or no conversation —a thing which surprised Palfrey and enabled him to understand how the visitors from the skies had affected them.

Towards the end of the meal the tension relaxed a little. Palfrey and Drusilla, sitting at a small table in one corner, heard their neighbours talking more freely. They were speculating on whether von Runst would address them. Apparently that was a custom when anything untoward happened, and the hall at lunchtime was the chosen place. Eyes were turned towards the open doors.

Footsteps on the wooden steps were followed by the tall shadows of three men. Von Runst, von Klowitz and von Marritz entered and marched straight to the dais where the orchestra had played the previous night. Then von Klowitz coughed, raised his hand and said: 'Your attention, please, immediately, for His Excellency the Field-Marshal.'

'You are doubtless wondering who has come to visit us,' said von Runst, in a tone of gentle irony. 'I have come to set your minds at rest. In fact, we are to be congratulated once again. The aeroplane was one which had been forced off its course by a thunderstorm which raged yesterday evening to the west. It contained two Chinese and two English officers, returning to Europe for consultations with the authorities, and a prisoner—a German prisoner who had been caught while attempting to reach us here. The name of the prisoner some of you may know. It is Goetz—Hans Goetz, one-time Gauleiter for Amsterdam.' Von Runst paused. 'I would like to hear from anyone who knows Hans Goetz,' he added.

Palfrey tried to see every corner of the room. If there were a single person here who knew the man, then Stefan's deception would be doomed to failure from the beginning. A chair scraped on the floor, and his heart missed a beat. Someone coughed. Von Runst's mild blue eyes roved about the room, and then he shrugged his shoulders.

'That is to be regretted. I wished that Goetz would have a friend among us. However, I have no doubt that he will soon make friends. You will be glad to hear that he is a clever man. It is true that he was once a fanatical Nazi. We here are not fanatical Nazis, we are Germans. Goetz will come to understand that Germany is more important than its one-time rulers.'

Back in the bungalow, Drusilla said: 'It means that he will mix freely with us.'

'When his Nazi ideas have been drummed out of him,' said Palfrey, with a grin. All we have to do is to hold on for a bit.'

'I don't follow you.'

'Stefan didn't come by accident,' Palfrey told her simply. 'The whole thing was a put-up job.'

'But how can we get in touch with him? How can we talk in confidence? I never feel that we're safe, even in here.'

'Safe!' echoed Palfrey. 'I'd rather be sitting on the edge of a volcano! We mustn't forget that the notorious Dr. Palfrey was known to work with Drusilla Blair and Stefan Andromovitch, a Russian of great size. They may not know it here, but if they do, von Runst will probably see through it.'

'Which means we're in a worse position than ever.'

'I don't think so,' said Palfrey. 'I don't think we were ever expected to get out of here under our own steam. I think we've been delivered here to find information, and that when the time is ripe the valley will be attacked. Our job is to stay alive until that happy day!'

'Sap—do you thing that Japanese you saw has anything to do with the mystery?'

'Karl, you sap—or have I said that before?' joked Palfrey. 'I wouldn't be at all surprised, my sweet. I wish I knew where the Japanese is now, and who else knows that he's in the valley, and above all I wish I knew the name of a Japanese of some importance who has only one hand. Stefan might know.'

'You talk as if all he has to do is to come here and knock

at the door,' said Drusilla. 'I——'

She broke off, for one of the little electric cars pulled up outside. Palfrey saw von Klowitz climb out of it, as his chauffeur stood stiffly to attention by the open door. The General took his monocle from his eyes, seemed to sniff the air, and then walked swiftly towards the door. He thundered on it, and was in the tiny hall when Drusilla reached it.

'My dear Baroness!' cried von Klowitz, delightedly. 'I am fortunate to find you in! I know your husband will forgive you if you spare an old man an hour of your time,' he added. 'I think you will enjoy a drive through the valley, my dear!'

'I—yes, very much,' said Drusilla, hastily.

'Excellent!' Von Klowitz turned to Palfrey. 'You will not object, my dear Karl?'

'On the contrary, I am delighted,' said Palfrey.

'Excellent!' Von Klowitz beamed. 'Come, my dear!'

There was a devil in the man! By his gestures, by the glint in his eyes, by the little movements of his thin lips, he implied that he was baiting them, that he knew the tension which his invitation created, that he enjoyed making them suffer the agonies of uncertainty. There was mockery in his eyes as he bowed to Palfrey and slipped an arm through Drusilla's. He led her to the car, and Palfrey stood watching as they were driven off towards Headquarters.

Palfrey felt much as he had done when he had been taken off that morning—except that his fears for Drusilla were greater. He was agitated, and smoked heavily for the next hour. His enforced inactivity got on his nerves, and suddenly he tossed a cigarette away and stood up.

He had plenty to do: he had instructions to be a Paul Pry!

Apparently the settlement enjoyed an afternoon siesta. He saw no one except men who were obviously doing guard duty, although they did not carry guns. Why was it necessary to watch the people so closely? It was a crazy situation!

He soon gave up the hopeless quest; von Runst had given him work which he could not do, it was all part of the effort to play on his nerves, but why did the man not come out with an open accusation? Palfrey's idea that the Field-Marshal was not sure of the justice of the accusation began to fade.

He walked along a narrow path beneath a copse. In different circumstances it would have been delightful, for it was cool and the birds made music.

He came unexpectedly upon the river.

It was no more than twelve feet wide, and flowed slowly

through the valley. A little further along there were small rocks, and he walked to them and sat on the lower ones, the sun hidden by a rock which towered above him.

Into the quiet of the afternoon, a cool voice came.

'You are wishing you had changed your mind,' said Laughing Fragrance. 'No! Don't look round!'

He stared at the water, his body tense.

'Where are you?'

'In the woods behind the rocks. I cannot be seen. It is not wise to be seen together. Doctor——'

'*Baron!*' exploded Palfrey.

'I shall not speak when we might be overheard,' said the woman, lightly. 'I came a different way and have seen no one for some time, no one will dream that we are together. Doctor, do you know who has joined us?'

Palfrey said nothing.

'It is Andromovitch.' Laughing Fragrance waited. When he made no comment, she went on: 'So you do know. There is a danger that he will be identified, and if that is done there will be no possible hope for you. You are at the outskirts of the village. You can walk through these woods behind you and disappear. You may not get another chance.'

'Look here,' said Palfrey, and added weakly: 'Don't talk nonsense!'

She laughed. 'You are stubborn—I am beginning to understand why Orishu showed such pleasure when he learned that you were coming to help us.'

'Did he?' asked Palfrey, perfunctorily. 'For all the good I can do, I might just as well not have come. I——' He broke off, and had to exert himself not to turn his head. 'Laughing——' He stopped. 'Is that your only name?'

She laughed again.

'Most Europeans think it is delightful! I have another name, however—Min Shu.' On her lips the syllables were like softly-running water. 'Min Shu,' she repeated, 'but do not use it when anyone else is near, only my husband is aware of it.'

'Why did you marry——' Palfrey began, and then stopped abruptly. 'I'm sorry. Min Shu, do you know of a Japanese with only one hand?'

'One hand?' she repeated.

'Yes. A tubby—that is, fat—little fellow, bald-headed and with his left hand missing. He was with von Runst this morning and said something about "nothing being started yet". I didn't gather why.'

She did not reply.

He waited for so long that again he was sorely tempted to look round, but he restrained himself and spoke more sharply.

'Did you hear me?'

'Yes,' she said. 'And you ask what good you are doing!'

'For the love of Mike, don't make more mystery!' snapped Palfrey. 'Who is he?'

'Hiroto,' she said, very softly. 'Hiroto, the Emperor's most trusted confidant, *Hiroto!*'

'Well——' began Palfrey.

'Do not pretend that you do not understand!' snapped Laughing Fragrance. 'The Government has refused for a long time to come to any agreement with Germany, and was against giving sanctuary to any of them. I have never known why it was persuaded. Now I think I see a reason. Hiroto arranged it—the man has the cunning of a thousand serpents, he has seen some good reason for bringing the Emperor and von Runst together. Out of the very jaws of defeat they hope to snatch some share of victory.' Her words were scarcely audible. 'Do you want to hear more about Hiroto? He is the liaison between the Cabinet and the Emperor. He was instrumental in bringing about Tojo's downfall. He works behind the scenes but his influence has never been greater. It is said that he has been known to defy the Emperor in person. If Hiroto is here, then there is some scheme of greater importance than I ever dreamed.'

Palfrey said: 'There must be something of the kind. This place is a problem in itself, it's more like a home for lost souls than for scheming *Junkers*.'

'Oh, that!' she said. 'You would never expect von Runst to care for anyone who could not do exactly what he wanted. Most of the women are here simply because men cannot do without them. Do not harass yourself with wondering why there are such queer things happening.'

'We're talking for the sake of it, Min Shu, and I must get back.' He stood up. 'Is there anything else you want to talk about?'

'Not for the moment. Why are you in such a hurry? Do not imagine that your wife will be waiting for you.'

Palfrey caught his breath.

'I warned you about her,' Laughing Fragrance reminded him.

'What do you mean?' he snapped, and when she did not answer at once, added fiercely: 'Do you know what is happening to her?'

'I know that she was taken away by von Klowitz,' said Laughing Fragrance, very softly. 'Such sacrifices are necessary,

Doctor. I allowed myself to *marry* von Marritz. You . . .' her voice trailed off, for Palfrey began to walk away. He did not look back, he did not hear her again as he sped on. He passed through the copse, looking neither right nor left, with no idea of what he would do if he reached the house and found it still empty. He burst through the trees, and saw the little house a hundred yards away; the shadow of a great chestnut fell upon its roof.

He made for it, but had not gone a dozen yards before he heard the report of a shot; a second followed, and they came from his house.

Palfrey raced across the grass, and saw no movement from any of the other little houses. As he drew near his own, one of the guards from the street approached. He hurried through the back door into the passage—and then he stopped dead.

Drusilla stood on the threshold of the living-room, an automatic in her hand. She glanced round at Palfrey but kept her gun trained into the room.

'This man is a thief!'

On one knee in the corner of the room was a man whom he did not recognise. He was a German, dressed in a khaki linen suit. On the floor was a heavy automatic, just out of reach. He looked up malignantly, his broad, red face flushed with rage. There was a wound in the back of his right hand.

The guard came hurrying through the front doorway.

'What's the matter?' he demanded.

Drusilla said: 'I returned home and found this man searching my rooms. I called to him, and he drew a gun. I shot him.'

'Where did you get the gun?' asked the guard, stretching out his hand for it.

'It is a gift from General von Klowitz.' Drusilla kept a tight hold on it, 'I shall give it to no one but the General!'

The guard looked startled, and drew back.

'I understand, Baroness.' He turned to the kneeling man and snapped: 'Come, at once!'

'Wait,' said Palfrey. He drew himself up and looked angrily into the eyes of the thief. No one could have played the part of an outraged German officer better than Palfrey did then. His cold gaze, his curling lip and the tone of his voice made the guard stiffen and brought the kneeling man to his feet hurriedly.

'Secure the gun,' said Palfrey, and the guard hastened to obey. 'Give it me!' snapped Palfrey, and glared at the thief. 'Why did you come here?' He stepped forward and slapped the man on the face—and along the narrow path from the road came General von Klowitz and his aide, von Marritz.

Palfrey screamed: 'Open your mouth, you sullen pig! Open your mouth and talk!' He struck again, hard enough to knock the man against the wall. 'Answer me! Why did you come?'

'You seem excited, Baron,' said von Klowitz, with exaggerated casualness. 'What is the matter?'

Palfrey swung round on him.

'This pig dog was in my house and attacked my wife, and now will not answer my questions. What happens here when a woman is insulted, what happens to a thief?'

Von Klowitz stared at him from narrowed eyes, but did not interfere. Palfrey stood over the man with his fists clenched, livid with rage and trembling from head to foot. There was a moment of uncertainty, and then the victim gave way.

'I—I had orders to come——'

'Whose orders?'

'I—I am not free to say, I——'

'Name the man,' ordered von Klowitz.

'It was *Herr Oberst*—Colonel Barlack.'

'Barlack!' exclaimed Palfrey, genuinely surprised. 'Why should a man of whom I know so little send a thief to my house? Why did he send you? What did you seek?'

The man gasped: 'Any—any papers, any evidence that——'

Palfrey drew himself up and sneered:

'So the thoughtful Colonel Barlack sent you from the front fortress to explore *my* belongings, to find evidence—evidence of what, you swine? Evidence—or *money*? Evidence—or *jewels*?'

He thrust his hand into his pocket and drew it out, holding two diamonds on his palm; the sun caught them and brought a sparkling brilliance into the room. 'Admit it! You came to steal!' He drew himself up and bowed to von Klowitz, who continued to eye him with an air of mild surprise. 'His Excellency the Field-Marshal was good enough to entrust me with a commission. I believe that I have executed it. I must request an interview with the Field-Marshal, to discharge my duties and at the same time to give the lie to this dog's allegations. Evidence! Loot is the word!'

Von Klowitz said: 'Guard, take him away.' He waited until the wounded man was led out of the house, and then he smiled sardonically at Palfrey, adjusting his monocle absently. 'I must commend you for your method of interrogation,' he said, 'and I will arrange an interview with His Excellency. However, I would not, if I were you, *demand* such a privilege.'

'If in the heat of the moment I was impertinent, I apologise,' said Palfrey, stiffly.

'You are wise.' von Klowitz turned to Drusilla. There was no mockery in his smile now. 'I congratulate you also, Baroness, on the excellent use to which you put my little gift. It is obviously in good hands.'

He turned away.

Palfrey stood watching him, standing stiffly at attention, and did not move until he had disappeared. Then he relaxed and went into the sitting-room. He wiped the perspiration from his forehead and grinned at Drusilla.

'I came expecting to find you dead, and instead——'

'I think he would have killed me.' Drusilla ran her fingers through her hair distractedly. 'Sap, nothing goes as you expect it in this madhouse! I went along with von Klowitz, and I had my hand on one of the Professor's tablets all the time. He took me to Headquarters, and I thought I saw what he was after. I went with him into a room where Stefan was being questioned. He watched me closely all the time, expecting me to show some sign of recognition. Stefan was also closely watched, but of course neither of us winked an eye. Then'—she paused, as if she could not believe it—'von Klowitz took me along to von Runst; we talked idly for half an hour, and before I left with an escort von Klowitz gave me the automatic and told me not to hesitate to use it if I thought it necessary. What sense *is* there in it?'

'I give up,' said Palfrey. 'I—wait a minute, though.'

He took the gun from her, opened the chamber and shook the bullets into the palm of his hand. He inspected them closely, and obviously saw what he expected to find.

'Not bad,' he said, smiling faintly. 'Look—there's a little mark on each one of them, the bullets would be easily identified. If we had used it for a sly shot it would have been all up with you.'

'Be sensible.' Drusilla protested. "Why should they give me a chance to make a sly shot?'

'That's true,' admitted Palfrey, disappointedly. 'It almost looks as if they trust you.' He stared at her, with his eyes narrowed, and he began to twist a few strands of hair about his forefinger.

'Don't do that!' said Drusilla, sharply.

Palfrey drew his hand away. 'No, a bad habit here. Well, we're making better progress than we expected, there's no question of going backward! Laughing Fragrance, who is also known as Min Shu, told me that my little one-handed Jap is a person of some consequence behind the scenes in Tokyo—by name Hiroto. There is some pretty scheme afoot all right.'

A messenger came from the Field-Marshal an hour afterwards. Palfrey left Drusilla alone, not without uneasiness but less troubled because she had a gun. The entrance to Headquarters and the passages were now familiar, and he took careful note of them again.

A sentry was standing outside von Runst's door and forbade them to enter. Palfrey frowned as if annoyed, but the messenger did not seem surprised, and led him to the waiting-room. As he entered, another door opened further along the passage. He saw into a long room and he thought he saw a stage at one end of it. That interested him less than half a dozen men who streamed out of the room in some excitement.

Each was immaculately dressed, each was good-looking and wore make-up; that was less surprising than the fact that not one of them was of medium height; most were about five feet tall, and looked tiny against his German escort. They looked up at Palfrey incuriously, and filed past him. Had he seen them in a half light, he would have thought them Japanese, but there was no mistaking their white skin and he felt they were German. A coarse jest from one of them in German confirmed the impression. They went through another door and disappeared.

Palfrey looked at his escort with raised eyebrows.

'Who are they?'

'I must not answer questions,' said the man.

Palfrey shrugged his shoulders and settled down to wait. He could not get rid of the mental images of the little men, and was thinking of them when the door opened and he was bidden to hurry.

The two Prussians were in von Runst's room, and this time the Field-Marshal made no effort to impress him. He looked up with a broad smile, and Palfrey found it hard not to believe that the man was genuinely friendly.

'I am glad to see you, von Klieb. Sit down.' He pointed to a chair, and pushed a box of cigars across the table. Palfrey took one and bit off the end. Von Klowitz gave him a light, and in that atmosphere of concord von Runst said:

'I little thought that you would have such quick results, von Klieb. I will be a little more frank with you than I was before. The trouble here is pilfering—not on a large scale and not serious, but annoying. Small trinkets have been stolen, some food and wines.' He shrugged his shoulders. 'The man whom you interrogated has made a full confession. It appears that Colonel Barlack is not satisfied with the provisions which we gave to him at the outer fortress, and seeks to implement them by arranging foraging expeditions of his own. He uses men under his command.' Von Runst smiled gently. 'I shall have to sign another death-warrant shortly!'

Palfrey frowned. 'I am far more troubled by the wild accusations which Barlack's man made against me. He knew, it appears, that I had travelled in the guise of the notorious Dr. Palfrey, and made sarcastic references which made me think that he was insolent enough to disbelieve me. That, I imagine, is what his man meant.'

Von Runst spoke heavily.

'It is, von Klieb. You may know, now, that Barlack had sent a report expressing his suspicions.'

'The man is a fool as well as a rogue,' declared Palfrey.

'It begins to appear so.' Von Runst shot a quick glance at von Klowitz. 'Two people who knew you before have no doubt of your identity, so you need have no further anxiety on that score.'

'I am glad the matter is adjusted.'

'However, one thing has happened,' said von Runst, 'and it will be of particular interest to you. You heard me speak of Hans Goetz, who came unexpectedly this morning.'

'Yes.' Palfrey nodded.

'He is not Hans Goetz,' said von Runst. 'He is a Russian who worked for some time with the real Dr. Palfrey.'

Von Runst smiled with great satisfaction, and von Klowitz chuckled. Palfrey managed to save himself from showing any change of expression.

He said: 'That is remarkable—too remarkable for coincidence, Excellency. Has the man talked?'

'He admits nothing,' said von Runst. 'However, Hans Goetz was killed in a flying accident some months ago. There is no doubt of that—it was reported in the Berlin press just before the capitulation—we have a copy of the paper here as well as a photograph of Goetz.' He tapped a newspaper which was folded by his side. 'This man is the Russian. I am wondering if we can use him for our own ends or whether to shoot him at once.'

Palfrey shrugged eloquently 'I would shoot him.' The words nearly stuck in his throat. At all costs, he must not show the slightest sympathy for Stefan nor at this juncture do anything which might make them think he wished to save his life. A wrong step now might undo all the good he had done.

He thought that von Runst was satisfied with his comment.

'I would do so, normally,' he said, 'and yet it appears to me that we have an exceptional opportunity of learning *how* the Russian discovered where to come.'

Palfrey looked at him as if puzzled.

'So there are limits to your perception,' said von Runst with his deceptive smile and in a voice which was almost a coo. 'If you have successfully posed as Palfrey, my dear Baron, what is there to prevent you from doing so again? What is there to prevent you from discussing matters with Andromovitch?'

'It is impossible!' gasped Palfrey, in dismay. 'Impossible, Excellency! On the journey I met no one who was familiar with Palfrey. This man Andromovitch, you say, has worked with him. My voice, expression, mannerisms, all are different!' He cracked his knuckles explosively. 'I beg you to consider the folly of that, Excellency!'

'Folly?' asked von Runst. He seemed amused. 'What harm can come of the attempt? After all, you will tell him that you *are Palfrey,* disguised as von Klieb! I do not think that the prospects are as poor as you would like to make out, I have given this matter some thought,' went on von Runst, 'and have decided that Andromovitch shall have an opportunity to escape. He will find himself on the banks of the river—near the spot where you waited for Barlack's man to materialise,' he added.

Palfrey stared. 'Was I observed?'

'Everyone here is observed all the time,' said von Runst. 'In fact, your journey this afternoon put into my mind the possibility of a talk with Andromovitch. Did you know that you were followed, von Klieb?'

'Followed!' exclaimed Palfrey.

'By that very charming wife of von Marritz,' said von Runst, smoothly. 'She was within a few yards of you all the time, watching you closely. She is a comparatively new member of our little family,' he went on, 'and came here with a small party of Chinese women who, we believed, would be appreciated by our men. There have been indications that she is not what she seems. For one thing, she is known to be an acquaintance of a Japanese renegade who works for the Allies —a man named Orishu.' He uttered the name carefully, but appeared intent on his cigar and went on without a pause. 'We have watched her closely. We have come to the conclusion that, like Andromovitch, she is a spy. It is clear that she came to the conclusion that you *might* be Dr. Palfrey, and came to study you at close quarters. As she made no further approach, it can be assumed that she was not satisfied.'

Palfrey said: 'Then that——'

He broke off. He wanted to show astonishment, and a heaven sent opportunity was presented, he had no need to finish his sentence, for they would not suspect why his mind was suddenly in turmoil, grappling with an entirely new situation. One thing emerged: if they believed that Laughing Fragrance was a spy, and had seen her approach him without making her presence known, that was strong evidence in support of him as von Klieb; he was elated because she had been so cautious.

'You were about to say, perhaps, that if she was not satisfied that you are Palfrey, Andromovitch is not likely to be,' said von Runst. 'That is a good point! We must, therefore, arrange for your meeting to take place in a poor light. I think that can be managed. Now, von Klieb.' He leaned forward, and for the first time he seemed to take more than a casual interest in what he was saying. 'You have a great responsibility. We must find out from Andromovitch how he discovered where to come, and we must extort a full confession. By your success or failure on this mission your future position among us will be decided.'

'I will do my best, of course. When is this meeting to take place?'

'We will waste no time,' said von Runst. 'Andromovitch will be allowed to escape tonight. I will send a messenger for you during the evening. Be prepared, even if you have gone to bed. Say nothing of this to your wife.'

'Naturally not, Excellency,' said Palfrey. 'But I am alarmed by the suspicions of von Marritz's wife. She has been friendly to my wife, and von Marritz and I, of course, are old acquaintances. It is extremely difficult——' His voice trailed off.

'I do not think that it will give you further cause for anxiety,' said von Runst. 'The woman's interest in you is easily explained—it was noticed last evening that she took especial notice of you. She is not likely to continue to do so now that she knows that you are not Palfrey.' That little snake-like smile appeared again. 'Moreover, von Marritz will not be here and his wife will probably keep to her house.'

'Von Marritz——' began Palfrey.

'We think it better that he is not at hand for the next few days,' said von Runst, 'and as Barlack is to be removed from his post at the outer fortress, von Marritz will replace him. Orders to that effect are on the way to him. Have no fear, von Klieb, our precautions are not apparent but they are very thorough. You have a little time to prepare your approach to Andromovitch,' he added. 'You must begin at once.'

Palfrey stood up and saluted. 'I am grateful for the opportunity, Excellency.'

'Splendid! Oh, one small thing. I have been studying a dossier on Dr. Palfrey which was sent to me by some very good friends. It contains a summary of his mannerisms, his manner and a record of his known activities. You will familiarise yourself with the details.' He handed Palfrey a small folder filled with papers, and added: 'Be ready at any time after dark.'

10 : Stefan

'CAN we save Stefan?' asked Palfrey. His voice was subdued. 'I can carry a story back to von Runst that will probably satisfy him, but I can't be sure.'

'Supposing the circumstances were reversed?' asked Drusilla. 'Stefan would say: "First and last, Sap, comes the work we are doing. No individual life is worth saving at the expense of a cause."'

After a long silence, Palfrey gave her a bleak smile.

'Yes, you're right. He'd look on it that way.'

'So do you,' said Drusilla. 'I wonder if you'll be able to get any information from him for us?'

'It isn't likely,' Palfrey frowned. 'I'll have to guide the conversation somehow, warn him that we're being overheard. They'll have a witness who can understand English, and I daren't slip up. That in itself is the very devil of a problem,' he added. 'I—— Great Scott! Hark at that!'

They jumped to their feet as, loud and clear, there came the wail of the air-raid warning. It rose to a high-pitched note and fell again, rose and fell a dozen times while they stared at each other in the gathering darkness. The engine of an aeroplane started up, shattering the quiet. Palfrey hurried to the window and looked out, half expecting to see searchlights, but there were none, and he said:

'They daren't show powerful lights by night, of course.'

'No. I wonder——'

'If we're in for a raid,' said Palfrey. 'So do I.' He felt keyed up, less afraid of physical danger than of a development which would disrupt all his plans and hopes. All lights had gone out and when Drusilla pressed a switch, no light came on.

'General black-out,' said Palfrey. 'Listen!'

The faint drone of an aeroplane engine was clear enough; he thought he heard two or three, but could not be sure. The droning faded, and there was no shooting, no warning whistle of a bomb, no ominous crump. He stood away from the window and lit a cigarette.

Before he had finished it the 'raiders passed' wail went.

'I hope it doesn't make them alter their plans,' he murmured.

The light came on.

Drusilla was on edge, and he fervently wished it were not necessary to leave her behind. It was a pity that Laughing Fragrance could not keep her company—it did not matter where he turned, there were complications.

He smoked another cigarette as he looked through the dossier which von Runst had given him. It was very thorough, but it missed many human touches which Brett's dossier of von Klieb had included. It did, however, mention his habit of twisting strands of hair about his forefinger, and he read aloud, with some amusement:

'Listen to this: "Palfrey frequently pulls his hair, *from the left side of his forehead,* straight up and then, *invariably with the right hand,* twists some hair about his forefinger. When finished, he smooths the hair down and presses the palm of his hand against it." Not bad!'

Footsteps were followed by a sharp knock at the front door.

'This is it,' said Drusilla, with a catch in her voice.

It was a sergeant from headquarters.

Palfrey knew that he was in a dangerous mood of elation, and the bubble of it might burst at any moment, sending him into the depths of dark depression. While it lasted, he revelled in it. He settled down next to the driver of the car, seeing in his mind's eye the brief note written by von Runst, saying: *'This sergeant will drive you near the spot.'*

He broke the silence as they turned off the road which ran through the village.

'That warning was unusual, was it not?'

'We do get them,' said the sergeant, casually enough. 'Usually it is an aircraft flying near, and it is necessary to put out the lights. I myself have spoken to the pilot of the aircraft we sent up. The machines flew north, and not over the valley.'

'Good!' said Palfrey.

'They will never find us here,' said the sergeant. 'Never!' Judging from the blaze of his headlights, he was quite confident, and Palfrey wondered whether von Runst knew that they were so bright. There were no other cars about, and no other lights.

'How far are we to go?' he asked.

'Not far,' said the sergeant.

He slowed down soon afterwards, obviously looking for landmarks. At last he stopped, jumped out and opened Palfrey's door.

'His Excellency told me to leave you at this spot, *Herr Oberst*. You have a torch?'

'Yes,' Palfrey nodded, climbing out.

The sergeant handed him a sealed envelope, then climbed back into the car and drove off. Palfrey shone his torch on the envelope and took out the orders. They were also in von Runst's handwriting.

You will wait here for Andromovitch, who will be alone. You will tell him that you arranged for the door of his prison to be unlocked and for the passages leading here to be cleared of guards.

Palfrey switched off the torch, to let his eyes become accustomed to the darkness. He could pick out the shapes of rocks and trees, and, further away, what looked like a small hill. The night grew brighter as the mist cleared from the sky. He wondered whether there were many wild animals in the valley. Odd that he had not thought about it before; now, it made him jumpy, and he touched the gun in his pocket for reassurance.

Then he heard a rustle.

He stood quite still, peering towards the rocks, and the sound continued; he thought it was footsteps moving through long grass. His heart was beating faster, and he could hear its painful thumping.

Slowly a figure emerged from the shadow of the rocks, tall and unmistakable. As Palfrey stood watching, Stefan peered about him. The light was improving, the moon was rising above the distant mountains, and the stars grew pale.

Palfrey whispered: *'Stefan!'*

Stefan stopped moving, but remained a clear silhouette against the shining surface of the river. Somewhere near, Palfrey was certain, a man was lurking, ready to listen to every word. The next few seconds were vital.

'Stay where you are,' he said, in English.

He moved forward swiftly. Obviously Stefan saw him coming. He could hear the Russian's heavy breathing but no other sound. He prayed that he would be able to speak quickly and softly enough not to be overheard.

'Stefan! It is I, Palfrey!' Von Klieb would speak like that, just like that; he even managed to make his voice sound harsh, although he was quivering with excitement.

'Stay there, you German swine,' growled Stefan.

Palfrey thought: 'Does he think I'm von Klieb?' It was so utterly different from the greeting he had expected, but he was delighted; no one who overheard this encounter would have any doubt of Stefan's opinion. He stood quite still and added in a pleading voice: 'Do not make a mistake, Stefan. I—— You *fool!*'

His voice ended in alarm, for Stefan jumped at him. He backed away as Stefan closed with him and they crashed down. For a wild moment Palfrey was afraid that whoever was listening would come to his rescue, and then he heard Stefan's whisper in his ear: 'Keep struggling, Sap! It is a trick, of course?'

'Yes, but how——'

'They would never have allowed me to get out otherwise,' said Stefan. They were squirming on the ground, their bodies pressed close together, but Stefan managed to keep most of his weight off Palfrey. 'You have completely fooled them—is that so?'

'I think so. I'm here to get information from you.'

There was a laugh in Stefan's voice. 'I will give it you! Are we overheard?'

'Probably.'

'You had better succeed in overpowering me,' said Stefan, 'but not at once, Sap. Listen! There are several hundred Chinese in the valley.'

Palfrey gasped: *'What?'*

'Quieter! They descended by parachute a short while ago, during that alert. Do not ask questions now! They are in hiding for the time being, but it may be necessary for them to attack soon. Keep close to me if that happens.'

'Yes,' said Palfrey.

'Now,' whispered Stefan, 'overwhelm me!'

They pretended to struggle for a few seconds more, and then Stefan let out a convincing groan and fell back. Palfrey pushed him away, and slowly got up. Stefan lay on the ground, drawing in deep breaths, like a man suffering from great pain. Palfrey dusted himself down and stood looking at the Russian, trying to make up his mind what next to do. He was breathing heavily, and that was no pretence.

At last he said: 'Stefan, you should not have done that, I tell you that it is I, Sap!'

'You are a German swine!' growled Stefan. 'I have heard of you, von Klieb.'

'Be sensible!' pleaded Palfrey, and he hoped that someone was listening; to go through this without an audience would be intolerable. 'They *think* I am von Klieb, Stefan, I came here in place of von Klieb, they are convinced of my identity. Von Klieb is dead—don't you understand, *dead*!'

'It is so hard to believe,' said Stefan. 'I——'

Palfrey said: 'You must believe it! Stefan, how did you get here? How did you know——'

'The valley is known,' said Stefan. 'It has been suspected for some time. It was known that you were trying to get in but you were found dead—or so Brett told me——' He broke off, with a wondering air. 'If you are lying——'

'I am *not* lying!' snapped Palfrey, but he was suddenly alarmed, in case that statement was taken too literally; as far as he knew, von Runst had no idea that Palfrey had started out to come to the valley. 'It was not an accident, then, your arrival?'

'It was carefully planned. I was to try to convince them that I was Goetz, and stay for at least seven days. In seven days the valley will be attacked from the air, the Germans here will get no quarter. It is suspected that some of them may have a secret way out, and I was to try to find exactly what they are planning. Sap, *you* can do that!'

'It is why I am here,' said Palfrey. 'Listen to me—we may not have much time. How can I get a message out of the valley?'

'There is no way,' said Stefan, 'you will have to wait until you are rescued by the troops from the air, Sap. Get the information, and then hide—hide at the first sound of alarm. There will be bombing first, and then the attack from the air. At the first bomb you must get away from the village. Is not a week long enough for what you need?'

'It might not be,' said Palfrey. 'If only there were a way out.' After a moment of silence, he added: 'Is there anyone else here with whom we can talk?'

'There is a Chinese woman,' said Stefan. 'I do not know her name.'

Palfrey said, in a whisper which could only just reach him: 'They know her.'

'It is, in English, something to do with laughter,' said Stefan, as if he had not heard. 'I have not met her. She is supposed to be very clever, and she works with the Japanese, Orishu.'

'That man is masterly,' said Palfrey, in a loud voice, and then he added in a whisper: *'Hiroto has been here.'* If only he could talk for five minutes without the fear of being overheard! He wanted to know why the parachutists had come to the valley, and what they proposed to do—there were a thousand things he wanted to know, and all he could do was to interpolate a sentence here and there. His ears were strained to catch the sound of movement, but he heard nothing. 'I hoped you would know of a way out, Stefan.'

'I do not,' said Stefan.

'Then the best thing you can do is to hide in the valley and live on the countryside,' said Palfrey. 'If the Chinese come soon, you will be all right.' Hope suddenly flared up in his heart, and he whispered: *'Have a shot at that.'*

'Not I,' Stefan whispered back. Palfrey saw him smile, and knew that he was prepared to sacrifice himself to lend colour to Palfrey's story. *'If you let me go, they will have your head.'* Aloud, he said: 'I need most a cigarette, my friend.'

'You mustn't light one here,' said Palfrey. *'Don't be a fool. They trust me.'*

'They trust no one who fails them. Sap, is this the only place they have?'

'There is an outer fortress, near Hunsa.'

'I am not surprised at that,' said Stefan, 'I have always believed that village was in their hands.'

'Good evening, Herr Baron,' said a man at their side.

There had been no sound of his approach, nothing to indicate that anyone else was near. The voice came from the rocks, and Stefan swung round. In the strengthening moonlight a man in German uniform could be seen standing near the rocks, and a dozen men with rifles were moving away from it in a cordon which formed so rapidly that there was no possible chance of escape.

Stefan raised his hands, turned round and swung his fist at Palfrey. 'You swine! You are not——'

'The Baron has done very well,' said the officer, with a sneer in his voice. 'Do not try to get away, Andromovitch. You will be——'

For a terrifying moment Palfrey knew what it would be

like to face Stefan if the Russian went beserk. He saw his face twisted malignantly before Stefan closed with him. For added realism Stefan gripped his throat.

'Swine!' cried the German.

There was the crack of a rifle-butt on Stefan's head; his grip relaxed and he dropped down. Palfrey staggered away, clutching at his throat, but his chief emotion was fear that the blow had been hard enough to crack Stefan's skull.

The officer took his arm and asked solicitously:

'You are not badly hurt, I hope?'

'I—I am all right,' croaked Palfrey. 'It is a good thing that you came when you did!'

'I have been here all the time,' said the other with a laugh. 'You were never in great danger, Baron.' He motioned to his men. 'Take him away,' he said, pointing to Stefan. 'We can return by road, and you will be glad of a rest, Baron.'

'Very glad,' said Palfrey.

He now felt sure that no one would doubt that he was von Klieb, but the satisfaction which he derived from that was lost in his fears for Stefan. They had learned all they could reasonably hope to learn from him, as far as they knew, and were not likely to waste time. A firing squad—or perhaps nothing so formal, just a bullet in the back of the head—was Stefan's most likely fate.

He thought of the Chinese in the valley.

'You are to be heartily congratulated, von Klieb,' said Field-Marshal von Runst, rubbing his hands together. 'Your conversation with Andromovitch was recorded, of course! I have not yet heard it, although I have had the report from the man in charge of the apparatus.' He looked at von Klowitz, whose lumpy face was wreathed in smiles.

'Now we shall be regaled with a record of the masterly way in which that situation was handled!'

Palfrey stared at the leather-covered box on the desk.

He had arrived ten minutes before and been taken to the Field-Marshal's office immediately. He did not know where Stefan was, and there was no sign of panic or confusion at Headquarters; there was little likelihood that they suspected the presence of a powerful body of parachutists in the valley. Now he looked at the recording unit, and saw von Runst fit in a shellac cylinder, and his heart contracted. He had at most expected a written report; on this record *the whispered asides might come out*!

'Sit down, my dear Karl,' said von Runst, in an excess of geniality which made Palfrey more than ever suspicious that he was the victim of a gigantic hoax. 'Light up and enjoy your triumph!'

Palfrey smiled mechanically as he lit a cigarette.

'Now!' said von Runst, and pressed a switch.

The faint humming note which came first was interrupted by little cracks and a rustling sound which Palfrey thought was the clothes of the men who had been hiding in the rocks. If the recording gear were so sensitive that they could be heard, the whispers were bound to be audible. He sat back and tried to look at ease, with a smirk on his face. Then came his own voice as he called Stefan; von Runst took off his glasses and polished them. The conversation came back vividly, followed by the sounds of the struggle on the ground. There was no record of the whispered conversation then, but their laboured gasping for breath came clearly.

'You must teach me your close-fighting methods,' said von Runst.

'Quiet, please!' urged von Klowitz.

On it went, Palfrey's voice alternating with Stefan's, and the way Stefan had pretended to be gradually convinced of his real identity sounded so convincing that Palfrey almost forgot his own fears. If only he could remember when those asides had started.

'*There is a Chinese woman,*' Stefan said. '*I do not know her name.*'

'This is it,' thought Palfrey. He had whispered, 'They know her.'

'*It is, in English, something to do with laughter,*' went on Stefan, after a barely noticeable pause.

Perspiration broke out on Palfrey's forehead, but he did not wipe it off. The conversation sounded natural enough, the sequences were all normal and the whispers did not once come out. Now and again, as if one or the other had been weighing his words, there were pauses during which they had whispered, but that was all.

Von Runst put on his glasses. Palfrey dabbed his forehead, and hoped the room was warm enough to explain his perspiration. The record went on until the officer said: 'Good evening, Herr Baron!' Stefan's silence, followed by his malignant response, were alike impressive. Von Runst laughed, and switched the machine off.

'That is *most* satisfying,' said von Klowitz.

'We know so much more,' said von Runst. 'So they are

going to attack us from the air! They will have one or two surprises, I think.'

'I am puzzled by one thing,' said Palfrey. 'I did not know that Dr. Palfrey had started out to come here. That is completely fresh to me. I begin to understand why you had some doubts,' he added, with a mechanical smile.

'We would have had greater doubts but for the fact that we had a message about Dr. Palfrey,' said von Klowitz. 'He arrived in New Delhi about the same time that you did. He was seen by the Japanese agent, Orishu—but Orishu was unhappily unaware of the fact that another loyal Japanese, his second cousin Matsu—these Japanese and their relationships!—discovered it. Palfrey was dealt with there, according to reliable reports from Matsu.'

'I understand now,' Palfrey nodded, the dawning of real understanding in his mind. *Orishu had sent word to Tokyo, in Matsu's name*. Every conceivable thing had been done to establish his false identity. He dabbed his forehead again as he added: 'You have contacts with Japan, perhaps?'

'Very good contacts,' said von Runst. 'They are clever little devils.' He laughed, and there was something behind that laugh which made Palfrey suspect that the source of his amusement lay in the association with the Japanese. 'They will be very useful to us, Karl. Well, now, you will wish to tell your wife that you have been safely returned to her.'

'Yes.' Palfrey stood up, hesitated a moment, then said as if reluctantly: 'There is one other thing, Excellency. It occurs to me that Andromovitch might be persuaded to talk even more freely. If you were to offer him his life, for instance, he might make a full statement.'

Von Runst looked at him with a smile; Palfrey could almost see the words 'he is beyond making a confession' forming on the man's lips. He was wrong.

'That is being considered,' said von Runst. 'I do not think he will be able to talk until tomorrow, and you will be invited to attend the inquiry! After your treatment of Barlack's spy, I think we shall have to give you an opportunity to show your further ability.' The devil was still laughing, he was in a constant state of complacent amusement. 'Good night.'

Palfrey was opening the door when the telephone bell rang. Von Runst spoke softly into it, and then his voice grew sharper, and he snapped: 'Wait!' Palfrey closed the door and turned. Von Runst's expression had changed remarkably, and he was clutching the telephone tightly; it was the first time he had looked discomposed. He snapped: 'All forces, *at once*!' He banged the receiver down and stood up, and Palfrey saw him in a towering rage.

'The hospital is being attacked by Chinese,' he said. The words seemed forced from his lips. 'Andromovitch lied, they came tonight. And we were not warned, the observers declared that aircraft passed over! Get me the Air Kommandant!' he roared. He was transformed, his hands were clenched and raised and his face was livid. 'Bring him to me—and bring the pilot who was on duty tonight. Bring them at once!'

'At once!' echoed von Klowitz.

Palfrey hurried out of the room, seeing a gleam of hope for Stefan. Von Klowitz hurried along the passage and flung open a door. He roared instructions for the Air Kommandant and the pilot to go at once to the Field-Marshal, and then he took Palfrey's arm and said: 'We will see this thing finished.'

'They cannot rescue him,' said Palfrey.

'They can try!' snapped von Klowitz.

There was an atmosphere of bustle at Headquarters, but men moved aside quickly to let them pass. They hurried up the stairs and as they reached the open air, saw a stream of small cars heading for the hospital on the outskirts of the village. The rattle of small arms fire was constant, and now and again Palfrey saw flashes of flame. He heard the deeper note of a small gun, and thought he heard the unmistakable crump of mortar bombs. He joined von Klowitz in a waiting car, and in a few minutes was at the scene of the battle.

Two or three multiple mortars were in action. The hospital, a single storey building surrounded by trees, was ablaze with light. German forces were round it on three sides but enemy fire came from the far end, fierce machine-gun and rifle-fire. Occasionally hand-grenades were lobbed towards the German lines. Beyond the hospital, in the brilliant moonlight, Palfrey saw a rise of ground which gave the Chinese cover. He thought he saw one or two of the parachutists creeping towards the hospital.

A man appeared at their side.

'It is believed that they are attempting to take the man whom you sent, General.' It was Professor Kriess, his voice was unruffled as if there were no shooting; the moon gleamed on his white hair and his pale, apologetic face. 'We did not expect such an attack, perhaps?'

'It is prepared for and will be beaten off!' snapped von Klowitz. 'Karl, wait here!' He went stalking off, and was lost in the shadows of a copse. The firing grew sharper, but there were fewer mortars. Two white-clad nurses came like ghosts from the hospital, and Kriess called to them. They told him that the prisoner had been released and was being taken away.

'I wonder if you will be interested to know that von Marritz's wife visited the hospital just before the attack,' said Kriess. 'That is not unusual, she is a frequent visitor, for she is an excellent nurse.'

Palfrey dared not move away against von Klowitz's orders and yet he knew that if a well-directed burst of fire could come from behind the Germans the Chinese would have a better chance of getting away from the village. Once in the foothills they might find a place where they could hold out. His hands were clenched as he watched, and he saw that the battle was moving away from the hospital.

'They have lost the hill,' murmured Kriess.

The firing was still audible, but out of sight. The dark shapes of men were moving forward and disappearing over the brow of the hill. Von Klowitz appeared suddenly.

'We shall soon have them,' he growled. 'Come with me, Karl.'

'Goodnight,' said Kriess, softly.

The man's voice was echoing in Palfrey's ears as he drove with von Klowitz back through the village and then on to a road on the other side. He saw the river ahead of them. The hospital was several miles away. He saw several other cars approaching a bridge; it was the attack in the rear which would surely prove fatal to the Chinese. He saw the cars slowly crossing the bridge, like great black beetles; it was a swing-bridge not meant for wheeled traffic.

One reached the other side . . .

A flash gave Palfrey a second's warning. He flung himself to the ground and felt von Klowitz tumble on top of him. Before he could cover his head with his arms there was the terrific roar of an explosion. He literally bit earth, and, as the booming echoes faded, he heard the thudding of débris hitting the ground. He waited there for a few more seconds before scrambling to his feet. Von Klowitz did not move.

He stared at the river.

There was nothing left of the bridge, nor of the line of cars. Only one, far back, remained in sight, and that was on its side with the bodies of two men lying beside it. He saw men on the other bank standing and staring across the river, and he knew they were the Chinese who had made their way to the bridge and set this trap.

About him there was a scene of great desolation; pieces of

cars, the bodies of men, wood from the bridge, small arms and ammunition.

Von Klowitz did not move; no one moved this side of the river. He looked back towards the village, two or three miles away, and saw no sign of movement. Then the sharp crack of a shot startled him. He caught a glimpse of the flash—it was from the far side and he was the target, so he dropped down quickly. Two more shots were fired at him. He raised his head cautiously after a spell of silence. The men on the other side obviously thought that he was hit, for they were moving away at a fast walk; there were five of them in all.

Von Klowitz did not stir. Palfrey knelt beside him and turned him gently on his face. He saw the ugly wound in the side of his head and another in his arm, above the elbow; both were bleeding freely. Only an expert could hope to stop that bleeding; minutes counted, even seconds.

He set to work, using strips of von Klowitz's shirt to make a tourniquet and then padding the wound in the head and binding it skilfully—nothing else would serve. There was no likelihood that von Klowitz would come round for hours yet. He finished and stood up, then lifted the man gently. He staggered with him to the bank of the river, and put him beneath the rocks which bordered it. Then he stood up and looked towards the village. No one was coming; obviously no one knew of the disaster which had overtaken this force. He turned back and went through the German's pockets, taking everything and thrusting them into his own. He tucked all papers into the breast-pocket of his coat, without glancing at them. When he was finished he took off his coat and kicked off his shoes; then he waded into the river.

It got deeper with every step until, near the middle, the water was up to his neck. He held his coat above his head all the time. The bitterly cold water rippled in the moonlight, like a mirage. It lapped against his chin and lips, but soon he reached higher ground and in a few minutes he was on the opposite bank.

He began to run in the direction of the five men whom he had seen walking swiftly across the valley. He did not doubt that they would be waiting, not far away, to make sure that no one crossed the river and came in pursuit. As he drew nearer a little ridge he put both hands up, holding the coat in one, and slowed down. He was near the ridge when he saw a man appear and heard a command in Chinese. He stopped immediately.

He said, in English: 'Who speaks English? Please?'

A man asked, carefully: 'Who are you?'

'I am Palfrey—a friend of the Russian. Palfrey.'

'*Palfrey!*' said the man who could speak English, and drew nearer. He turned Palfrey's face towards the moon and stared at him. 'Most good!'

Going hot with relief, but acutely aware of the need for speed, Palfrey began to take the things out of his coat pocket.

'Understand, please, that these are important,' he said. 'They have been taken from a German General here. General von Klowitz—von Klowitz, do you understand?'

'Yes. General von Klowitz.'

'If there is a chance, take them out of the valley,' said Palfrey. 'They are papers of importance.'

'Yes,' said the Chinese. 'We take them.'

'Can you get out?'

'There is a way over the mountains. It will take three—four days.' The man beamed. 'There is always a way.'

'Good!' said Palfrey, fervently. 'I am staying here. I have much to do. Tell the Russian that—and also tell Min Shu.'

'We go.' The Chinese drew himself up, to Palfrey's surprise, and saluted. 'Wish luck, Dr. Palfrey!'

He did not watch them go, but turned back towards the river. They disappeared on one side of the ridge, and he the other. He faced the river again, feeling too weak to try to swim; he had not realised how much the journey had taken out of him. He reached von Klowitz and sat down by the man's side; von Klowitz was breathing but unconscious. Kriess would probably examine von Klowitz's wounds and would not betray the fact that only a man with medical knowledge could have saved the man's life. He must get him to the hospital within an hour or two, and a car was needed.

He shook off his overwhelming fatigue and stood up, looking towards the village. For the first time he saw movement along the road; small cars were travelling towards him. It was lucky that they had not started before. Now he would be able to claim the privileges accorded a man who had saved so important a person as von Klowitz.

11 : Von Runst Springs a Surprise

FIVE cars were drawn up where the bridge had been and men were searching among the wreckage. No one appeared to suspect that he was near. He climbed over the bank and walked towards a copse, frightened lest one of them should catch sight of him. They seemed intent on their grim task; probably they were looking for von Klowitz.

He reached the trees, made for the road along which the cars had passed, and then broke into a run, shouting at the top of his voice. Several men looked up, and as he ran one hurried to meet him.

'General von Klowitz!' gabbled Palfrey. 'Badly injured—by the river—Professor Kreiss, quickly. *Quickly!*' he repeated, and got a bark of authority into his voice.

The man turned and shouted orders.

Palfrey walked slowly from the underground headquarters to his house. The moon was at its brightest and cast a ghostly light upon the village. Palfrey went on through that milky whiteness every step betraying his utter weariness. It was past four o'clock; the operation on von Klowitz had taken five hours and he believed it would be successful; he had never seen a man work more skilfully and confidently than Professor Kriess. Von Klowitz would probably recover, after a long period of convalescence.

He reached his own gateway; the front door was open, and before he was half-way along the path Drusilla came out half running towards him.

'Are you all right?' she demanded, gripping his arm tightly. 'Are you——' She broke off, and he heard her catch her breath. He put his arm about her waist, and not until they were indoors with a light switched on did either of them speak. There were tears on Drusilla's eyelids and others running down her cheeks, but she was smiling through them and dabbing at them with her handkerchief.

She stared at him with increasing incredulity as he told her what had happened. He closed the window of the bedroom and drew the curtains, talking in an undertone to make sure that there was no chance of being overheard.

'I went back to headquarters with von Runst. He is a changed man. At the hospital he was more the Junker officer you would expect, but something has affected him. It might have been the sight of the operation, which was pretty grim. It sickened him, of course, but he made himself stick it out. We went straight back to his office and he sent for whisky and drank half a bottle in half an hour, without uttering a word. I think he's forgotten how to smile. He became almost maudlin, although not to the extent of giving anything away. All he did was to talk about losing a powerful friend at a vital time. The odd thing is,' added Palfrey. 'that he doesn't seem alarmed at the fact that the valley is known. He seems indifferent. It might be confidence that he can handle any attack, although after tonight's show you'd think his confidence would be pretty severely shaken, wouldn't you?'

Drusilla nodded: *He* was safe and nothing else mattered.

'It beats me,' said Palfrey. 'He knows the situation at its worst—always excepting the fact that I'm what I am!' There was a flash of humour in his eyes, which looked heavy with sleep. 'The Chinese withdrew to the foothills and lost half a dozen men out of a force of at least fifty. We—he!—lost a dozen killed and as many more wounded. His intelligence system let him down, his airmen let him down, his radio-location failed him—and yet he doesn't turn a hair about that, just sits at his desk tippling and talking about von Klowitz. I felt almost sorry for the devil!'

'Nonsense!' Drusilla protested. Then:

'I'm only telling you the facts,' said Palfrey. 'On the whole, I'd say that the thing which affected him most was that von Klowitz had been robbed. We were in the theatre when he remembered that, and asked me to explain what happened. I told him that I was knocked unconscious by the blast and when I came round the Chinese were bending over von Klowitz. I said I feigned death, and it seemed to satisfy him.'

'Unless someone saw you, he can't very well doubt it,' Drusilla's voice was still shaky, 'you look as if you've had a rough time.'

'I'm all right. I've found out that everyone of the little convoy was killed.' Palfrey shrugged. 'Well, that's that. I know I ought to be rejoicing,' he added, 'yet something's missing. If you ask me whether I think Stefan and Laughing Fragrance will be all right I can only tell you that the Chinese I spoke to seemed pretty confident. Some time during our trek west,' he mused, 'they discovered a great deal of information, and Chunking is fully acquainted with the position of the valley. Von Runst knows that as well as I do, that's the astonishing part about it.'

'From what you say, he's drinking himself blind because of it,' Drusilla suggested.

'I just don't believe it,' Palfrey insisted. 'I'm probably crazy, but I just don't believe it. Von Runst doesn't *mind* whether there is another attack or not—that's the truth. After tonight's show there isn't likely to be any faulty intelligence, either. I'll tell you another thing I've discovered,' he added. 'They've a dozen fighters, built to look like Jap *Zeros* but a darned sight better armed and faster, in underground hangars. A small airborne force would have a bad time unless it were well protected.'

'The Chinese won't play at it now.'

'No.' Palfrey shrugged again. 'Well, you know all the answers. We've no friends left—except Professor Kriess,' he added with a rueful smile. 'The old boy spotted me first go and hasn't let me forget it. What do we do next?'

'Get into bed,' said Drusilla.

'To tell you the truth,' mumbled Palfrey, as he obeyed, 'I'm tired of being Karl von Klieb. I don't like von Klieb at all and I don't like his friends.'

Stefan turned his head and discovered for the first time that it was heavily bandaged. A Chinese woman was sitting cross-legged on the grass by his side. They were on the grassy slopes of a hill, and behind her a small stream was falling over some rocks, caught by the sun and shining like liquid diamonds. Men were sitting on boulders or grassy banks and looking across the river. Not a half a mile away a wall of rock rose sheer towards the sky, its top a razor-edged ridge on which several men were standing. The rock made a half-circle about him and the girl, and the only way to the main valley seemed to be through the river, which appeared to cut the ridge in two.

'Min Shu,' Stefan spoke in a bewildered voice. 'Min Shu—Laughing Fragrance.' He tried to get up. 'I did not know——'

'You will have a severe headache unless you lie quiet,' said Laughing Fragrance. 'There is nothing you can do and nothing to worry about. Perhaps you would like a drink?'

'I would like one very much.'

She leaned forward and poured a little water from a flask into a tin mug. She held it to his lips and supported his head so that he could drink in comfort. The cold water tasted very sweet.

'You were unconscious when we brought you away,' said Laughing Fragrance. 'Professor Kriess, the doctor who attended you, gave you a sedative. You are not badly hurt. Later in the morning I will dress your wounds.'

'Thank you.' Stefan closed his eyes, for the brilliant sunlight made them painful. He continued to turn his face towards her, with her image vivid on his mind's eye. 'When was I brought away?'

'Last night. The hospital was attacked.'

'Was that wise?'

'The flying men had instructions,' said Laughing Fragrance, 'and that is all I know of that. One of them came to see me and I told him that you were in hospital. It appears that they had instructions to rescue you unless you succeeded in representing yourself as Hans Goetz. You did not have much success,' she added, and there was a laughing note in her voice. 'Much less than your doctor friend!'

'Where is Palfrey?'

'Still in the village.'

'Is he safe?'

'I do not know. He was safe until after the main attack, and he brought us some documents and personal belongings of General von Klowitz, who was severely hurt. Then he went back, so it is likely that he expected to be safe.'

'He is capable of anything,' said Stefan, opening his eyes and smiling. 'He might even walk into this camp now, and apologise for interrupting—it would not surprise me!'

She laughed. 'It would surprise me, because between us and the village there are several hundred very angry Germans. They are searching for us, but I do not think they have yet discovered where we are hiding. If they should do so, they will suffer severely. I do not think they have the numbers or the equipment to force a way in here.'

'So this place was known and selected beforehand?' Stefan looked thoughtful.

'It was known. High in the mountains, unknown to the Germans, there is a Llama temple. The priests do not often interest themselves in the affairs of the world,' said Laughing Fragrance, 'but they approached the settlement at a time when three people were murdered—wandering Chinese, murdered by Germans. So one of the priests crossed the mountains and visited Chungking—which is why you were able to fly across the valley and how it became known. It was not discovered until after Palfrey and his wife had started on their long trek, of course, and I believe that the authorities considered it wise to allow Palfrey to continue, in the hope that the thousandth chance would succeed—as it appears to have succeeded.'

'How do you know all this?' asked Stefan.

'There is Kao Lun, a well-informed major in command of these troops,' said Laughing Fragrance, 'and he had instructions to tell me or you or Palfrey. I have been in the valley for over five weeks,' she added, 'and I did not expect ever to get out again. Now I think that I may be able to see my father once more, for the priest who gave the information is now back in his temple and will show us the way to get out of the mountains.' She spoke quietly and closed her eyes, so that Stefan could look at her, with his expression hardening, and without fear of giving his thoughts away.

'Tsui Lin,' said Stefan, softly.

'Tsui Lin,' said Laughing Fragrance. 'Is he not a grand old man? For a year he has been deceiving the Germans and still they continue to trust him!' She opened her eyes suddenly, and saw his face; her expression changed remarkably, the smile disappearing, her lips suddenly parted. 'Why do you look like that?' she demanded harshly. 'Why do you look like that?'

'Tsui Lin was a very brave man,' said Stefan.

She sat like an image carved from alabaster, staring at him without moving a muscle of her face and without closing her eyes.

'So,' she said flatly. 'How did you learn of my father's fate?'

'I was there,' Stefan told her. 'It was quick, Min Shu.'

She said: 'What of my sisters?'

'It was quick, Min Shu,' repeated Stefan.

She rose and walked away from him, towards the river. She stood there, motionless, for long minutes. When at last she turned and walked back there was no sign of grief on her face: she had struggled successfully to suppress her emotions.

'I think I can lead the Germans here,' she said. 'I think if they were to come into this place by the river and we were to hide in the hills and behind the rocks on the ridge we might kill all of them who venture in.'

'Perhaps they know who you are,' Stefan protested.

'They do know who I am.'

'Then you would needlessly sacrifice your life,' he told her, quietly.

'I shall allow myself to be captured,' said Laughing Fragrance. 'I shall tell them that I was turned loose by the men here because they did not know me. I shall tell them that I am filled with hatred and thirsting for revenge, and they will believe me,' she added simply. 'They will believe me. Have you a message for Dr. Palfrey?'

'If you intend to go,' Stefan demurred. 'I think you should discuss it with the major whom you mentioned. He will know, perhaps, when it is planned to make a strong attack on the valley.'

'He has sent word to Chungking,' said Laughing Fragrance, 'together with von Klowitz's papers and he has requested the other forces waiting to attack to wait until further instructions come from Chungking. There is, however, no reason why *he* should not attack again if I can lure the Germans in.'

Palfrey did not sleep the clock round, but it was after midday before he woke, to find himself alone in the little bedroom.

He got out of bed, put on a silk dressing-gown, and went into the kitchen. Drusilla was not there, nor in the bungalow. He called '*Hilde!*' but there was no answer, and he was getting in a panic when he heard footsteps outside. He looked out of the window and saw her with Professor Kriess, who barely came up to her shoulder.

Palfrey relaxed, and kept out of sight.

'So I can assure you that the Russian is not in the hospital and has not been found,' said Kriess, softly. 'In fact the search is failing, for no reports have come in. I believe it will cause great anxiety. My advice to you is—do nothing and say nothing. Good morning, Baroness!'

Palfrey showed himself as soon as Kriess had gone, and Drusilla's eyes lighted up.

'We are doing well this morning,' said Palfrey. 'White linen with a pleated skirt—where did you get your wardrobe?'

'A case arrived this morning,' she told him. 'I think it was from von Runst. You look as if you were drunk last night!'

'That was certainly von Runst,' said Palfrey. 'What an incredible place this is—and already we accept it without the slightest question. I think I'll have a bath. Can you fix a cold meal—I don't particularly want to go to the hall today.'

'We've had instructions not to go to the hall,' Drusilla reported. 'Why don't you have a cup of tea first?' She walked to the little kitchen. 'You heard what Kriess said about Stefan?'

'Yes. Any news of Laughing Fragrance?'

'She disappeared, presumably with Stefan.'

It was early evening when the summons came; Baron and Baroness von Klieb were invited to dine with the Field-Marshal. It was a very formal invitation.

'I haven't seen von Runst in his living-quarters,' said Palfrey. 'This looks as if we're still in favour, my sweet! I wonder if there's to be a party?'

There was no one else in the small dining-room, which led off the black-walled office. Palfrey started and then stared with great curiosity at a dozen grotesque masks which decorated the walls.

'Like 'em?' he asked.

'No,' said Drusilla, 'but they're clever.'

Palfrey studied them with his eyes narrowed. 'Perhaps you're right, but it's not my taste.'

'I, on the other hand, think them remarkable,' said von Runst.

He must have been standing with the door slightly open, listening to the conversation. Palfrey was heartily thankful that they had made it a rule to speak in German even when they were on their own. He looked round with a smile.

'My wife was agreeing with you, Excellency!'

'It has long been apparent that she has excellent taste.' Von Runst bowed. He seemed in an amiable frame of mind—showing no sign of his overnight weakness.

The door opened suddenly, without a knock. One of the little men whom Palfrey had seen a few days before stood on the threshold. He wore a robe which reached the ground, but his face was not made up and there was something about the features which was incongruous against the robe.

'What is it?' snapped von Runst.

'If your Excellency could spare a few moments, we would be grateful,' said the little man.

Von Runst snapped: 'I will come.' He glanced at Drusilla and, obviously annoyed, said: 'I will not be long.'

He was away for some time, however. There was a small alcove with easy chairs, and Palfrey and Drusilla were served with strong Manhattans by a smiling barman, dressed in white.

A door opened, and the Field-Marshal came back.

'I live very humbly, as you see,' he said, 'but I think I can assure you that I have the best chef in the Fourth Reich!' He laughed. 'How are you, von Klieb? You look remarkably fit after your misadventures.'

'I slept until midday,' Palfrey told him.

'The advantage of an easy conscience! I also slept. You will be delighted to know that there is good news of the General. In fact, he will be able to start a journey in a few days.'

'I am very glad to hear it,' said Palfrey. 'You are sending him away to convalesce, perhaps?'

'It can be called that.' Von Runst seated himself at the table and rang a small bell. A waiter came in, soft-footed, and began to serve the meal. The Field-Marshal applied himself to his victuals with a heartiness which told Palfrey that his improved frame of mind was not assumed.

After the meal, he led the way through yet another door into a long, narrow room, where the lighting was like artificial sunlight and where the easy chairs and settees were dreams of comfort.

All the time, Palfrey felt instinctively that the man was watching them carefully, as if for any slip which would betray them. Yet he was in excellent humour and cracked one or two poor jokes. Then came a sudden change of mood. He frowned and thrust his legs out in front of him, saying:

'I do not think that it will be wise for us to stay here for long.'

Palfrey looked startled.

'I thought——'

'You thought that we would stay here for a long time,' said von Runst. 'Of course, my friend! That is exactly the impression which I have been at great pains to create. It is certainly implanted on the mind of the Russian and also on the Chinese woman—both of whom made good their escape—there is no need for alarm. We can leave at very short notice, and a small party of us can reach safety without the slightest risk. Very few people here realise it, of course—you see that I repose great trust in you.'

'I warmly appreciate it,' murmured Palfrey

'You have done well,' said von Runst, 'and I need good men. The General will not be able to serve for some months to come . . . About the General,' he added, with surprising casualness, 'I think I forgot to tell you that I was relieved. When you told me that he had been robbed, I was apprehensive because I knew that he had papers which gave an outline of our plans. He was wise enough not to carry them with him, however; I found them in his room—and there is no fear of the real truth being learned.' He laughed. 'So I am in a very different frame of mind from last night, Karl!'

Palfrey smiled mechanically.

'I will admit one thing,' went on von Runst. 'I am not fully satisfied even now that all the Chinese agents who found their way into the settlement—I do not mean the airborne troops—have yet been found. I do not propose to tell you where we are going, but I want to warn you that you will probably both be called, in the near future, to make a journey with me. I shall take two or three officers for whom I have respect, Professor Kriess, who is invaluable, and perhaps one or two of the women. The others——' He laughed. 'They will stay here.'

'Here!' ejaculated Palfrey.

'Where they will doubtless be found by the Chinese and will be put to death,' said von Runst, casually. 'It will be assumed by the Allies that I have been driven away and that I have gone to Japan, perhaps, and my last sanctuary. They will have a shock, one day—after my death, perhaps after your death.

The time it takes does not matter—what matters is the rebirth of the Reich, Karl—do you not agree?'

'Fervently!' Palfrey assured him.

'It was obvious to me that this valley, although so well hidden and so remote, would one day be found,' said von Runst. 'It was not the location which I would have chosen myself. However, I made the best I could of a situation with which I was confronted. But soon after taking up my command here I began to look for another place, even more remote, even less likely to be discovered. For it was immediately apparent, as I am sure you will agree, that we must settle in a place where no one would dream of looking. A few generations in the life of a nation is not important, it is the ultimate triumph which counts.'

'You are inspired!' gasped Palfrey.

Von Runst beamed.

'Fortunately a number of us were inspired. I return, then, to the obvious need—a colony in a secret place, unsuspected by the rest of the world. This one was badly chosen. At first I was angry. Then I saw that it would be a very good thing to *allow* the Allies to find this place! It would satisfy them that they had, once and for all, destroyed us. When I came it was peopled with brilliant men and women; now, most of the inhabitants are of little account, they will be no great loss to us. The *real* representatives of the new Germany are certainly not here—they have gone elsewhere. Within ten minutes we can be on our way from here to a place of great safety—and, as you will already understand, I shall be glad to have you with me.'

'You are very good,' murmured Palfrey.

'I am a judge of men,' said von Runst, blandly. 'From the first I paid little heed to the suggestion that you were, in fact, Dr. Palfrey. It had to be put to the test, and that has now been done. You will not be surprised,' he added gently, 'to know that no one who reaches the next colony will leave it until the time comes to spread our new gospel. A few will come in from the outside, but very few, and they will be carefully selected.' He laughed again. 'There is only one drawback, my dear Karl. Several of our most brilliant men are ill. We cannot afford to lose them. Professor Kriess is an excellent doctor and surgeon, as well as a brilliant psychiatrist, but he cannot do everything. Many of these brilliant people were forced to live underground for some time, and such living conditions give rise to dangerous diseases. One of those which causes most anxiety is tuberculosis.' He took off his glasses and polished them. 'Dr.

Palfrey, before he was persuaded to become a spy, was perhaps the greatest living authority on the scourge. Some time ago I discussed it with Professor Kriess, and he told me that if we could get Dr. Palfrey it would probably add many years to the lives of those men whom we can ill afford to lose. Sit down, my dear Doctor,' added von Runst, without raising his voice. 'Sit down, my friend! You are in no danger. I wish you to live. Do not look so alarmed, my dear Mrs. Palfrey! I have outwitted you, that is all. There is no reason why we should not remain good friends.'

Neither Palfrey nor Drusilla spoke.

Until the last minute, until the first time the world 'tuberculosis' came from his lips, he had completely deceived them. The shock was the greater because it was created by that soft-voiced, smiling man who had pretended to take them so fully into his confidence. Palfrey stared at him, hardly able to believe the truth. Drusilla sat quite still. Von Runst chuckled, leaned forward and pressed a bell-push in the wall. After a short pause the door opened and Professor Kriess came in.

'I think perhaps your services are required, Professor,' said von Runst. 'Two cases of shock! You might care to tell Mrs. Palfrey what was really in those little tablets which you gave her.'

Kriess spread out his hands deprecatingly and his apologetic smile looked to Palfrey like the leer of a satyr.

'A little sedative,' he said, 'a gentle one which would send her to sleep—I was most anxious that she should not be distressed or think that she was without friends.'

'You see how thoughtful we are,' said von Runst. 'Sit down, Kriess! Well, Dr. Palfrey, why do you not say something? You have been most talkative in the guise of Baron von Klieb, and I am sure we would all like to hear what you have to say now—especially the Professor. Eh, Kriess?'

'Provided it is not abusive.' Kriess smiled.

'Come, Doctor!' encouraged von Runst.

Palfrey pushed his chair back and stood up. The others watched him closely and von Runst's right hand moved towards his side. Palfrey went to Drusilla's chair and sat on the edge. There was a vacant expression on his face but his stupefaction was fading. Slowly his right hand strayed to his hair and he began to twist a few strands round his forefinger.

Von Runst cracked his knuckles in triumph.

Palfrey smiled.

'Very clever,' he murmured. 'Very clever indeed! And why

should I be abusive?' He looked at Kriess thoughtfully. 'You outwitted me completely—I should not have come to you last night, of course. I should have let von Klowitz die.'

'You should,' agreed von Runst. 'It was that, naturally, which finally convinced us.'

'Oh, well,' said Palfrey. 'You may as well do a good job while you're about it.' He released the hair and patted it against his forehead, where it stayed flat, a little kiss-curl which made him look even more vacant. 'Why didn't you stop me from going with von Klowitz?'

'I came to the conclusion that while your wife was here you would return,' von Runst was at his blandest.

'I see. A demonstration of your ability to judge character. Well, that's that.' Palfrey pressed Drusilla's shoulder and smiled wryly. 'Lead us to the padded cell.'

'We do not propose to deal harshly with you,' said von Runst. 'Contrary to the general impression in Europe, all Germans are not beasts who desire only to cause pain. In fact we can and do admire a courageous adversary, and in defeat you prove your courage even more than in an imagined triumph. You will come with us, Palfrey, and you will help us to mend the lives of the men whom we need so badly. That shall be your punishment. For the rest . . .' He shrugged his shoulders. 'Provided you behave well, you will be able to live in peace with your wife. In fact, she will be protected, I assure you—you need have no fear. You will not even have to give your parole, because there will be no chance for you to escape from where we are going.' He smiled broadly.

'Why did you let Andromovitch and Laughing Fragrance go?'

'To enable them to carry the story of our valley to Chungking,' said von Runst. 'I told you that I was not satisfied that all the agents had been found, did I not?' He laughed again. 'I have greatly enjoyed the little joke, my dear Doctor! I have a great sense of humour. If you had killed von Klowitz I might not have been so amused—by saving his life, you saved your own. Now, what will you have to drink? Brandy? I can recommend——'

'From now on I shall be a teetotaller,' said Palfrey, firmly. 'An old English custom—no drinking with Huns.' He laughed. 'I'm afraid my feelings got the better of me for a moment. But you wouldn't expect me to be pleased.'

'Kriess warned you not to be abusive,' said von Runst.

'Oddly enough, I don't intend to take much notice of the

Professor,' Palfrey told him. 'How sick are your brilliant men, von Runst? Very sick? Badly in need of my help? I think perhaps I could be allowed a little freedom of speech in return for my services.'

'Do not be too free,' von Runst warned, coldly.

'Oh, come,' said Palfrey. 'What can you do, at worst? Kill us, that is all. There may be a painful interval, but no more. Do you want me dead?' He looked from Kriess to von Runst, and stood up, his voice sounded almost gay. 'What a peculiar position, Excellency! You need my services and you need them badly. With the best intention I warn you—if you lay a hand on my wife, if you cause her a moment of unnecessary pain. I shall do nothing to help you. Nothing, do you understand?' He beamed. 'You see, the cards aren't all in the same hand.'

'You take great risks,' said von Runst, harshly.

'Oh, no greater than I've taken before,' Palfrey assured him. 'Do you mind if we go, now?'

'If you should try to escape——'

'Don't be absurd,' said Palfrey, with a touch of acerbity. 'While there's life there's hope. If I get a bullet in the back, that will put paid to hopes and ambitions.' He put a hand at Drusilla's elbow and helped her to her feet; she still seemed dazed. He lit a cigarette and smiled at von Runst. 'On the whole I think it's a relief. I didn't enjoy it, and I wasn't sure from one moment to the next whether you knew the truth or not. And you would be surprised what a burden the simple "von" can be!'

12 : The Return of Laughing Fragrance

APPARENTLY they were to be allowed to stay in the house on their own. Palfrey whistled softly as he helped Drusilla to an easy chair, then sat on the foot of the bed and looked at her smilingly. 'We're alive,' he reminded her.

Drusilla shivered. 'Alive!'

'It's bad,' said Palfrey, 'but it's almost comic. Shall I get some tea?'

'Yes. I'll be all right here.'

He nodded and left her, whistling under his breath. It would be better, perhaps, if Drusilla wanted to do something. He himself found a great relief in the prospect of putting on a kettle, getting tea-cups, watching the kettle as it began to steam. There was something reassuring about the ordinary actions. He smiled as he pushed open the kitchen door. He had not yet really felt the effect of the shock, of course.

He opened the door.

It did not go right back against the wall, and he was immediately wary. There was no telling what the devils would do. They might decide to strike at once, after all; they might think that a knife or a bullet would be better used now than later. He stepped in cautiously and then jumped further into the room, pushing the door to.

'*You!*' he exclaimed.

He hardly knew how he managed to keep his voice on a low key as he stared at Laughing Fragrance.

She stood against the wall with a hand at her lips. He stared for an appreciable time—and then he heard Drusilla's footsteps. He opened the door a little and held up a hand in warning; she came in quietly and cautiously, and was as startled as he had been.

Laughing Fragrance said: 'Why are the men outside?'

'It didn't come off.' Palfrey told her. 'Kriess let us down.'

'Kriess!'

'My sentiments, entirely,' said Palfrey, recovering from this fresh surprise and going to the small electric stove. He filled a kettle and plugged it in. 'Is there anyone outside this window?'

'Probably, but they can't hear through the shutters.'

'I hope not.' Palfrey smiled gravely 'Well, what gave you the bright idea of sacrificing yourself?'

'I came to——' She hesitated, and stepped closer to him. 'I think I can lead most of the forces they have here into a trap. I was going straight to Headquarters when I saw the men here and wanted to find out what was happening.'

'How did you get in without being seen?'

'It was very dark,' she said, 'and all the houses have the same keys.' She leaned against the sink, looking at Drusilla, and she gave Palfrey the impression that she understood what an ordeal Drusilla was undergoing. 'Will you try to get away?' she asked.

'Not yet.' Palfrey shook his head.

'Why have they let you come back here?'

'They feel quite happy about us,' Palfrey assured her, 'and on the whole I think they've reason for it. You're a complication,' he added, and then he stiffened and eyed her eagerly. '*Are* you, though! Can you get back to the others?'

'I think I could, but——'

'You must!' said Palfrey. 'Listen . . .'

He told her all that von Runst had told him. She stood quite still, her eyes shining, and when at last he had finished she said: 'I will get to them, somehow!'

'There is no way,' Drusilla broke in sharply.

'We'll have a shot at finding one,' said Palfrey. 'I suppose you can stay here in hiding,' he went on, looking thoughtfully at Laughing Fragrance. 'The real danger is whether they saw you come and didn't stop you, but are listening now.' He began to twist hair about his forefinger, and his expression was vague. 'Well, let's have some tea!'

Drusilla said: 'Sap——'

'Tea,' repeated Palfrey, firmly. 'Not another word until we've had it. Make it, will you, and I'll go round the windows and doors and make sure that they're shut as tightly as they can be.'

Drusilla brushed the hair back from her forehead and picked up the teapot, while Palfrey made a quick tour of the house. Drusilla was probably right, although when she had recovered a little she would be as eager as he to seize a forlorn hope. If he were to try to escape . . .

'Got it!' he said aloud.

The women were drinking tea when he got back to the kitchen, and even Laughing Fragrance looked startled when she saw his broad smile. He sipped appreciatively, then put his cup down on the stove as he told them:

'They know there are forces in the hills. They'll guess that we'll try to get to them. They're all ready for our attempt to break out. It wouldn't surprise me,' he added, 'if they don't let us get a little way so as to find out where the forces are. So—we'll try to lead them!'

Drusilla stared at him.

'You and I,' said Palfrey, gaily, 'will leave in about half an hour, before the moon gets up. The chief risk is that they will start shooting the moment they see us, but we'll have to chance that. If they let us get even a few hundred yards from the house, Laughing Fragrance can escape—they only expect to see two of us. Yes?' he added, beaming.

'You will be caught,' Laughing Fragrance objected, 'and——'

'Why worry about that?' asked Palfrey. 'We've got to forget ourselves. If we can get that information out, it will be more than useful. We've already sent word of Hiroto's visit, and with this second spot of information we won't have done so badly.' He lit a cigarette. 'Agreed, 'Silla?'

'Of course.' Drusilla smiled wryly. 'I feel as if I'm living in a dream, though—nothing really makes sense.'

'It all makes a great deal of sense,' said Palfrey. 'I might make a start by trying to bribe one of the fellows outside,' he added, and he took out the crumpled handkerchief, selected a diamond, and tossed it in the air. 'Wish me luck!'

He went out of the front door.

There was a man standing a few yards away. He stood to one side as Palfrey appeared, and did not seem in any way disconcerted when Palfrey approached him.

Palfrey asked, in German:

'Are you a rich man, my friend?'

The man did not answer.

'Because, if you're not, you could be,' Palfrey persisted.

The man said: 'This will be reported.'

'Oh, come!' Calmly, Palfrey took the diamond from his pocket, holding it in the light; it lay on the palm of his hand, sparkling brilliantly.

'This will be reported.'

Palfrey shrugged his shoulders and put the stone into his pocket. Then he went towards the back of the house. Three men were in the shadows, each standing about ten feet from the house itself, and other men were stationed at the foot of the ridge.

He walked back, whistling to himself.

When he reached the road in front of the house the man whom he had tried to bribe followed him. So did two others. Apparently those watching one side of the house followed if he appeared there, but those on the other side stayed at their posts. He strolled back, whistling aloud. There was an eerie quality about the silence.

The man whom he had tried to bribe stood in the same place.

'Don't forget to report it,' said Palfrey, and went in and closed the door.

'Report what?' asked Drusilla, appearing from the kitchen.

'I think I probably chose the wrong man.' Palfrey explained exactly what had happened. He went on: 'I'm going out first—I think I'll go to von Marritz's house. You follow, 'Silla—and go in the opposite direction.' He looked at Laughing Fragrance. 'The front of the house should be clear then, and with luck you'll make it. Are you still prepared to try?'

'I am in a hurry to try,' said Laughing Fragrance. 'I have only one regret: that I cannot make sure that they will follow me—there was to have been a reception for them.' She did not smile. 'Will you start at once?'

'Yes,' said Palfrey, and pressed her hand in farewell.

He could not be sure that the guards would use the same methods the next time he ventured out, and as he walked across the grass he was looking right and left, his ears strained for the sound of creaking boots or a rifle being cocked. He knew that the men were following him. He did not look round until he reached the road outside von Marritz's house, when he turned and peered towards his own little place. He thought he could just distinguish Drusilla's light suit. That faded. He stood in silence before he snapped his fingers and began to walk swiftly towards the hospital. It would be better to pretend to have a reason for the excursion.

He was not challenged even when he reached the hospital and went along the passage towards the operating theatre. Suddenly a door opened and one of the assistant doctors looked out.

'Good evening, Herr Baron.'

'Good evening,' said Palfrey. 'I wish to see Professor Kriess.'

'He is dining with the Field-Marshal, Herr Baron.'

Palfrey frowned. 'That is a pity, I have an urgent message for him. I will wait!' he said, grandly, and looked towards a door with Kriess's name on it in small black letters. 'Shall I wait here?'

'I do not know when the Professor will come back,' said the doctor uneasily, 'I will ask him to come to see you, Herr Baron.'

'I will wait!' barked Palfrey.

He thought that it would be a good notion to try to get into the laboratory; it would probably be thought that he was looking for a poison which Kriess had failed to give him. The doctor looked uncertain:

'The waiting-room would be best, Herr Baron.'

'As you wish,' said Palfrey, grandly.

He was left alone in a small waiting-room, where he waited until he thought the doctor was safely in his room, then tiptoed out. He had seen the word '*Laboratory*' on one of the doors near the operating theatre. He found the door, glanced quickly right and left, and then thrust it open.

'Good evening, Doctor,' said Professor Kriess.

He was standing by a bench, wearing a white smock, and his gentle smile was much in evidence. He had a small bottle in his hand, which he replaced on a shelf with great care.

'I am not surprised to see you here,' he added, 'but I warn you that you are being very foolish, Doctor. The Field-Marshal needs your services. I may say that it was his intention to execute you forthwith and to amuse himself with your wife, but I pointed out the great advantages of having such a renowned physician as yourself in our little colony.'

'You are a liar,' Palfrey said, flatly.

Kriess shrugged. 'I cannot hope to convince you that I acted in your interests. I *like* you, Doctor. I did from the moment I saw you. It is true that I remained loyal to His Excellency, but you should be the first to admit that loyalty is an admirable quality. Stop being angry, Doctor. Wait until we send for you, then settle down comfortably with your wife and do service to humanity—and at the same time, Doctor, rear a family! How pleasant it will be for you to think that your children will be trained as *Herrenvolk*.' He beamed.

Palfrey hardly knew what happened to him.

He saw Kriess as if through a mist. He felt a sudden, furious anger against this man whom he had trusted and who had proved a traitor to his own race. He stepped forward with his clenched hands raised—and it was not until he heard Kriess speak in a sharp voice, with a note of genuine alarm, that he stopped moving. The mist cleared; and he saw the automatic in the Professor's hand.

Kriess said: 'I will overlook this, Doctor, but if it reaches the ears of the Field-Marshal you will be killed and your wife will bear children for another man. Go back to her. Try not to be a fool. I have done my best for you.'

Palfrey stared at him for a long time—and then he swung round and groped blindly for the door. It was the first time he had fully realised what was in store for them, the first time the real truth dawned on him, and he saw the future as an illimitable stretch of time spent in the company of such men as these, without recourse to ordinary civilisation, without hope. The depression dropped upon him like a blanket. As he walked swiftly along the road to the little house, he was in a mood of blind fury—a fury made worse by the knowledge of his own impotence. He did not even see whether he was followed: he had almost forgotten what he had set out to do.

There were two men near the front door of the house.

He let himself in and saw a light beneath the door of the sitting-room. As he went in, Drusilla jumped to her feet.

'Did they catch her?'

'Her?' echoed Palfrey. He drew his hand across his forehead and sat down. He said: 'No, I haven't seen her. I saw Kriess. I think I came close to killing him, but I don't know what good that would have done. No, it's all right,' he added, when he saw her expression change, 'I did nothing, and he said that he would not report it.' After a long silence, when he felt more normal although he was still cold, he went on: 'I must be touched with the madness which affects everyone in this loony-bin! I've never known myself behave like it before.'

'You were so sure that we have a trump card,' Drusilla said, 'and I think Laughing Fragrance got away. There was no cry of alarm, no shooting, no scene of any kind—and surely there would have been, had they seen her?'

'I suppose so,' said Palfrey.

He tried to convince her that he was feeling better, but it was not easy. He was consumed with a flame of despair which exceeded his worst imaginings.

By the following morning Stefan was declaring that he had never felt better. It was an exaggeration: he was weak and knew he would not be able to walk any great distance. But his head was not aching. The Chinese who had taken off the bandages that morning, in place of Laughing Fragrance of whom there were no tidings, had been reassuring. The wound would soon heal. He was the man to whom Palfrey had talked and to whom von Klowitz's papers had been handed.

By then, Stefan knew that they were thirty miles from the village, the last fifteen of them over a difficult road. This little spot where they were hiding was a valley within a valley, and well-nigh impregnable.

The men had been busy. Fish had been caught in the river and one or two small pheasants had been shot. The appetising smell coming from a little group of men near a fire by the water's edge made Stefan's mouth water. He strolled down.

As he joined them a man of medium height, well-built and with a cheerful smile, came from the rocks—it was the major, Kao Lun, with whom Stefan had spent most of the previous day. Kao Lun felt sure that no further action would be taken until word was received in Chungking from him, and his messengers would take three or four days to reach the nearest military depot, from where a radio message could be sent. It would be a week, therefore, before they could expect instructions. Meanwhile, they would wait here, where they felt quite safe.

'We shall have word today,' said Kao Lun, spearing a small fish and eating it off the knife with relish. 'That woman is capable of performing any miracle.'

'I believe she is,' Stefan assured him.

They concentrated on their breakfast and were nearly

finished when a shrill whistle came from one of the men on the ridge. He was standing up, and beckoning. Stefan jumped to his feet, and Kao Lun ran towards the ridge. The others left the fire and before Stefan had caught up with Kao Lun, all were carrying their guns.

A sound came faintly to Stefan's ears; it was the rattle of rifle-fire. He thought he saw the flashes of the shots.

'Can you see what it is?' he demanded.

'There is one person ahead of several others, who are shooting,' said the major, calmly. 'We will go to meet him.' He shouted orders, and a jeep appeared on the hillside. It was pushed on to a raft moored close to the river bank and then guided by four men who waded nearly shoulder deep to make sure that it did not get out of hand. Stefan and Kao Lun hurried back to the river, then waded in the wake of the jeep. Four men on foot were already going towards the scene of the shooting.

Kao Lun, Stefan and two others crowded into the little motor, Stefan head and shoulders above the others.

Kao Lun handed Stefan his glasses.

'It is not a man,' he said, 'it is Min Shu. I think perhaps we shall just be able to reach her first.'

As Kao Lun spoke, Laughing Fragrance was looking over her shoulder towards the men behind her. Three men fired; the woman staggered and lost her footing, then regained it.

There were a dozen men in sight behind her now, and the shooting was coming more frequently. They could see bullets hitting the rocks and giving off little clouds of dust from the trail. The hillside was so uneven and rocky that there was no hope of accurate marksmanship; the men often slipped as they fired.

Laughing Fragrance left the narrow trail. Stefan saw that she was making for a small ridge of rock; if she could reach it before she was hit again she would be safe until they joined the fight.

Heavy boulders in their path forced them to make a detour. Bullets struck the earth near them and one hit the side of the jeep. Most shooting was directed towards Laughing Fragrance, who, still on her feet, was within a few yards of the protecting ridge. From the main party of Germans, three men broke away and approached the ridge from the other side.

Stefan said: 'We must split up.'

The words were hardly out of his mouth before Kao Lun gave orders. The two men behind jumped from the jeep as it rocked from side to side and made their way swiftly towards the far side of the ridge, to meet any attack from there. The major and Stefan faced the bulk of the Germans, more of whom were appearing behind rocks and lower down the trail. The stuttering note of a machine-gun added to the din and bullets carved a straight line on a rock not thirty yards in front of the jeep.

Stefan stood up; for a moment his huge figure was a clear target. Bullets hummed past him as he stepped over the side, leaning backwards as his foot touched the ground. The jeep lurched forward at a faster pace the moment he left it. He caught a glimpse of Kao Lun, smiling as if this were exactly what he wanted, and saw the bullets striking the front of the vehicle, without stopping it. He himself moved to one side, approaching the ridge and Laughing Fragrance. Two or three Germans, crawling up the slope, were nearer her than he was. They could not see her, and they were obviously nervous in case she fired if they showed themselves. They were so intent on her that they did not see Stefan.

He took careful aim and fired three times.

One man fell backwards and began to roll down the hillside. Another sprang to his feet and turned and ran pell-mell, dodging out of the way of the falling body of his companion. The third lay quite still.

A burst of shooting came from the far end of the ridge, fifty yards or more from Stefan—a signal that the men who had tried to outflank Laughing Fragrance were being met by the two Chinese. Stefan reached the ridge and the girl. Her face was ashen, and he saw blood on her shoulder and her side. She looked at him with a tight-lipped smile and then moved forward so that she could see behind the ridge to the scene below.

There the jeep was careering down as if Kao Lun had lost control. He was past some of the leading Germans, driving straight at the machine-gun post. The bullets must have passed within inches of him, and most of them were flying high; they were tracers which Stefan could see clearly. Suddenly the men manning the gun turned and ran and the jeep crashed into and over the machine-gun. It looked as if the little car would be turned over. It righted itself, and Kao Lun continued to drive furiously downhill. The men further down were firing at him frantically, but they were between rocks which made it impossible for them to move to the right or left. There was only just room for the jeep to pass between the rocks.

Had they been prepared, they could have stopped him

without difficulty. Instead, they were taken by surprise by his daring and they turned tail, those in front cannoning into those behind. In a few seconds they were jammed between the rocks, struggling and fighting among themselves. Stefan could hear them cursing, their voices sounded above the roar of the jeep's engine. A few of the men were firing from high ground on one side. Stefan began to shoot, to distract their attention from Kao Lun.

The Chinese stopped the jeep some twenty yards in front of the Germans, who were jammed inextricably, making the situation worse with every moment.

Bullets struck the jeep and the rocks on either side but Kao Lun seemed not to notice them. He stood behind the jeep, and every movement was as cool and deliberate as if he were on a practice range. They saw him take the pins out of hand-grenades and toss them, one after the other; two were in the air at the same time. As the first landed close to the jammed soldiers, Kao Lun ducked behind the jeep.

The explosions followed so fast upon each other that they seemed like a continuous roar. Flame and smoke and then a cloud of billowing dust hid the men from sight, but did not hide Kao Lun. He lost no time in turning his attention to the men among the rocks on either side. He was still a target for desultory shooting, but Stefan's fire was keeping most of the men quiet.

Kao Lun began to climb up the rocks.

'Come back!' cried Laughing Fragrance. 'Come back!'

For answer, Kao Lun tossed a grenade towards two crouching men who were firing at him at almost point-blank range. He lost his footing, as if he were hit. The grenade exploded and the two men disappeared in the billowing smoke.

A sudden cry of warning from behind made Stefan swing round. In his tense interest in Kao Lun's magnificent attack he had forgotten the possibility of danger from the rear. A bullet struck Laughing Fragrance on the arm, another passed within a few inches of his own head. The two Chinese were on the ground, one of them still shooting. Two of the Germans who had tried the outflanking move were approaching, one badly wounded, the other apparently untouched.

Stefan aimed, but his gun was empty.

He dodged to one side and flung himself flat, stretching out one arm and bringing Laughing Fragrance down with him. He tried to reload, but the gun jammed. A rock gave him shelter but it would not serve for long; the man was getting nearer, and he saw his head, then his shoulders. The German crept along by the wall of rock which formed the ridge, obviously expecting a volley of fire. Stefan worked desperately at the gun, but he could not open it to reload.

Laughing Fragrance lay very still.

Stefan saw the German's face light up; as the man saw what had happened he jumped into the open. Stefan flung the useless gun at him and leapt forward. There was just a hope that he would crash into the man before he was shot. He expected a bullet in his chest, but instead he saw the man crumple up in front of him. The other wounded German was lying on his back, his face turned towards the sky.

Stefan drew back, gulping in great breaths. He looked behind him and saw that the Chinese who had come on foot were within easy rifle range and were hurrying towards him. He looked down the trail. Kao Lun was sitting at the wheel of the jeep and pulling calmly at the self-starter. There was no sign of opposition from either side.

Stefan dragged himself wearily towards Laughing Fragrance. His head was splitting and the pain was so great that he could hardly see. He bent down beside her, seeing the pallor of her face and the spreading patch of blood at her shoulder. He cut her linen shirt away, but as he worked there was a mist in front of his eyes; he staggered and nearly fell across her.

She opened her eyes.

She said: 'Palfrey discovered. Von Runst other hiding-place. Going soon. Do not know how leaving—needed as doctor. Needed as doctor,' she repeated, and added: 'All understood?'

'Yes,' said Stefan. 'Be quiet, now.'

Before anyone else reached him, he knew that she lost consciousness.

They were back at the valley within the valley.

Stefan had been brought by a second jeep, Laughing Fragrance had been taken ahead in Kao Lun's jeep. When Stefan arrived, badly shaken by the jolting but in better shape than when he had tried to help the girl, he saw that she was lying on a bed of grass with a blanket stretched over her. Kao Lun and two others were washing the wounds in her shoulder, chest and arms. She was still unconscious. Kao Lun's face was set, and as Stefan looked at him he realised what had inspired him to that mad drive. It was not simply a desire to kill every German within sight; it was something deeper, apparent in his gaze as he stared at Min Shu's pale face.

Stefan touched his bandaged head, and his fingers came away wet with blood. He was afraid that if he moved he would lose consciousness, but he was desperately anxious to find out whether Laughing Fragrance was fatally injured. He got to his knees.

Kao Lun turned towards him. 'We have got the bullets out,' he said. 'I think perhaps she will live.'

'She will live,' said Stefan, confidently, and was astonished at the relief in the man's eyes, proof that he was prepared to clutch at any hope. 'She gave me a message,' he went on, and repeated it. 'That information must be sent to Chungking quickly—it is even more urgent than the other.'

'At once!' Kao Lun called to two men who were standing nearby, and spoke swiftly. He made them each repeat the message three times before he ordered them to start over the mountains on that dangerous journey to take news which was of such vital importance.

Stefan found himself, now, thinking less of Laughing Fragrance and more of Palfrey and Drusilla. . . .

There was no summons during the night at the little house where Palfrey and Drusilla were captives, and when they woke up everything seemed normal—that false appearance of normality which was the most unnerving feature of the village.

They were allowed to wander about their own little garden at will, but were stopped directly they tried to go further.

After lunch Palfrey declared himself calmer.

'The portents for Laughing Fragrance are good,' he said. 'She probably got away. The longer we're left here, the better the prospect for us, too.'

'It means that von Runst isn't going to panic,' Drusilla agreed.

'Yes—he has a quite unnerving confidence. He obviously means to make this as nerve-racking as possible, of course. I rather expect that we'll be separated before long.'

'I'm waiting for that,' admitted Drusilla.

'I don't think we have too much to fear at the moment,' said Palfrey. 'I think he was quite serious when he said he wanted my services, and he probably knows that I meant it when I told him he could sing for them if he harmed a hair of your blonde head. Which reminds me . . .' He stood up, and looked at her hair intently. 'Darkling shoots among the gold,' he announced, 'but that stuff lasted well. At least you won't have to try it again.'

'I think I *am* less on edge, now that the strain is over,' said Drusilla.

'That's the ticket! Shall we take the air for half an hour?'

They walked round the house, watched but unmolested, and then went to the back and peered towards the distant mountains.

A guard came and stood nearby.

Palfrey, staring longingly towards the hills, saw something move. It was a long way off and he thought it was a bird or an animal—but, narrowing his eyes and with the sun behind him, he changed his mind; it was more like a man.

He turned to the guard: 'Have you field-glasses?'

'*Ja.*'

'Lend them to me.'

The man hesitated. Palfrey glared, and the fellow took a pair of small field-glasses from his knapsack and handed them over. Palfrey put them to his eyes, adjusted them, and saw the rugged rock formation coming much clearer; at last he focused on the man and saw him walking unsteadily. He could not see his face clearly, but he could see that one side of his trousers was darker than the other, and there seemed to be a dark patch on his coat.

'Please!' said the guard.

Palfrey handed him the glasses.

'A wounded man is approaching the river; if I were you I would report it.'

The guard did not speak, but peered through the glasses for a long time. He put them down and called to one of the others, who came hurrying up.

Soon an electric car was being driven along the road towards the river, the road along which the ill-fated convoy had travelled a few nights before. A small wooden bridge had been slung over the river, although it was out of sight. The car disappeared for a while, but came into view again not far from the approaching man—or woman.

It stopped alongside the wanderer, who was helped in.

The car disappeared in the direction of Headquarters.

'We may as well go in,' Palfrey suggested.

'Yes.' They walked back, to the guard's obvious relief, but had not been inside long before footsteps heralded a caller. It was the lieutenant who had allowed Palfrey to see the one-armed Japanese, Hiroto. He clicked his heels and saluted formally.

'You will come with me, please.'

'Where?' asked Palfrey.

'His Excellency wishes to see you.'

Palfrey shrugged. 'All right. 'Silla——'

'You only,' the lieutenant interrupted.

Palfrey said, coldly: 'Wherever I go, my wife will go with me. If you have instructions to the contrary you may take my compliments to His Excellency and tell him that I am unable to come alone.'

'Is that wise?' asked Drusilla, uneasily.

'We've got to try our luck sooner or later,' said Palfrey.

In his office, von Runst looked at Drusilla coldly, but made no comment.

Sitting in an easy chair which had been brought in from the lounge was the man who had been wounded. He was dirty and haggard, and his eyes were twitching. Kriess stood by von Runst's side; the little Professor's lips were set tightly and for once there was no smile on his face. Von Runst seemed to have forgotten his great satisfaction at the huge joke which he had perpetrated.

He barked: 'Palfrey, I want the truth!'

'About what?' asked Palfrey.

'When did you last see the Chinese woman, Min Shu?'

Palfrey's heart missed a beat, but he kept his face set and forced himself not to glance at Drusilla.

'Some days ago,' he said.

'I want the truth!' roared von Runst. 'Have you seen her since you were put under arrest? Answer me! Have you seen her?'

13 : Von Runst Gives an Entertainment

'No,' said Palfrey.

His eyes did not flicker, but he was praying that Drusilla had given no sign of alarm. Kriess was looking at her; von Runst was paying full attention to him. The office was quiet, only the heavy breathing of the injured man sounded clearly.

'I believe you are lying!' snapped von Runst.

He turned savagely to the wounded man. 'Pretzer—the truth! This woman was coming from the village?'

'From the direction of the village, Excellency.' The man's words were hardly audible.

Von Runst turned baleful eyes on Palfrey.

'Understand that none of my promises hold if you are

lying to me. *Hold the woman!'* he added, and the two men stepped smartly to Drusilla's side and gripped her arms. *'Bring her here!'* They marched her to the table, where Palfrey stood only two feet away and Kriess was immediately opposite her, at von Runst's side.

'Have you seen this Chinese woman?' von Runst thundered.

'No.' Drusilla's voice sounded refreshingly quiet and controlled. 'I have not seen her for some days, Herr Field-Marshal.'

'You are lying!' Von Runst pushed his chair back and stood up. He picked up a round ebony ruler from the desk and hit the side with it heavily. 'Tell me the truth! She came to your house! You told her what I had told you!'

'Your Excellency forgets himself,' said Drusilla, coolly.

'I forget! I will show you, you English slut, what——'

'I think, Excellency, that I can find a way of making her tell the truth,' said Kriess, gently. 'If you will allow me to take her to the hospital, where it is much more convenient.'

'This matter is urgent!'

'I will lose no time,' Kriess assured him, 'and you have much to do, Excellency.'

'I have too much to do!' snapped von Runst. 'Take her away. Palfrey will stay here.'

'I——' began Palfrey.

'You will stay here!' roared von Runst.

Kriess took Drusilla's arm and walked to the door with her and the two guards. Their heavy footsteps had an ominous ring, and Palfrey felt on the verge of defying the man and going after her; but it would serve no purpose. Sooner or later, something had been bound to happen. He felt a deepening hatred for Kriess.

Then he found himself alone with von Runst and the wounded man.

The Field-Marshal looked at him steadily, more composed now. He pressed the bell again to summon more men in. He pointed to the wounded soldier and, as the fellow was carried out, he took a heavy automatic from his desk and put it in front of him. Then he pulled open a drawer of the desk and took out some green folders. By his side was a large, steel waste-paper basket.

'I am preparing to leave,' he said, putting some of the papers aside. 'There is a risk that an attempt will be made to rescue you, Palfrey. I do not intend to allow it to succeed. How many Chinese are in the valley?'

'I know nothing more about them,' said Palfrey.

'Did Andromovitch pass on a message which was not recorded on the machine?'

'No.'

The German looked up. 'I am not yet sure whether you are to be believed, Palfrey. I give you my word that if you or your wife are lying to me you will deeply regret it. I will not waste time in elaborating my threats. You are not a man without imagination. We shall know, soon, whether you have lied; Kriess will get the information. Have you seen the Chinese woman?' he added abruptly.

'No,' Palfrey repeated.

A buzzer sounded on the desk, and von Runst looked up sharply, then pressed a bell-push. A door behind him opened and a little man came through, one of the immaculate creatures whom Palfrey had seen several times before. He said: 'We are ready, Excellency.'

'I will come at once.' Von Runst picked up the automatic and dropped it into his pocket. 'Come with me, Palfrey.'

There were guards outside the door; any wild thought of attacking von Runst faded at the sight of them. Palfrey walked by the man's side, absorbed with thought of Drusilla —it was all he could do to retain his composure.

He was led along passages which he had not visited before, and then into a large room with a stage at one end. It was a small private theatre, with rows of comfortable chairs, none of which was occupied. Several little men were standing in front of the stage, and one escorted von Runst and Palfrey to front-row chairs.

The unreality of the situation did nothing to soothe Palfrey's nerves. His mind kept straying to Drusilla and Kriess, and he kept clenching and unclenching his hands.

Two of the little men took seats immediately behind him and gradually the room filled up. Several higher officers came in, sat down, and ignored both Palfrey and von Runst. Where his staff were concerned, the Field-Marshal seemed to hold himself aloof.

Faint music began to fill the room. Subdued lights appeared in front of the curtains, and then the main lights went out, leaving only a faint glow from concealed lamps. Palfrey could just see one of the little men by his side; another was immediately behind von Runst.

The music grew louder. It was strange and reedy; something Eastern, with a mournful air. It increased the strain on his nerves. Von Runst was staring at the curtains, which moved suddenly with a soft, swishing sound.

The stage was set in exotic fashion, with rich, colourful carpets, lacquered furniture and vases, a low divan and rich silk cushions—Japanese fashion, Palfrey noted with a sudden deeper stirring of interest.

There was a movement in the room. A man came walking softly towards von Runst, accompanied by several others who kept a respectful distance behind him. Palfrey glanced up and saw that he was a Japanese; old, thin, dressed in a flowing gown of royal blue, wearing a tiny cap on his greying hair. He stood in front of von Runst and bowed. The Field-Marshal rose from his chair and returned the compliment. Accompanied by his retinue, the Japanese took chairs along from von Runst, and he himself sat next to the Field-Marshal. He did not appear to notice Palfrey; his gaze was fixed on the stage.

The music softened. One of the curtains moved and a man or woman, face covered with a grotesque mask, appeared on the stage and held the curtain to one side.

Another masked figure appeared.

No longer did Palfrey seek an explanation of the masks in von Runst's rooms. This man was wearing one, more grotesque and much more elaborate than the first. The man began to talk in a low-pitched monotone which conveyed nothing to Palfrey, yet there was a quality of fascination about it; it reminded him of English mummers, for it had the same tonelessness and the same intensity.

Other figures appeared.

They moved with smooth, appealing grace, and all were clad in gorgeous robes. As they entered they began to chant on a low-pitched monotonous level.

A woman appeared.

There was no ugliness and nothing repulsive about the mask she wore. There was a quality of beauty about it which made Palfrey catch his breath. She was dressed in a robe of soft pastel shades, more beautiful than any of the others. She walked with ineffable grace towards the centre of the stage, and then she began to sway from side to side.

Slowly, so slowly that at first it was hardly perceptible, her movements grew faster. She seemed to revolve at the hips, her head moving in ever-widening circles. On and on she went; the music faded and there was a deathly silence in the room—and then, abruptly, she began to sing, on a high-pitched wailing note.

Louder and louder grew the music and the singing, louder and louder the wailing from her lips . . .

Then she collapsed.

She sank to the divan with the folds of her gown falling about her, covering all but her mask. She lay back with her head upon a cushion; the singing began to fade and the music softened. Very slowly, until at last Palfrey was not sure whether they were singing or whether the sounds were in his ears, the music faded.

There was no sound; no movement.

It was von Runst who broke the tense silence, and there seemed nothing strange to Palfrey in the fact that he spoke in stiff, stilted English.

'Is it satisfactory?'

'Yes,' said the Japanese. 'Yes. Quite satisfactory. Very good, Excellency. Very good. I congratulate them.'

Von Runst stood up, and led the way back to his office, and when they reached it Palfrey saw that although he was pale there was a smile on his lips. The memory of the massacre of his men, the problem of Laughing Fragrance, no longer seemed to affect him. He looked at Palfrey with mockery in his expression, and then turned to his Japanese guest.

'This is the eminent Dr. Palfrey, of whom you have heard.'

'Delighted to meet the honourable doctor.' The Japanese bowed. 'You have just seen——'

'We do not intend to tell Dr. Palfrey what we have seen, yet,' said von Runst.

'I beg your pardon, Excellency.'

'Dr. Palfrey is not a willing guest,' added von Runst. 'He once thought that he knew what we are doing. Can you guess now, Doctor?'

Palfrey's hand strayed to his forehead and played with his hair. 'No,' he said.

'You would be a clever man if you could! This time, at least, I believe you.' He smiled at the Japanese. 'Is there need for another rehearsal?'

'All possible rehearsals are wise, Excellency. None you need attend. You wish further talk?'

'I will come to see you later,' von Runst told him.

He bowed when the Japanese backed towards the door, and when it closed he and Palfrey were left together in the office. 'I should soon hear from Kriess,' he announced. 'Tell me, Palfrey, did I not enable you to forget?'

Palfrey said: 'Yes.'

'You have seen a performance of the famous *No,* the Japanese drama which has been performed for countless generations,' said von Runst. 'What you saw was one of the greatest tragedies known to Japanese drama—far more famous in their eyes than *Hamlet* or *King Lear*. There is no reason why you should not know that much, Doctor——'

The telephone bell rang.

Palfrey was perspiring freely, but the worst of the tension had gone.

Von Runst said, with a glance at him:

'Yes, Professor—yes.' He listened, his head on one side. 'Are you sure? In that case, Professor, you may return Mrs. Palfrey to her house. Is she hysterical? Not hysterical? Excellent!'

He broke the spell which held Palfrey as he went on speaking into the telephone:

'How far was it necessary for you to go? . . . I see . . . You are quite sure that she has told you the whole truth? . . . Yes, yes, excellent, Professor . . . I will deal with Palfrey myself!' He replaced the receiver and stared into Palfrey's eyes.

'She has admitted that she saw the Chinese woman,' said von Runst. 'Confess fully, Palfrey, and tell me all that you told Min Shu. Otherwise . . .'

He stopped, and held a gun pointing at Palfrey's stomach.

The mist in front of Palfrey's eyes cleared. He knew that had von Runst been a moment slower he would have flung himself at him. It was the same wave of blind insane fury which had overcome him when he had seen Kriess in the laboratory. He knew that he was deathly pale—yet there was an urgent warning in his mind. If Drusilla had confessed, why did the man want confirmation from him? *If* Drusilla had confessed . . .

Coldly, he said: 'If my wife made a "confession" it was not true. There is no knowing what she may have been driven to in an excess of pain.'

'A likely story!' said von Runst. 'It does not matter, Palfrey. The story is known. It is a great pity. Go and look at your wife,' he added abruptly. 'It will, perhaps, teach you to understand that in future you must not hold out against me.'

He pressed a bell-push; the young lieutenant came in, and he snapped: 'Take Dr. Palfrey to his house. Have a strong escort. If he leaves the house without orders, shoot on sight. You understand?'

'Perfectly, Excellency.'

The men took Palfrey's arm and led him out; he walked mechanically, and his heart seemed to have stopped beating.

Darkness had fallen and lights were showing from some of the windows. The lieutenant guided him towards the gate of his house and he saw the light shining from the window. No one appeared against it. He reached the front door, and the shadowy figure of one of the watching men appeared.

'Your key,' the lieutenant demanded.

'Key,' said Palfrey. He fumbled in his pocket and produced it. The lieutenant opened the door and stood aside.

'You understand the orders—you will not move from the house except with permission.'

'Yes.' Palfrey nodded bleakly.

As he stepped inside, a figure appeared in the doorway of the bedroom. He stared incredulously. His heart began to race and there was a mist in front of his eyes—but not a mist of anger now; one of incredible relief. Fantastic relief! Here was . . .

'Sap!' cried Drusilla.

'Don't move!' Palfrey said softly.

He stared at her fixedly. The mist cleared from his eyes and he saw every feature of her dear face. It was unscarred; she did not look as if she had suffered, nor as if she had come from some hellish torture chamber. Her hair was freshly groomed and she had just made-up. Except for the brilliance in her eyes, a brilliance born of anxiety because of his pallor, she was normal, natural.

'Sap, what is it?'

'Von Runst said——' He took a step towards her, and his voice broke. 'Oh, my dear!'

'Sap, what have they done to you?'

'Nothing, nothing at all.' Laughing, Palfrey took her arm and gripped it tightly. 'You're real. This isn't another damnable trick, you're real!' He laughed again. 'I'm going mad! I think that's what he wants—to drive me mad. One of these days,' he added, much more gently, 'I will really let myself go, without being able to help it, and with these delicate fingers I will throttle the gentleman.' He raised his left hand, with the fingers bunched, and there was a quality in his voice which Drusilla did not recognise.

'You almost sound as if you mean it,' she protested.

'He has reduced torture to a fine art. He gave me the most gruesome word-picture of what had happened to you——'

'*Nothing* happened to me,' said Drusilla, 'except . . .' Her anxiety for Palfrey had eased and now she was able to give full rein to her own memory. 'They took me to the hospital,' she went on, 'and in the room next to the laboratory there is a steel chair, a kind of hot-seat, I think, judging from the wires leading to it. I was in a frenzy for a moment, I thought they were going to electrocute me. Kriess held my hand. Do you know, Sap, there is a queer quality in that man—it actually soothed me.

'He had something that looked like a seismograph on a bench, and he adjusted it and then began to ask questions—the same questions. It was unnerving, and yet—well, I wasn't frightened at all.'

'Triumph of curiosity,' Palfrey suggested.

'Do you think so?' She was absorbed in her recollections. 'Whatever it was, I watched him and answered him promptly. He asked the one question—had we seen Laughing Fragrance since our arrest—in different ways. I kept answering "no"—just that, not another word. Sometimes he glanced away from me and looked at the instrument by his side. It had a small needle which made a fairly smooth red line. If it was a lie-detector, it didn't work!'

'Did they inject anything into you?'

'No.'

'What happened then?'

'Nothing. It lasted for the better part of an hour, I suppose, and then he seemed satisfied and went out of the room. I heard him talking on the telephone, I think.'

'To von Runst, probably,' said Palfrey. 'Hum! Von Runst thought it would be a good idea to have a little joke, and nearly drove me off my head.'

'You looked *ghastly,*' Drusilla told him.

'I looked as I felt, only less so! It's a curious business,' Palfrey went on. 'Laughing Fragrance was seen and hunted by a patrol looking for the Chinese force. She was coming from the direction of the village, but they aren't sure whether she came from here or whether she had been in hiding and was trying to get in touch with her friends. All except one of the Huns was wiped out, which is quite a feat. Von Runst said that he was planning to move pretty quickly.'

'What made him tell you all this?'

'Partly because it amused him and partly, I think, because he hoped that he would catch me out if he told me half a story. I think we can be sure that Laughing Fragrance got through, anyhow, and that the Chinese taught them a sharp lesson.' He lit another cigarette, watching Drusilla closely. 'I know the secret of the masks and the little men, anyhow.'

'Seriously?' she demanded.

'I think so. Part of it, anyhow.'

He told her all that had happened, and so great was the effect on him of what he had seen that he brought something of the atmosphere of the little theatre to the room. He could almost hear the reedy music and the wailing cry of the woman dancer, and when he finished the room was very quiet.

'Japanese tragedy!' said Palfrey. 'If you can tell me why von Runst should want to see it, why he should ask whether another rehearsal were necessary, why he should have a Japanese in to see it, I don't know. Except——' He paused, and his eyes lighted up. 'Sweet, I see a gleam of light!'

'Go on!' cried Drusilla.

'Japanese are little men,' said Palfrey in a faraway voice, 'and all the actors were little men—presumably the fellows who once caused me such bewilderment. Sooner or later that drama, acted by Germans who cannot be told from Japanese because of their masks, is going to be played before a Japanese audience.' He looked at Drusilla blankly. 'Question—*why*? It could explain the Jap—he was there to make sure that the Germans did the job properly. Apart from that, it seems only like a gigantic hoax—there *must* be something more behind it.'

'Didn't he give you a hint?'

'No. He told me just enough to put me on edge, and then left me,' said Palfrey. 'Von Runst is a cunning devil,' he added, slowly. 'He and Kriess make a fine pair.'

More people were about next morning than usual, all hurrying. Palfrey wondered if there were any significance in that, and then forgot it when the familiar sight of an electric car appeared outside the house. The equally familiar face of the young lieutenant appeared from it. The man brought a summons. Palfrey raised no objections, and expected to be taken to the underground headquarters. Instead, they were driven in the opposite direction, past the hospital and towards flat, even countryside from which all trees had been cleared. There were some mounds of earth, which he realised were covered dug-outs. With quickening excitement, he whispered:

'The airfield, I think.'

'So we're off,' said Drusilla.

She looked over her shoulder towards the village.

Palfrey saw the expression in her eyes, half wistful, half regretful. He knew exactly what she was feeling: this place had suddenly become desirable. They had found it eerie and at times hostile; they had been through mental agony every day since they had arrived there, but it was infinitely preferable to the unknown destination for which they were bound.

They pulled up beside a mound much larger than the others, and were led on foot to the front of it. It astonished them. There was a wide, narrow hole in the ground, with the roof of the 'dug-out' forming the top; it was like a great, gaping mouth. Men were turning handles on each side of it, and the ground itself slowly sank lower, enlarging the hole until they could see the front of a tri-engined monoplane. The great hangar, so effectively hidden, was filled with men.

The engines started up and the machine was taxied out. As if moved by clockwork, other machines appeared about the field—Palfrey counted five. Men emerged from the hangars, and he saw the 'actors' climbing into the cabin of an aircraft; there were twenty men, all told. Another cabin was filled with officers from Headquarters. A third appeared to contain mostly luggage, a fourth, airfield personnel. A smaller machine appeared, a twin-engined monoplane which was obviously much faster than the others. In it von Runst was sitting with the Japanese of the theatre, and by standing on tiptoe Palfrey saw that von Klowitz, on a stretcher, was also inside. Kriess appeared and entered von Runst's plane; Palfrey and Drusilla, with several more members of the Headquarters staff, were ushered aboard a machine standing near it. The field was loud with the roar of motors and busy with the preparations for departure.

The first machine taxied forward and was airborne in a few seconds. The others followed swiftly, Palfrey's the last to leave the ground. The moment or two of bumping over the grass was soon over and almost before they realised it, they were airborne, unaware of movement until they looked out and saw the countryside streaming by. Palfrey turned to peer back and was astonished; even from a few thousand feet it was impossible to see the buildings of the village.

They flew north.

He tucked Drusilla's arm into his, and they stared down into that incredible valley, so serene and lovely in the sun. As they gained height it seemed much smaller than when they had been walking about it. The foothills were insignificant, too, completely lost in the mighty grandeur of forest-clad mountains whose barren peaks were covered with a mantle of virgin snow.

There was another valley between the topmost peaks, a place where shadows lurked and where the beauty was lost in a terrifying mystery of jagged rock and mighty caves. Parts looked dark as pitch, and all looked hostile. They could see the same terrain stretched about them on all sides. Only when they looked back towards the valley did they see the smiling green, a tiny patch which seemed an infinite distance away. It was easy, now, to understand why it was difficult to see the valley from the air.

No one spoke.

Palfrey leaned back against the comfortable upholstery of his seat. Drusilla had her eyes closed, as if she wished to get through this stage of the journey without looking about her. The other aircraft were flying in loose formation in front of them, the small 'plane with von Runst leading the way.

Something dark flashed across its nose.

Palfrey thought at first that it was a gigantic bird—until he saw bright lines of light flash above the leading machine and then drop down towards the rocks.

''Silla!' he gasped.

There was a sharp crackling sound, and as Drusilla opened her eyes and sat upright, a voice came over the radio. There were ceaseless atmospherics, but the words were audible enough.

'The formation is being attacked. Split up. The formation is being attacked. Split up.'

Suddenly, their machine banked steeply. Palfrey caught a glimpse of several Typhoons, with Chinese markings, and one or two smaller machines with Allied markings. He also saw the bright streaks of tracer bullets. Then the machine seemed to lurch and lost height rapidly, and he saw that the port engine was on fire.

14 : The Baron Gives Advice

THE aircraft banked again. Drusilla was thrown against the window with Palfrey's full weight pressed tightly against her. The flames from the engine were yellow streaks which swept back as far as the windows, and smoke made the cabin dark. Palfrey tried to ease himself away from Drusilla, but the machine was moving too fast and banking too steeply. He could just see the rocks below through gaps in the smoke.

Slowly, the pilot straightened out.

The port engine was burning more fiercely, but the others seemed all right. Palfrey saw two small fighters flying almost alongside, and suddenly the radio crackled again.

'Make for the valley—make for the valley!'

The pilot weaved this way and that, but whether to try to avoid the fighters or whether to put out the fire, Palfrey did not know. A man crawled towards them along the cabin and thrust two packages into Palfrey's hands; they were parachutes. He fastened Drusilla's mechanically; there was little room to move, and it seemed to take a long time.

'Be ready to jump!'

They were losing height rapidly. Now, the fighters were flying above them, as if they dared not go so low. They sped past a hilltop and for a moment Palfrey thought that the wing would crash into it; they could not have missed by more than two or three yards. Then they gained a little height, and Drusilla said: 'I think the fire's out.'

Smoke was still pouring from the engine, but there were no flames. The two remaining engines seemed to be turning over evenly enough. They gained more height. The worst danger seemed to be past—but suddenly a second engine faded and they heard the third missing.

'Be ready to jump!'

They had lost more height, and were less than a thousand feet above the rocks, themselves thousands of feet above the green valley. If they could fly for another five minutes they would be over the valley, where they would have more chance of making a safe descent.

Further along the cabin there was a trap-door in the floor; it was opened by one of the officers. The blast of cold air made them gasp and again, Drusilla was pressed back against the window, this time by the force of the inrush. The roaring noise was unnerving, and drowned the sound of the engine; for a few seconds they thought that the final engine had failed them. They were flying fairly smoothly, however, and Palfrey gave her a smile.

'He'll make a forced landing,' he assured her.

In spite of his words, he was not at all convinced. Sometimes the rocks beneath seemed only a few feet away, and he knew that if they had to jump at this height they would crash to death. The pilot managed to gain a few feet, and then they flew over the valley of the river, with grassland on either side. There the earth was several thousand feet beneath them.

The man in the pilot's cabin called:

'Jump!'

The last engine was missing frequently. The aeroplane was

swaying from side to side, and Palfrey felt a desperate eagerness to get to the door. The others seemed to take an age. One after the other they jumped; one after the other, the white silk envelopes of the parachutes opened out.

The man in front of Drusilla went.

'Off you go,' Palfrey urged.

He squeezed her arm and helped her to climb through; she sat on the floor of the cabin for a moment, and then edged herself off, and fell into space. Palfrey caught a glimpse of her hair streaming in the wind, and then she fell behind and he started to climb through the hole.

The aircraft lurched and flung him back against one of the walls. He heard the scream of the wind but no sound of the engine. Then the aircraft went into a crazy spin. Palfrey could not save himself from being thrown this way and that; he had no control over his movements, and the blood drumming through his ears was filling his head with blinding pain. Yet his thoughts were crystal clear. The attack proved that Allied forces had hemmed the valley in, and Drusilla had a great chance of finding safety.

He was going to die.

A new sound came; at first he did not realise what it was, but the wild revolutions of the aircraft steadied a little, *and then he heard the even throb of an engine*.

The aircraft steadied and flew on a straight course.

It happened as quickly as it had gone into a spin, and was far less easy to believe. They were only a few hundred feet from the ground, following the course of the river. Breathing heavily and leaning against the door, Palfrey looked out. Only the pilot remained in the aircraft with him; he could just see the man through the door leading to the front cabin. He was sitting at the controls and calmly putting the nose of the aircraft down. The wheels touched the ground, the machine rose a few feet and dropped again, and then began to taxi along. When it came to a standstill, Palfrey saw that it was within a few yards of one of the underground hangars, from which men were already hurrying.

The pilot sat back in his seat. There was something about his attitude which made Palfrey squeeze through the little door and hurry to him. There was a taut smile on the airman's face, and his eyes were narrowed with pain. The whole of his right side was soaked with blood.

Men appeared at the cabin door, and Palfrey called for a stretcher. Two men came in and helped him to move the pilot, who was ashen grey, and unable to move on his own. They eased him through the door and on to the stretcher, which was pushed into a small ambulance driven up from the hangar.

'To the hospital,' said Palfrey, mechanically.

'At once, Herr Baron.'

Palfrey started and looked hard at the speaker, a sergeant. He caught a glimpse of the pilot's face and saw the way his lips turned down. Their eyes met, and there was a great deal in that brief exchange, bringing to Palfrey the bewildering realisation that the ground staff did not know that he had been taken away under arrest. The pilot knew, and he was well enough to be able to betray him; instead, he gave that twisted smile.

The ambulance was driven off.

The men crowded round Palfrey, asking urgent questions. Soon it transpired that they had been told that the aircraft would return. None of them knew that their leaders had deserted them, nor had any of them seen what happened at the start of the attack, but they had seen the two Allied fighters following the returning aircraft. Men were manning ack-ack batteries, and two fighter aircraft were getting ready to take off.

No airborne machines were in sight, but in the distance, along that forbidding valley, there was a tiny blaze and a column of smoke which went straight upwards; one of the escaping aircraft had crashed in flames. Palfrey saw a second blaze, further away; it was no more than a flicker of red light.

He answered the questions mechanically and tried to decide what he should do. Drusilla was only a few miles away, but he could not see any of the parachutes; they were too far off to be seen by the naked eye. A captain in summer uniform barked a comand, and the crowd of men pressing about Palfrey thinned out. The captain looked harassed and bewildered. Was it possible, wondered Palfrey, that he did not know the truth about the 'Baron von Klieb'?

Apparently it was, for the man asked:

'Will they ever get back, now?'

'They did not intend to get back,' said Palfrey.

'They did not . . .' the man's voice trailed off.

'It was desertion and betrayal,' said Palfrey. 'I knew, and was taken away under arrest—I was not allowed to speak. All of us were to be betrayed. Von Runst knew that our days in the valley were numbered, and hoped that he would be able to save his own skin.'

'It—it is incredible!'

'It is true,' said Palfrey. 'Only junior officers and men were left behind. For some time I have been trying to warn them, but I had no opportunity.' The story offered the one hope of saving himself from interrogation, and it would depend on whether the men who had parachuted from the burning aircraft returned soon to tell the whole truth. He elaborated on the theme when the captain summoned other junior officers. One or two looked dazed, but some of them admitted that they had been puzzled by the fact that no senior officers had been left behind.

'What are we to do?' asked the captain, helplessly.

'We have two alternatives,' said Palfrey, harshly. 'The valley will undoubtedly be invaded, and we can fight or surrender. Von Runst would not have deserted us had he believed that we had any chance of success. I think the time has come when we should stop fighting hopeless battles—that is Nazi folly. There are Chinese forces in the valley now, who will accept our surrender.'

'They kill all prisoners!' said a young lieutenant.

'Nonsense!' barked Palfrey. 'But I will, of course, abide by the decision of the majority.' He stalked away, and stared towards the tiny fires, not much larger than the flame of a match from where he stood. He heard the officers talking agitatedly among themselves, and wondered if, in this topsy-turvy situation, they would decide to take his advice, and surrender.

His first inclination was to organise a small party to search for Drusilla and the other officers, senior men who would, no doubt, tell the truth about him. He doubted whether they would have much fight in them, and if he handled the situation dexterously he could make sure that they carried no influence. By far the most important thing was to persuade the men here to give up the thought of making a last fight. There was no telling how soon the valley would be invaded.

'Herr Baron . . .'

He turned to see the captain just behind him. The man saluted, and went on formally:

'I am Captain Walheim, Herr Baron. It has been decided not to offer resistance if you are sure that the Chinese do take prisoners.'

'I am *quite* sure,' said Palfrey, emphatically. 'I was a prisoner in their hands for several weeks. I had excellent treatment. You are very wise, Walheim,' he added, with a smile, and then said briskly: 'A few of the senior officers parachuted to safety when we were forced to turn back. They may wish to force us to resist. I advise you to send a patrol, to disarm and arrest them. I myself am prepared to lead a patrol to the Chinese force in the valley.'

'I will lead the other,' said Walheim, quickly. He looked relieved. 'It will be a good thing finished,' he declared, 'it has been a great ordeal here.' He clicked his heels and saluted, and then turned with Palfrey to join the rest of the officers.

Little groups of men were gathered together some distance away, watching the officers closely. Palfrey thought that he saw signs of rebellion in their attiude. Walheim went towards them; most of them drew themselves to attention, but some of them stood at ease, regarding him insolently. Walheim began to speak and as he told them what had been decided, Palfrey saw the delight in their faces, and knew that they had been ready to refuse to fight.

He stopped thinking of them.

In the distance there was a dull rumbling sound. It had been in the air for some time, but he had not noticed it consciously; now he realised that large formations of aircraft were approaching, and the noise rapidly grew louder.

The wail of the air-raid siren broke the hush. The village siren joined in. Walheim hesitated, looking to Palfrey for guidance. Palfrey said sharply:

'Man the guns! If they bomb we must defend ourselves!'

Any other decision then would have been fatal. If bombs came, thought Palfrey, the whole plan might fail; if the crews started to fight they might continue to the last man. He uttered a silent prayer that this was but a show of strength to frighten the people in the valley.

Something dropped from the aircraft.

A non-commissioned officer shouted an order.

'Stop!' roared Palfrey. 'Stop, they are not bombs!'

Parachutes were opening as the aircraft roared over, and at first he thought there were men attached to them; then he saw canisters and, immediately afterwards, some of them opened and leaflets began to flutter through the air. The aircraft roared overhead and then began to wheel and go back. Palfrey watched that storm of fluttering paper, saw men jumping up in the air to catch them as they fell. One touched his head, and then he seemed to be enveloped in them.

He clutched one, and read:

Overwhelming forces are ranged against you. Resistance will only end in death for every individual. You have no chance, except in surrender. Prisoners will receive good treatment, by order of the Chinese Government and the Allied Far Eastern Command. Signify your willingness to surrender by painting white crosses large enough to be seen from five thousand feet on all open spaces near your airfield.

Before Palfrey spoke men were hurrying to the hangars, and while he talked to Walheim, pots of whitewash and brushes were already in use.

. . . . . .

After the leaflet raid, two aircraft flew at three or four thousand feet, and saw some of the crosses already marked out and others in preparation. Within an hour there was another dull rumbling of approaching aircraft, this time carrier 'planes with fighter-escorts. Instead of leaflets, parachutists came down, and a few gliders were brought in and landed with perfect precision in the valley.

Walheim and his men appointed Palfrey as their spokesman. He spoke in German, and formally surrendered the valley to one of the colonels who had dropped with the airborne troops. He was on edge to send help to Drusilla. As the Chinese colonel talked, it occurred to him that the men who had dropped from the aircraft before Drusilla might determine to try to make a suicidal stand; and they might force Drusilla to go with them. The thought made him interrupt the man.

'There is a small force to the north,' he said; 'they should be rounded up quickly. They——'

The Chinese turned and pointed towards the forbidding valley, and Palfrey saw parachutists dropping from aircraft several miles away, tiny specks floating beneath the billowing parachutes. He wiped his forehead, and then pushed back his hat and began to twist a few strands of hair about his forefinger. He was looking vaguely at the Chinese colonel, trying to marshal his thoughts—but the astonishment on the man's face startled him.

'What . . .' he began.

'*Dr. Palfrey!*' exclaimed the colonel. 'You are Palfrey!'

Palfrey said, hesitantly:

'I don't want the others to know yet, they might take it badly. Er—how did you know?'

'That trick of yours!' said the colonel, lowering his voice. 'I was warned to watch for it. A man representing himself as Dr. Palfrey might not betray it—I am delighted that you are safe. Doctor! You need not worry about the others, they are being rapidly disarmed.' He laughed. 'Where is your Russian friend?'

'Holding out, to the west.' Palfrey patted the hair firmly on his forehead and reflected that it was a habit which might one day cost him his life. 'I think he's all right. I—by George!' he exclaimed. 'I'm not quite sane! There's another force in an outer fortress——'

'The outer fortress was stormed before we started off,' said the colonel mildly. 'You need have no worry about that, Dr. Palfrey. The chief anxiety is—which of the aeroplanes got through our fighters. Two of the aircraft succeeded in getting away to the north, they were extremely fast.'

'Was one a twin-engined monoplane?'

'That is so.'

'So von Runst got through? That's a pity.'

'It is not a pity,' said the colonel, confidently. 'It was hoped that he would escape. Even had he been captured, I had instructions to *allow* him to escape. You see, Dr. Palfrey, only he can lead us to his next destination. Perhaps I should not tell you this,' he added, 'I believe that Orishu wishes to talk to you as quickly as possible.'

'Is he here?' asked Palfrey, eagerly.

'He is due here soon,' said the colonel. 'I believe there are comfortable quarters in the village, Dr. Palfrey, perhaps I would be well advised to make them my headquarters.'

• • • • • •

Within ten minutes of each other there arrived Drusilla, unscathed, Stefan, heavily bandaged but obviously not seriously hurt, and Laughing Fragrance, on a stretcher which was immediately taken to the hospital. Palfrey went with Drusilla to see her; the doctors left behind by von Runst were already operating, and he had no fears for her recovery. A bright-eyed Chinese major, whom Stefan called Kao Lun, stormed into the hospital as Palfrey was leaving, and demanded to be taken to Laughing Fragrance. Stefan explained who he was.

'I wonder what happened to von Marritz?' Palfrey mused.

'If you mean the commander of the outer fortress, he was killed in the attack,' said the colonel, promptly.

'Oh,' Palfrey smiled happily at Drusilla. 'What the eye doesn't see, they say——' He broke off, as the colonel eyed him curiously, and gave a little vacant smile. 'Do you know,' he said, 'I think I'm tired. Or dreaming. I hope. . . .' His voice trailed off.

'You will wake up,' said Stefan, with a broad smile. 'I have the same feeling of unreality, Sap—I had given up all hope of seeing you again.'

'Yes. The problem is, have we finished all that we can do?' asked Palfrey. 'There doesn't seem a lot left for us, does there? And I should like to see the end of it,' he added, reflectively. 'It would give me all the pleasure in the world to see von Runst under arrest.'

'I suppose that whatever he is planning *will* fail?' said Drusilla.

Palfrey stared at her, and began to twist hair about his finger.

'That's the trouble,' he mumbled. 'I don't know.'

15 : Orishu Returns

LATE in the afternoon, reports came in from the rocky valley. The wreckage of aircraft had been discovered and one or two wounded men had been rescued. All of them were officers; there was no trace of the little men.

'So the actors got away with von Runst,' said Palfrey. 'The beggars probably had their 'plane specially armoured, like his own, to allow for accidents. Somewhere that grotesque drama is going to be staged again, and somewhere von Runst thinks he can stage a really big show.' He rubbed his chin. 'I wish to heaven I had second sight!'

He was in the little dining-room leading off von Runst's office. The masks were still on the walls, and he peered at one —a duplicate of that which the woman had worn on the stage. As he looked at the set features, with their hint of tragedy, the reedy music seemed to fill the room and he remembered every incident of the play. He tried to read significance into the actions of the actors, but he knew that if there had been any significance it was in the words which he had not understood.

The door opened, but he did not look round.

'I wish you could talk, my beauty,' he told the mask.

'I have no doubt that she can,' said a soft voice.

Palfrey turned abruptly—and Orishu stood in front of him, smiling faintly.

They shook hands warmly.

'You have been through much since we last met,' said Orishu. 'I for one, did not expect to see you alive again, Doctor!'

'You've got some explaining to do,' Palfrey chided him. 'Why didn't you tell me that you knew all about the valley?'

'I did not,' said Orishu, 'and nor did Chungking. It is a very great mystery, my friend. There was, it is true, information from a Lamaist priest, which helped a little, but that was not how we learned so much. We learned much more even after Andromovitch had dropped down with the first parachutists.'

'Now what are you driving at?' demanded Palfrey.

'I am telling you, as simply as I can, that we were sent full information about the valley,' said Orishu. 'We thought that perhaps it came from you. It was delievered by an aeroplane to the nearest airfield to the valley. It was immediately acted upon. Full instructions were given as to the site of the airfields, the strength of the defences, the position of the village *and* the plans to leave the majority of the people to our mercy.'

'You're fooling!'

'I am not, Doctor! I have with me a copy of the message and the plans of the valley.' He took a paper from his pocket and smoothed it out, and Palfrey stared in astonishment at a carefully drawn map. There was nothing missing, as far as he could see—in fact, there was more information than he had been able to get for himself.

'The only clue, you see, is that the writing is in Japanese characters,' said Orishu. 'I like to think that one of my country-folk realised that von Runst is evil, and that his plans must not be allowed to mature. I will translate the most important passages for you, Doctor.' He spoke swiftly, as if he had learned them off by heart. 'We are warned to act swiftly if we wish to prevent von Runst from escaping. We are warned that he believes that he can succeed in his main purpose, which is the establishing, in Asia, of an outpost of what he calls the Fourth Reich. We are warned that his plans are connected with a company of German actors of diminutive size.' He paused, and his eyes were so narrowed that they seemed to be closed. 'It is possible, of course, that Hiroto, the renegade minister from Tokyo, is in von Runst's power and tried to prevent him from succeeding. If that is so, it can be assumed that the plans have some connection with Japan.

'We have to admit, also, that several of the higher officers who have flown with von Runst came here from Tokyo. That does not mean official collaboration, of course. Hiroto himself is sufficiently powerful in Japan to be able to arrange that, but—*why*, Doctor?'

Palfrey shrugged. 'The colonel told me that von Runst's 'plane would be shadowed. We should know where he goes.'

'He will probably expect to be followed,' said Orishu. 'I

would not be surprised if he has not another trick prepared, like the one in the valley. We cannot be sure that where he goes next will be his final destination. Nor can we be sure that it will be so easily raided as this valley. I do not like the situation,' he admitted. 'It troubles me greatly. And yet, Doctor, I think that you have a vital clue, if only you could give expression to it.'

'You mean the drama?'

'Yes. Von Runst told you that it was a performance of *No*. Can you describe it?'

'It beggars description!' Palfrey grimaced. 'I can try, but'—he smiled—'if I saw it again, or even heard it again, I wouldn't take long to recognise it!'

'I have been thinking of that,' Orishu nodded. 'Do what you can to describe it, Doctor.'

Palfrey did his best, but knew it to be inadequate. At last Orishu said:

'I do not think we shall succeed this way, Doctor. The words and the form of the chanting and the music make up the widest differences between one rendering of *No* and others. To your eyes, perhaps, it would not look very different, but to ours there is a great difference. I wonder', he added softly, 'if you would recognise *everything* if you were to see it again.'

'I haven't much doubt of that,' Palfrey assured him. 'But where can I see it?'

'They still perform tragic drama in Japan,' said Orishu.

• • • • • •

'On the one hand,' Palfrey told Stefan and Drusilla, three days later, 'we can all leave here and get back to Europe. We've had a message from Brett, bless his heart—we're free to do what we like. Stefan's heard from Moscow to the same effect. If there is a German military clique still in Japan it's fairly safe to say that von Runst is in or has been in communication with it, and they'll be on the look-out for us. The odds are against us, and there's no demand being made on us.' He paused.

'That is, as you say, on the one hand,' smiled Stefan.

He was leaning back in an easy chair, into which he was tightly wedged. His head was still bandaged, but the wound no longer bothered him. Three days' rest had made a great difference to it. He was cheered up, also, by the knowledge that Laughing Fragrance, although still seriously ill, was out of danger.

'Yes.' Palfrey frowned. 'Well, we can nobly refuse to go

back to peace and quietness. We can be very foolish and say that we started this business and we intend to try to see it through. Orishu, confound him, has pointed out that I might be able to help by identifying that drama. Morally, how can I say that I won't?'

Neither of them answered him.

'I was afraid you wouldn't be able to give me a satisfactory reason,' said Palfrey, sadly. 'I don't want to go, but I fear I've got to do it. I know one thing,' he added, with a sudden illuminating smile. 'This time, I leave my wife behind!'

Drusilla said nothing.

'That is essential,' Stefan agreed.

'I'm not sure that I oughtn't to leave you behind, too,' said Palfrey. 'That statuesque figure of yours is a dangerous thing to have about.' He laughed mirthlessly. 'I don't know why I'm talking. I've never been the leader of this outfit, that place goes to Orishu. He wants me to say that I'll have another shot, although he hasn't put it into words. He'll accept my offer, and say whether there is anything for either of you to do.' He lit a cigarette, and stood up abruptly. 'On the other hand, I can tell him what I will do and what I won't—and I will not let you do anything more, 'Silla. Sorry. You can stay in Chungking and spend a week or two learning how the Chinese live when they are not in isolated villages or wandering tribes. Wandering tribes,' he added, looking out of the window towards the road. 'How long ago that seems now!'

'So you've decided to go,' Drusilla asked, quietly.

'Yes.'

'When are you likely to start?'

'It's up to Orishu,' said Palfrey.

. . . . . .

Palfrey reached the entrance to the underground headquarters, smiling faintly. Already the possibility of success was in his mind; already he was looking forward to the final act. An hour before, it had been the last thing he wanted to do; now . . .

He supposed that he was relieved because Drusilla had shown no desire to stop him, and was not hoping to come with him.

He entered the office. Orishu was sitting in von Runst's chair, and the Chinese colonel was with him. The colonel rose and saluted. Orishu smiled at him, and said softly:

'I have been waiting for you, Doctor.'

'Well, I'm here.' Palfrey smiled back.

The colonel said: 'I know you will excuse me, gentlemen.' He went out, and Palfrey sat down in front of the Japanese and began to toy with his hair.

'If I come to Japan,' he queried, 'is there a reasonable chance of success?'

'It depends what you mean by success,' said Orishu. 'I think I can undertake to get you to Japan and keep you there unsuspected by the authorities. I can make arrangements by which you can study the drama. Beyond that, of course, I cannot go. What you know may prove the key to the great mystery. You will, of course, have to come alone.'

'Of course.'

'Your—wife——' Orishu hesitated.

'It is settled, she is not to come,' said Palfrey.

'She is a remarkable woman,' declared Orishu, with his faint smile, and then asked a strange question: 'Are you a Christian, Dr. Palfrey? And is she?'

'I try to be,' Palfrey told him, mildly surprised.

'I would like you to know,' said Orishu, 'that I am, also. There are others in Japan who are also followers of Christ, and at all times in Japan there has been a measure of tolerance for Christians. You think, perhaps, that what I say is irrelevant. It is not. Religious beliefs make us do strange things. Sometimes they fill us with prejudice.' He paused, and watched Palfrey steadily, and now Palfrey was genuinely puzzled.

'Not far from Tokyo, near the shores of Lake Yamanaki, which is at the foot of Mount Fujiyama,' Orishu explained carefully, 'there is a little wooden house. It is next to a wooden church—a Christian church. Its minister, a missionary, has always been highly respected, even by the authorities. I cannot explain why, except that his good works are legion and he has never allowed himself to take part in political affairs. He is a very fine gentleman,' Orishu continued. 'One of the few Englishmen who was not interned in Tokyo; in fact, in all Japan. Other missionaries, English, Americans, Danes, Swedes, Germans—a strange mixture of races to meet together in amity—visit him from time to time. They are allowed to pass. They are, of course, questioned, but few of them are *known* by the Japanese in Tokyo. They come from all parts of the island, from north and south, even from occupied parts of China. From time to time, when they have gathered together, the little church and the wooden house beside it have been visited by members of the police and secret service, but never have they been taken off, nor has any action been taken by the Japanese Government. Yet I have often been there and talked to the missionary,' Orishu went on softly. 'I have told him that one day I may call on him for help. He has promised me that help. I have assured him that I would only call on him if I were convinced that it was in the best interests of my country. He trusts me, Doctor, and I trust him. I wish to take you there, but you may feel that you cannot pose as a Christian missionary.' He paused again, and, when Palfrey did not answer, added: 'I have been completely frank with you. I wish you to know the whole truth. I do not wish to take advantage of you or to bring you suddenly face to face with the need for adopting a disguise which may be—repugnant to you, Doctor. You understand, I am sure.'

Palfrey nodded: 'Yes, fully. Of course I will come.'

'I will make arrangements for the journey at once,' said Orishu.

• • • • • •

Palfrey stood at the door of the little wooden house, and looked across the lake. It had a beauty and a serenity which held him enthralled. He had been enthralled, and not quite balanced, since he had come to Japan. He had not known anxiety or fear; there had been no alarms on the journey, no hint that he was suspected. The little party of Japanese with whom he had travelled since he had descended from an aeroplane over the wooded mountains of Honshu, the main island of Japan, had been unmolested.

He had seen the strange, fragile, cold beauty of Japan; of the people, the flowers, the waters and the woods; it was a new and different world.

Now, Palfrey stood looking over the lake. He could see the huddled buildings of Tokyo, which he had not yet visited, for the church and the house were on the lower slopes of the great mountain. He had been there for three days, and had been to the edge of the lake and talked to the fishermen and the children, a surprising number of whom spoke English. No one seemed to suspect that he was more than another visitor to the missionary who was now sitting at a low table, writing industriously. Palfrey had not been surprised to find an old, bearded man, in whose eyes there burned an unquenchable fire and in whose frail body there was the strength of eternal youth. He had come to see that the man was almost worshipped by many who listened to him or whom he helped.

Orishu had been in Tokyo since early morning. He had been every day, without explaining what he did—he kept his own counsel, as if he did not trust even Palfrey with the details of his activities. He was always the same. In Japan he wore badly fitting European clothes and loose-fitting canvas shoes, and he always carried a pair of slippers in his pocket. Carefully, he had rehearsed Palfrey in the essential customs of the country, putting him through an oral test each day. There was little that Palfrey forgot; a single slip, when the great moment came, might damn him.

Figures of men and women moved by the shores of the lake, and along the road which led to the top of Fujiyama, the vast mountain which cast a shadow over Tokyo and was the Mecca of all Japanese.

Palfrey picked out the figure of Orishu among a file of men walking towards the wooden house. The others went on up the mountainside, but Orishu, impassive and quick-moving, came towards him.

He bowed, spreading his hands palms downwards.

'All is well,' he announced.

Palfrey's heart leapt.

'When?'

'Tonight, my friend. We shall go to the main theatre and you will be welcomed; no one will be surprised to see you there. The authorities will allow you to enter and you will be quite safe. I shall, of course, come with you.' He led the way inside, and made obeisance to the old man who sat writing and looked up with a vacant smile. There was an unearthly quality about the missionary, and Palfrey was not altogether at ease in his company.

'You must understand that the theatre in Japan is very different from that in England,' said Orishu. 'A performance is very, very long. The theme is usually tragedy,' he added softly, 'but it is broken by farces which come immediately after tragic dramas, and you will find it very strange. I have been able to arrange for *five* dramas, which have scenes similar to those which you described, to be played in the late evening. I think you will find that one of the five is the one you saw.' He smiled. 'That is good, Doctor?'

'Yes,' Palfrey smiled wryly, in return. What if he could not, in fact, help?

'We travel from here after dark,' said Orishu, 'because it will be wiser not to be seen by too many people.' His manner suggested that he was not so confident of safety as he pretended. 'Hiroto is in Tokyo.'

'Oh,' said Palfrey.

'He has been away for some time,' said Orishu, 'and the rumours which I have heard suggest that he has been on some secret mission. In fact, the strongest rumours are that he has been in touch with the Allies, trying to find a formula for peace which will help to save the Emperor's face. I do not believe it. I believe that he has, once again, been with von Runst.'

'You never told me where von Runst went,' Palfrey put in.

'For a very good reason—I do not know,' said Orishu. 'It is hardly remarkable that there are times when the best plans fail, Doctor. Two extremely fast, powerfully armed fighters with highly-trained crews, all with great battle experience, followed those aeroplanes, but heavy cloud over northern China made it impossible for them to trace their destination. The only indication that we have is the range of the aircraft and the direction of the flight—north-westwards. The range would take von Runst into Manchukuo, southern Russia, or to Japan. It can only be said with certainty that he is in one of those three places.'

'You can rule out Russia,' Palfrey assured him.

'I am not so sure,' said Orishu. 'It would not be impossible, I think, for him to hide himself for a short while in the vastness of that country. I can tell you this: I believe that von Runst and certain elements in Japan are planning to present the Allies with a situation which they cannot overcome. The question is, what does he propose to do there, and what part is Hiroto playing in the plot?' He gave his faint, oblique smile. 'I think we shall have to talk to Hiroto, before long.'

'We?' asked Palfrey, startled.

'Yes. I hope to kidnap him,' Orishu explained, simply . . .

It was almost dark when they were carried by sedan chair into Tokyo. There were many people about; Palfrey could see their vague shapes passing.

Now that he was in the middle of Tokyo, he was struck by the strange hush which spread everywhere. It was possible to feel the tension, to know that they were going about their business in the fear of a sudden attack from the air.

Orishu took Palfrey's arm.

He led the way through a door which was well shielded against light from inside the building. Once the door closed he turned along a narrow passage. There was a glimmer of light; Palfrey could see men and women, some in native dress and some in Western, moving to and fro. Soon they were in the entrance hall of the theatre; they were expected, and taken to a door flanked by two guards in uniform.

As Palfrey stepped through, he heard a sound which had never wholly faded from his ears—the eerie, reedy music of the theatre. They were in semi-darkness; most of the light came from the stage. They were led to one of the boxes.

Palfrey sat on a wicker chair, and Orishu took one beside him. He watched the stage, but hardly had he settled down than the curtains fell.

Had it not been for the hope that he would recognise the drama he had seen before, the next two hours would have been unutterably boring to Palfrey. Farce and tragedy followed each other, each scene taking about half an hour. Then the lights began to fade again and, after a brief interval, the curtains were drawn back for the next presentation.

He gripped Orishu's arm; the setting was exactly the same as it had been in the valley.

Within a few minutes he was sure this was the same drama. The music came back to him; he seemed to remember every chant, every beat.

. . . . . .

Not until the next interval, when there was a general relaxation among the audience, did Orishu take Palfrey's arm and lead him out of the box. Many others left the auditorium at the same time, so there was nothing noticeable about their own departure. Palfrey tried to calm himself, hardly able to understand why he was so agitated. He hated the thought of the lonely journey in a sedan chair back to the little church.

'This way,' whispered Orishu.

So they were not going back immediately!

Orishu held his arm as they threaded their way through the crowds and turned down a side street. He stopped, hesitated a moment, then turned into a doorway.

They went up a flight of narrow stairs and along a passage carpeted in red. Then Orishu opened a door and ushered Palfrey into a small room, where three Japanese were sitting. They rose immediately. Palfrey forced himself to respond to the inevitable, excessive exchange of courtesies. All these men spoke English, and pitched their voices on a low key.

'These are our friends,' said Orishu, at last. 'They have helped me for many years, Doctor.'

Palfrey bowed yet again. 'I'm very glad to hear it. Orishu, you know that we saw——'

'We saw the royal version of *No,*' said Orishu, softly.

Palfrey was looking at the others. He saw them stiffen, saw incredulity on their bland yellow faces.

'Is there no doubt?' one asked softly.

'No doubt at all,' said Orishu.

'What *is* so remarkable about it?' asked Palfrey, with a touch of impatience.

'We are surprised and yet not surprised.' Orishu was speaking with an obvious effort. 'It has been discussed as possible, and yet we could not really believe that you had seen this particular version of the drama, Doctor. You see, it is the favourite version of the emperor's.'

'Well?' Palfrey was still no wiser.

'It is played to him and his Court once every year,' said Orishu. 'The company which you saw perform tonight will give the performance at the Royal Palace.' He closed his eyes, while the others continued to stare at him, as if numbed by the effect of his words. 'Very few strangers ever enter the Palace, Doctor—very few indeed. Hiroto is one of them. Hiroto, we know, is in touch with von Runst. Von Runst has with him a compnay of German actors trained so as to give a performance of *No* exactly as you have seen it tonight. It becomes apparent, then, that von Runst's men will play before the Emperor.'

'But——' began Palfrey.

'Never in the history of Japan have foreigners gazed upon the Emperor in such a fashion,' said Orishu, and Palfrey realised that he, as much as the others, was affected by the thought that unclean eyes were to gaze upon their Emperor. 'There will be a small audience, Doctor—it is always very small. Never before have unauthorised people entered the Palace—*never* before. I think,' he added, in a voice so low that Palfrey could hardly hear the words, 'that von Runst is planning *to kidnap the Emperor*.'

16 : The Great Adventure

FIELD-MARSHALL VON RUNST was gifted with a sense of humour. It enabled him to avoid feeling ridiculous in circumstances which would have been unbearable for many of his fellow *Junkers,* and in the days after he had left the valley it had stood him in good stead.

Now, in a small room inside the Shinto Temple, which was near the Imperial Palace of the Mikado, he was dressed as a priest in a flowing robe, more than a little dirty and smelly. His head was shaved, his face was stained a dark, sickly yellow, but he stood the discomfort of the facial disguise well. His eyes were pulled up at the corners, giving them the oblique, upward slant characteristic of Orientals: he had sat for hours while an expert worked on him. His eyelashes were stiffened with gum; instead of shooting outwards from his eyelids, they converged and made a curious ellipse through which the pupil of his eyes could be seen. He kept his hands inside the flowing sleeves of his robe; he wore sandals; and kept his lips set tightly.

With him was the one-handed Japanese whom Palfrey had seen in the valley, the notorious Hiroto. Hiroto looked uneasily at the Field-Marshal, who was staring towards the Imperial Palace. He could see the roofs, odd-shaped, some glittering with lacquer, some drab, behind the high wall. He could see the Imperial Guards, and to von Runst they looked absurdly small and incapable of withstanding an assault. He found the whole situation amusing, yet he realised that all the hopes and plans of many years would succeed or fail according to what happened on the following day.

'I cannot repeat it often enough, Excellency,' said Hiroto, 'it is a mistake for you to be here. If it should be even whispered that a strange priest is in this temple, then you would be examined and taken off. It was a mistake, Excellency. It was——'

'You are far too nervous,' von Runst rebuked him calmly. 'It is all very simple—and I like simplicity. I cannot see how it can fail. This will be a sensation for the world, Hiroto!'

'It will cause heartfelt relief in Japan, certainly. The knowledge that the holy person of the Emperor is safe will sustain the people in the adversity which will follow defeat, Excellency. If the Emperor were to become a prisoner in the hands of the enemy, then . . .' Hiroto paused, fingering the stump of his wrist nervously.

'I am not unaware of the consequences,' said von Runst, with great self-satisfaction. 'In future, Hiroto, Germany and Japan must fight as one, not as Allies with different objectives, jealousies, rivalries and the absurd hatred between races of different colour. We will fight as one, Hiroto—and the only way to be sure of that is for the Emperor to be safe in *our* hands.'

'The only way,' murmured Hiroto.

'I do not think the Allies realise that if the Emperor is safe and able to speak to his people, as he will speak in due course—the people will remain loyal to him at heart.'

'Nothing is more certain,' Hiroto agreed. 'When they realise what has happened, when they come to see the advantages it will bring, then they will join you.'

'I know,' said von Runst. 'I know, Hiroto. The people of Japan will await the return of their Emperor! The people of the Reich will await the return of their real leaders! The time will come when it will be possible to overthrow the effete democratic Governments which the United Nations will set up in our great lands. The dream of Germany will be the return of the Generals; the dream of Japan will be the return of the Emperor. We shall work ceaselessly to prepare them for the Day of Restoration!'

'Please, Excellency,' Hiroto tried again. 'Most humbly I beg you to reconsider your decision to stay here to receive the Emperor. It will be better if you go to safety before he comes. I beg you——'

'*I shall stay!*' roared von Runst.

'As you say, Excellency,' murmured Hiroto, and he bowed himself out.

Von Runst followed him out, then walked over the matted floor of the temple towards an inner room. He went in, and from a low stool, where he had been sitting smoking, Professor Kriess rose to greet him.

Nothing could disguise the fact that Kriess was a European Jew; he wore priest's clothes, but far less successfully than von Runst. He took the pipe from his lips and smiled gently.

'Is all ready, Excellency?'

'Yes.' Von Runst stared at the Professor for a long moment, obviously thinking of something else. 'Yes,' he repeated, 'according to Hiroto. *Can* we trust that man, Kriess?'

'We could not have worked without him.'

'I did not ask that—I asked whether we could trust him.' There was no harshness in the Field Marshal's voice. He sat down slowly. 'He has persisted in trying to make me go away. It is obvious that he wants to know where we propose to take the Emperor.'

'You have refused to tell him, Excellency?'

'Of course,' said von Runst. 'When we've got the Emperor, then we can tell them where to find him. Until then I would not trust a single Japanese.'

'You are wise,' murmured the Professor.

Von Runst sat brooding for a while, and then he shrugged his shoulders. 'I think he will be reliable. He is desperately anxious that the Allies should not capture the Emperor—the man is loyal to his monarch, if to no one else.'

'And, therefore, he will be loyal to us,' Kriess nodded. 'I am in full agreement, Excellency! When is it to be?'

'Tomorrow.'

'And after tomorrow,' said Kriess, softly, 'we can really rest. I have not wished to alarm you, but I can tell you now that you are in urgent need of rest—*urgent* need, Excellency. I have seen it for some time.'

'I am well enough,' growled von Runst.

'You have been carrying a great burden, and since the injury to the General you have not been able to share it with others,' said Kriess. 'No human being could stand the burden for long, Excellency. But there will be rest! We shall reach our destination by tomorrow night, you say. We shall, of course, be expected.'

'Of course,' Von Runst laughed. 'There is no further reason why you should not know where we are going.'

'I do not wish Your Excellency to divulge any information which will cause you anxiety,' Kriess protested, quickly

'It will cause no one anxiety,' said von Runst. 'We have performed a miracle, Kriess! A town has been fashioned out of the uncharted wastes of the Gobi Desert. No place on earth is more inaccessible. No place on earth has better natural defences than the place we have chosen. It was made for us, Kriess, created for us by a Providence which has always guided us, *always* guided us!'

• • • • • •

Palfrey sat cross-legged on a stool in a little wooden house, on the morning after the drama in Tokyo; the morning after Orishu's awestruck announcement of his theory. Throughout the night, during which he had been restless, lying awake for long stretches, he had tried to understand the immensity of von Runst's project.

Orishu had told him:

'I am not sure, Doctor, that it would not be better to warn the Diet of what is going to happen, rather than allow von Runst a chance of success. The Emperor must not be allowed to leave the country.'

Palfrey had not known what to say.

As he looked across the lake towards the city, he was in two minds. He was not certain that Orishu would consult him again before warning the Japanese Government; he was not sure that anything remained for him to do. He was on edge, watching for Orishu, who had left the wooden house before he had woken from the deep sleep into which he had fallen towards dawn. He was afraid that when the man returned he would face him with a *fait accompli*.

He saw Orishu leave the path up the mountain and come towards the house, and he was waiting for the little man on the threshold. Orishu did not smile, but bowed and waited for him to turn inside.

'Well?' Palfrey asked, abruptly.

'We have reached no decision,' said Orishu. 'My friends are trying to get together enough men to oppose von Runst's plans but there are few who can be trusted with the knowledge that this is to be an attack upon the person of the Emperor. It will strike them all as the ultimate crime, Doctor. Even I cannot bring myself to believe that it is really contemplated.' He looked steadily at Palfrey. 'In the past I have told myself that the Emperor is but a figurehead of no importance, and yet now that it comes to the test——' He broke off.

Palfrey said slowly: 'I have been thinking, Orishu.'

'I shall be more than grateful for any expression of opinion,' Orishu assured him.

'We would have to have enough men to defeat von Runst,' said Palfrey, 'but he can't have many at his disposal here. Twenty would probably be enough.'

'So far, we know only of seven. What would you do then, Doctor?'

Palfrey said: 'Wouldn't the Emperor be welcome in Chungking? There would be great scope for Allied negotiations if they held him as a hostage; great bloodshed could be avoided, and the future might be controlled with greater ease.'

'I agree with you,' replied Orishu slowly. 'The Emperor will be safe and the Allies, by judicious handling of the situation, can plan the future. *Yes,* Doctor. We will find enough men.'

'And make sure that we can get him to Chungking?'

'That will not be difficult. Preparations have been made to take *you* to Chungking directly the need for your services is over. I will go.' Orishu went to the door, then turned back. 'I should have told you this, Doctor. We have made a most careful investigation, and have found that there is a strange priest at a Shiba Temple, the nearest building to the Imperial Palace. It is almost certain that their attempt will be directed from there. We have taken no steps, of course, except to watch the temple. We have found one other thing,' he added softly. 'The performance at the Imperial Palace will, without doubt, be tonight.'

• • • • • •

Not far away, just visible against the night sky, was a small building with the familiar pagoda-shaped roof. They had stopped perhaps fifty yards away from it.

Orishu whispered: 'There is the Palace.'

He pointed beyond the temple, where the outlines of the many roofs of the palace were just discernible. Now it was possible to hear men walking about the wall. Palfrey felt suddenly appalled by the magnitude of the task confronting them—and not only them, but von Runst. He knew something of the precautions taken to guard the Emperor. He knew nothing of the arrangements for escape, and had to trust Orishu; he had never been more ready to place implicit faith in the little Japanese.

Suddenly, Orishu said: 'The actors are coming, Doctor.'

Palfrey strained his eyes but could see nothing; then he heard the sound of motor engines and, before long, dark, sleek shapes appeared below him. He could not see the gateway to the Palace, but he saw the cars disappear and his heart began to beat uncomfortably fast.

After a long time, Orishu whispered: 'Men are leaving the temple, Doctor!'

He could see them; there were three, who left the temple and stood not far away from it, staring towards the Palace. Palfrey wondered if von Runst were among them.

• • • • • •

Inside the Imperial Palace, the quiet was broken only by the weird sound of the reedy music and the chanting of the actors. On the stage, they were performing with the unnatural calm which had so affected Palfrey. The girl was dancing, and the hush was intense—even the breathing of the watching men and women was hardly discernible.

The Emperor sat apart from all the others. Seated behind him were his sons and daughters, the sons and daughters of his brothers—the whole Imperial household was gathered in that one room.

The Emperor watched with narrowed eyes and without expression. He held himself completely aloof; none looking at him could have doubted that he believed in his divinity. Yet although many of those about him were dressed in fine clothes, although the soft light shone on priceless jewels and costly ornamentation, the Emperor was plainly dressed in a blue robe; and he was bareheaded. His hands were folded over his stomach and he sat without moving or blinking.

The play went on, the dance of despair waxed faster and faster; the chanting and the music stopped; the dancer fell.

The silence which followed lasted for a long time. There was no sound, no sign of movement; all present were waiting for an indication of approval from the godhead. He was looking towards the prostrate dancer.

Suddenly, he rose.

With a rustling sound all the others rose and stood quite still, and he approached the stage and stared at the girl, then at the men. He did not speak; no expression was on his face. Yet those with him knew that he was satisfied; this was the sign of his approval.

He turned to go.

He would be led from the room by the Captain of his Guard, and the others would follow him into the wide passage where guards were stationed at every door and corner. But he would only cross the passage and enter his own chambers, where he would give audience to the leading dancers, attended by the Captain of the Guard.

He went out.

The doors of the theatre closed, so that he should not be closely followed—and as they closed the actors moved, not through the doorways to the back of the stage but downwards to the auditorium. It was perfectly done; one moment they were still, the next they were among the audience, and from their hands dropped little glass phials of gas which rose in clouds and set the royal entourage gasping and swaying; and it acted swiftly. The actors did not move their masks—and with good reason, for each was fitted with a gas-mask, completely concealed. They reached the doors and stood guard over them. But there was no sound of alarm from outside, and inside only the sound of men and women falling to the floor as if struck dead in those few, devastating seconds.

The leading dancer hurried to the stage and through the doors to the passage where 'she' would be expected; 'she' was a man. Men were waiting to take him to the door of the royal chamber, the audience which set the seal of fame on any actor in Japan. He entered, and saw the Captain of the Guard with his sword drawn, the Emperor sitting on a stool piled high with cushions.

The Emperor opened his lips . . .

He took the full force of the gas which 'she' sent into his face from a small gas-pistol, and he was still staring incredulously at the masked man when the Captain of the Guard moved towards him. The Emperor fell as swiftly as his family, and the Captain of the Guard saved him from falling and lifted him shoulder high. From the folds of his dress the 'actress' took another mask, which he fastened over the Emperor's face, while another man came forward and replaced the blue robe with one of many colours.

The door opened and the actors, still in their grotesque masks, took possession of the Emperor. In the passage the guards were lying on the floor, all of them unconscious. The cars were waiting for them inside the gates. They entered them, and the Emperor was placed in the first. The Captain of the Guard gave orders to the men on duty inside the walls, and the gates were opened. The cars moved forward and, once outside, the gates were closed. The cars went for a little way along the road to Tokyo, and then turned down the narrow road towards the temple.

Palfrey saw them coming.

Von Runst, standing with Kriess and Hiroto, also saw them coming. Kriess moved away from the others, and went into the temple. The cars drew nearer. Von Runst stepped forward as the first pulled up, and asked in German: 'Have you got him?'

'Quiet, Excellency!' gasped Hiroto.

'Yes,' said the leading actor, 'we are ready to go. Hurry, please——'

Palfrey heard the words, carried on a gentle wind, and was filled with something approaching panic.

He whispered: 'Orishu, quickly——'

'Hush!' said Orishu. 'Something is wrong.'

Palfrey stood straining his eyes through the darkness. He wanted to see Orishu's men go forward; there would never be another chance like this to capture both the Emperor and von Runst; he believed it could be done; the Germans were not prepared for an attack. He gritted his teeth as he peered through the darkness . . .

And then he saw a multitude of figures rise from the ground about the cars. He saw a party of them plunge towards the first car and he sensed that the Emperor was in it. The others . . .

Machine-guns suddenly opened fire.

The cars were riddled with bullets in that first terrible fusillade. The actors tried to get out, and as they came they were set upon with knives which glistened in the searchlights. Except for the one burst of machine-gun fire there was little sound, but the quiet made the whole scene more ghastly. Not a man was to be left alive.

Palfrey heard von Runst's voice: 'Hiroto! *Hiroto!*'

'Be calm, Excellency!'

Palfrey saw men come from the massacre near the cars towards Hiroto and the Field-Marshal; only then did he realise that the gaunt-looking priest was von Runst. He saw the men surround him, saw two of them take his arms.

Von Runst said in a strangled voice: 'Hiroto——'

'You would not seriously expect me to deliver the Emperor into your hands,' said Hiroto. 'He will be taken to a place of safety, Excellency, where the Allies cannot capture him. That is what you desired, is it not? You would not seriously expect me to deliver him to *you,* Excellency.' He spoke in English, which had always been the common language between the two men, and Palfrey heard every word. He felt a dawning understanding which almost stupefied him; Hiroto had never contemplated treachery, *and he had completely deceived the German*!

'*I* am the authority now, Excellency,' said Hiroto. 'All of your friends here are dead, except the little Professor, and he will not live for long. He was seen to hurry into the temple. Where is your hiding-place?'

Von Runst turned on his heel.

For a moment it looked as if he would be able to drag the two Japanese with him, but they stopped him, and Palfrey heard him gasp with pain.

'Please!' said Hiroto, as if distressed. 'Please understand I do not wish to cause you pain, Excellency, but we must know where you wish to go. We must get the Emperor away to safety quickly and we have not much time. Members of the Cabinet are with me in this very humble plot, but the Army does not know—the Generals would not like it!' He laughed. 'Nor would the Liberals and the industrialists, Excellency. You see, I make these admissions to you!'

Orishu gripped Palfrey's arm.

'We are going,' he whispered. 'Do you wish to stay here?'

'Yes,' Palfrey told him.

'We will return,' said Orishu, 'but I beg you, do not move, do not allow them to see you. They may search the trees, and here, by your side, is a place to hide. On your right. Lie down, roll over, and then do not move—that is if they come to search. We shall be back soon,' he added.

Palfrey stood alone among the trees.

He did not hear Orishu and the others turn and hurry back; and it was impossible for anyone else to hear them, for all were further away. The temple was surrounded; the lights showed the men standing about it, as if they were waiting for the order to attack.

The lights began to go out.

At last only one small beam of light shone on von Runst and Hiroto and the men about them. Von Runst's face was unrecognisable, only the voice convinced Palfrey that it was the Field-Marshal. Hiroto was grinning, and so was a little man who approached with a knife in his hand.

'Please, Excellency,' said Hiroto. 'We must know the place where you plan to hide. We do not wish to cause you pain, it would be greatly regretted, but—tell us the name of the hiding-place, Excellency, *quickly*.'

Palfrey watched, hardly daring to breathe. If the place were named and if he could get away, any danger from von Runst's fantastic scheme would be removed. About the Japanese and this cunning plot his thoughts were less clear—Orishu would do what thinking was necessary about that. He had come from England to find out where the Germans planned to have their hide-out, and now he knew for certain that there was another place besides the valley. He did not think that von Runst would be easily persuaded to talk.

As von Runst stood there, without speaking, two more Japanese stepped forward. They seized his hand and thrust it forward. The man with the knife, whom Palfrey could see clearly, was grinning broadly. He moved the point from von Runst's stomach to his hand. Palfrey saw the knife pushed down a fingernail!

Von Runst gasped and writhed; there was a swift turn, and Palfrey saw the blood dripping from his finger. He tried to wrench his hand away but it was held too tightly. The point touched another nail.

'Excellency!' wailed Hiroto.

Then von Runst broke away.

How he did it Palfrey did not know; one moment the man seemed helpless, with the blood dripping from his finger and the knife against another; and then there was a flurry of movement and von Runst got free. There was a gasp of surprise from the men, a squeal from Hiroto. A sudden burst of machine-gun fire raked the ground into which von Runst was running, but he seemed to be unhurt.

He made for the trees!

Palfrey realised it after a moment of stupefaction; yet in spite of the realisation he seemed to be rooted to the spot. He heard machine-gun bullets tearing through the trees and the light was turned towards them. Von Runst reached the outer fringe.

Palfrey dropped to the ground and rolled towards the right. This dug-out had been well prepared, and the air was clear.

The sounds of tumult faded.

He lay quite still, and gradually he became aware of a sense of acute disappointment; he knew nothing of importance, and Hiroto's double-dealing would probably enable him and his small clique to get safely away with the Emperor. Cramped down there, not daring to move, Palfrey was vividly aware of what all this implied. The Emperor was the chief prize; if he were taken away, out of reach of the Allies, there could be no real hope of a complete change of policy on the part of the Japanese.

He thought he heard the sound of a car.

Cautiously he edged himself forward until his head was out of the little foxhole and he could see the shapes of the trees and above him, the faint peppering of the stars. The engine of a stationary car was turning over slowly.

Men were coming towards him. He ducked out of sight and lay with his heart thumping until they passed him. Then he dared to show himself again. He heard the whisper of voices and thought that there was an urgent note in them. He peered towards the cars, and he could see that some of the men were carrying a solitary figure towards the first car. He heard Hiroto urge the men to hurry. He saw a figure on the ground near Hiroto, and he thought it was von Runst.

Palfrey thought: 'If I could stop that car. . . .'

He had no doubt that Orishu had seen that the only way to prevent the kidnapping of the Emperor by his own people was to bring out the military, who would not permit it. Better that he should remain in Tokyo than that he should be got safely away. Hopes were fading of avoiding the inevitable bloodshed of the final assault on the main islands of Japan.

They must not get away.

He took out his automatic, but the range was too great. He moved forward cautiously. He was no more than thirty yards from the car when he raised his gun.

A cry from the temple made him hesitate. He saw men hurrying towards Hiroto, dragging another man between them. He did not know who it was, until Hiroto said sharply: 'Kriess'.

Palfrey stiffened. He did not shoot, there was no immediate hurry now, for he believed that Hiroto would try to make the Professor talk. He saw him dragged in front of the little Japanese.

Hiroto spoke in English.

'You will talk at once, Kriess. Von Runst refused—there is his body. Where was von Runst planning to go?'

'I—I do not know,' gasped Kriess, 'he would not——'

His words ended in a scream of pain, although Palfrey could not see what caused it. Hiroto began to talk more fiercely, Kriess was writhing in the grip of his captors—and then Palfrey heard the sound of motor-engines. Further down the road searchlights fixed on cars were moving up and down, casting a brilliant light about the countryside. There were a dozen cars or more, and their engines were very loud now.

Hiroto screamed an order.

Palfrey fired at the car.

The shot seemed very loud; he saw men turn towards him and he fired three times, towards the driver of the car, before he dropped to the ground. Bullets began to carve their way through the trees, but he no longer felt afraid; he saw the light of the headlamps already making the moonlight seem dull, and he realised that the party would have no chance to search the woods.

He saw shapes scuttling through the trees and others moving towards the temple. The first of the new cars was screeching towards the temple and men were jumping out of it. He saw Hiroto running and thought he saw Kriess fall to the ground. Everything was helplessly confused, but the one fact which emerged was that the Emperor's car did not move and the driver was leaning forward over the wheel.

Then the other cars arrived and the grounds of the temple became alive with men. There were others coming from the Palace now, and lights were everywhere. He thought he caught a glimpse of Orishu speaking to soldiers standing near the car. The doors were open. Men were lifting the unconscious body of the Emperor; all whom he passed bowed low. Then Orishu began to speak again, pointing to Kriess. Palfrey gathered that he was bargaining for Kriess's body. Agreement was obviously reached, for men dressed in civilian clothes came forward, lifted Kriess, and carried him to one of the cars.

It moved down the hill, its engine purring.

The sounds of pursuit after Hiroto's men were lessening, and the copse was quiet. Cautiously, Palfrey stood up.

He heard a movement close beside him, and his heart turned over.

A man spoke softly in English.

'Stay, please, you will be safe. Stay, please.'

Palfrey said nothing, but stretched himself at full length. So they had not forgotten him. He watched the whole scene as the moon rose higher, and its lovely light bathed the roofs of the Palace. He saw the gates open and the Emperor carried in. He saw the guard, obviously strengthened, patrolling the walls.

Nearer to him he saw the soldiers searching for the bodies of men who had been shot, and then some were brought in, prisoners who had failed in their wild dash for freedom.

He saw Hiroto.

While he watched, the man and his supporters were put to the sword, given no opportunity for *hara-kiri*; and the sight was such that he closed his eyes.

It was a long time before he heard the cars making their way towards the city. Before they left, others arrived and were admitted to the Palace. He could imagine the hurried consultations and the decisions which were taken. . . .

He could imagine what was happening in Tokyo.

. . . . . .

Death struck in Tokyo, silently, without warning. Cabinet Ministers, secretaries, intriguers known or suspected to work with Hiroto, fell before the knives which struck so savagely. As the night wore on, more and more men were murdered, and some, hearing that death was on its way, pushed swords into their bellies and twisted them.

. . . . . .

Orishu himself came for Palfrey before dawn, and led him through the trees and towards the city, but did not take him into it. He led the way across the fields on the foothills of Fujiyama towards the wooden church and the house nestling by it, and there he left him, warning him not to show himself until he received word that it would be safe.

He was not disturbed, and wakened of his own accord. He got up when he felt hungry, and went to the door. The room beyond, where the missionary worked, was empty; on the table was a bowl of rice and some coarse wheat-cakes, with a jug of water. He ate and drank eagerly. Then he heard a movement in another room.

He stared towards it, but the door did not open. The movement came again, accompanied by a curious, thudding sound. He opened the door.

A man was lying on a camp-bed in one corner. He kept raising a small table at his side, and letting it fall back on its legs, to attract attention.

'Kriess!' Palfrey gasped, hardly believing his own eyes.

Kriess was heavily bandaged about the head and shoulders and was bound to the bed so that he could not move. Palfrey needed no telling that he was grievously injured. He looked at the bandages, which had been put on by an expert, and from all he saw he judged that Kriess was bound to the bed because movement might be fatal to him, not to stop him from moving. Only his right arm was free.

'I am glad you are here,' Kriess spoke in a voice so low that Palfrey had to lean forward to hear. 'I wanted to see you before I died, Doctor. I have already told Orishu that von Runst had planned and built a city which he believed would never be discovered, somewhere in or near the Gobi Desert. I could not tell him more than that, because I do not know it.'

'You have told Orishu,' said Palfrey, speaking with an effort.

'Yes, Doctor. I do not think I shall live long,' went on Kriess. 'Hiroto's men have nothing to learn from—my country-folk. I am glad to have this word with you, before I die.' He closed his eyes as if the effort was too much for him, but he went on talking. 'I wanted to ask you to forgive me, Palfrey, but I had no choice. Von Runst would not tell me or anyone else where to find the last hiding-place. I—had to find out. I had to betray you, Palfrey, for only thus could I convince von Runst that I was worthy of his trust.'

He stopped again, and Palfrey did not move.

'I want you to believe,' Kriess went on at last, 'that it was I who persuaded von Runst that you would be of great service to him. But for that you would have died, and your wife——' He broke off, and his face, now wet with perspiration, twisted in a smile. 'Those little tablets, Palfrey, would have killed her. I did that for you, in spite of what I told von Runst. Perhaps

I was wrong, but I could not allow myself to think of her a the mercy of those creatures. Do you—do you understand, Palfrey?'

'Yes,' Palfrey spoke huskily. 'Don't talk any more now.'

'There is little hope for me,' said Kriess, 'and I will talk while I can.' He smiled again, and there was a haunting quality in it which reminded Palfrey of the time when Drusilla had spoken of the soothing power of his hands. 'I helped you a great deal, Palfrey. I took your wife away for questioning, having convinced von Runst that I was more certain to get the truth by my methods than he by his. She described the process, I have no doubt. I did not, of course, give her the necessary injection.'

'That should have told me the truth,' Palfrey murmured.

'I hoped that it would,' said Kriess, softly. 'You will think me a strange creature, Palfrey, but I did not wish to die with you thinking ill of me. Tell me, what happened to that brave Chinese woman?'

'She is recovering,' Palfrey assured him.

'And Andromovitch?'

'He is doubtless wishing he were here.'

'Yes, if he is alive, he will be. I am glad that things have worked out so well for you, Palfrey. I know that you have still to get out of Japan, but Orishu has arranged so many things so well that I do not think you have much to fear. Much to fear,' he repeated, and closed his eyes.

At first he gripped Palfrey's hand tightly, but gradually the fingers relaxed. Palfrey watched him, seeing the faint movement of his lips.

He died before Orishu returned.

. . . . . .

'I wish it were not so,' said Orishu, 'but there is some danger, Doctor. Yesterday I would not have said that. Today, the whole country is on guard. The purge during the night will continue during the day. Any kind of movement will be suspected, only fools will walk abroad. I have made arrangements to get out of the country tonight, and yet I do not advise you to travel.'

'Can I stay here?' asked Palfrey.

'Yes, but there is a risk. I do not think that this place will be visited, but it might be.'

'I'll stay,' Palfrey decided. 'I can't do much else! Did Kriess tell you everything?'

'Everything,' said Orishu. 'It was he who sent the reports about the valley, of course. He told us where we would find von Klowitz and the others who were in the aeroplane with him—they have been placed under arrest, and will be executed. Every other German in Japan has been executed.' He was quiet for a moment, but then he added: 'I think we were right, Doctor. Had Hiroto taken him away, had he been safe from Allied hands, there would have been a danger-spot in all the years to come. Now, when it is over, it will be the end in every way. I think we shall be able to build properly, next time.'

Palfrey stayed there for three days, until Orishu, smiling freely, came and told him that all was safe.

. . . . . .

There was some excitement in the Marquis of Brett's Brierly Place house, for the Palfreys and Stefan were expected. When they were a quarter of an hour later than predicted he began to fidget, but soon a taxi deposited the party outside the door.

Brett hurried downstairs to greet them.

Palfrey looked thinner, but brown and well. Drusilla looked tired. Stefan alone seemed exactly the same as when the Marquis had last seen him. They went upstairs, and Christian hurried to bring tea.

'I have all your reports,' said Brett, 'and I have also heard from Orishu—a very full despatch from Chungking. He was about to return to Tokyo, where he is now doing his best to strengthen the hand of those men who want to submit without further fight. We shall not know for a little while whether he has succeeded, but the final assault of the war will not be delayed much longer.' He glanced at Stefan. 'I was speaking on the telephone to Moscow last evening, Stefan, and I was asked to say that they will be glad to see you when you can return, but there is no hurry. Your wife is in London,' he added, and his eyes sparkled when he saw the way Stefan jumped up. 'She will be here later,' he said; 'she has been working and cannot get along until this evening. I thought it a good notion to get some work for her to do here.'

'A splendid notion!' declared Stefan.

Palfrey seemed to have forgotten his anxieties, and was soon talking.

'The last we saw of Laughing Fragrance, in Chungking, she was almost well again, and Kao Lun had managed, somehow or other, to be posted there. I don't think they have yet exchanged a word about getting married.' He laughed. 'We were seen off at the airfield by the Chinese colonel who arrested us, and I've never seen a man with a broader smile. We were fêted all the time we were there, not least by Wu Ling, and I was told that Ho Sun, who sent us to Hunsa, was arrested a few days afterwards. Oh—I think Drusilla broke one heart! Sing Quickly begged us to take him with us, but we persuaded him that he would be better off with Laughing Fragrance. Now that it's over, I wouldn't have missed it,' he admitted.

The Marquis smiled at that. 'Well, I have one or two things to tell you that you don't yet know. Chinese and American forces raided the Gobi Desert city. Von Runst was justified in hoping that it would remain undiscovered, I think. It was taken with little fighting, for they had no idea that they had been located. The arrangements were on the same lines as those in your valley—in some respects more thorough. Whether they would have lived to regenerate Germany and Japan as military Powers or whether they would have died out, we can only guess. It was undoubtedly a great danger.'

'Yes.' Palfrey looked towards the ceiling, and there was a vacant smile on his lips. 'I think I'll take 'Silla out,' he declared, looking suddenly at Stefan. 'You won't mind waiting?'

'I intend to wait until my wife arrives,' said Stefan.

'We'll be back some time tonight,' said Palfrey.

It was a calm evening, and the sky was free from clouds. Palfrey hailed a taxi, and when it pulled up, asked the driver: 'Will you take us as far as Kingston?'

'As far's you like,' said the cabby, promptly.

'Good! Then here we go, my sweet!' Palfrey climbed in after Drusilla, and as they were driven along, he said smilingly: 'I had an overwhelming desire to go to Kingston, to take a boat and to row as far as a little village where there is a Norman church. Does the idea please you?'

Drusilla's fingers tightened in his.